The magnificent Hotel Neversink is the crown jewel of the Catskills, a sprawling resort of unparalleled luxury that hosts athletes, actors, and even presidents. Owned and operated by the immigrant Sikorsky family, the hotel is a realization of their wildest American dream. But then a young boy disappears.

This mysterious vanishing—and the ones that follow—will brand the lives of three generations. At the root of it all is Asher Sikorsky, the ambitious and ruthless patriarch whose founding of the hotel in 1931 sets a fearful legacy in motion. His daughter Jeanie Sikorsky sees the Hotel Neversink into its most lucrative era, but also its darkest. Decades later, Asher's descendants grapple with the family's heritage in their own ways: grandson Len fights to keep the failing hotel alive, and great-granddaughter Alice sets out to finally uncover the identity of a killer who has haunted the hotel and family for decades.

Told by an unforgettable chorus of Sikorsky family members—a matriarch, a hotel maid, a traveling comedian, the hotel detective, and many others—*The Hotel Neversink* is the gripping portrait of a Jewish family in the Catskills over the course of a century. With an unerring eye and prose both comic and tragic, Adam O'Fallon Price details one man's struggle for greatness no matter the cost, and a long-held family secret that threatens to undo it all.

"Thoroughly absorbing. . . . Spanning almost a century, *The Hotel Neversink* is a multilayered tale of family, fortune, and fate that grows more eerily compelling with every passing page."

— LING MA, author of *Severance*

"A gripping, atmospheric, heartbreaking, almost-ghost story. Not since Stephen King's Overlook has a hotel hiding a secret been brought to such vivid life."

— LYDIA KIESLING, author of *The Golden State*

"*The Hotel Neversink* is an astounding literary feat—a murder mystery, a ghost story, a century-spanning family history, and a stand-up routine all in one, with dramatic variety to rival any Catskills floor show. Adam O'Fallon Price writes with the blackly comic energy of Philip Roth or Lorrie Moore, packing ten novels' worth of narrative into this compact knish of a book. I wolfed it down in a couple of bites."

— J. ROBERT LENNON, author of *Broken River*

"Like a heyday hotel, this vibrant novel teems with lives, stories, and dark secrets. With its large cast of characters, chilling crime, and haunted locale, *The Hotel Neversink* is a compelling and spooky mystery, but readers will also find it to be a perceptive and exceptionally well-written novel about the transmission of family trauma."

—CHRIS BACHELDER, author of *The Throwback Special*

"Adam O'Fallon Price's *The Hotel Neversink*, like its namesake, contains many rooms: behind this door, a tragic family saga; behind that one, a comic love story. And behind it all, a mystery that keeps you guessing until the very end. Book your stay soon."

—DANIEL WALLACE, author of *Extraordinary Adventures*

THE HOTEL NEVERSINK

Published by Tin House Books, Portland, Oregon

Distributed by W. W. Norton & Company

Library of Congress Cataloging-in-Publication Data

Names: Price, Adam O'Fallon, author.
Title: The hotel neversink / Adam O'Fallon Price.
Description: First U.S. edition. | Portland, Oregon : Tin House Books, 2019.
Identifiers: LCCN 2019005818 | ISBN 9781947793347 (pbk.)
Subjects: | GSAFD: Mystery fiction.
Classification: LCC PS3616.R497 H68 2019 | DDC 813/.6--dc23
LC record available at https://lccn.loc.gov/2019005818

First US Edition 2019
Printed in the USA
Interior design by Diane Chonette

www.tinhouse.com

THE HOTEL NEVERSINK

ADAM O'FALLON PRICE

 TIN HOUSE BOOKS / Portland, Oregon

For Elizabeth, for everything

A History

An article in the *Liberty Leader*, dated January 8, 1931, announced, in the breathless style of the times, "Local Tycoon Dies in Penniless Despair, Foley House to Be Pawned at Auction." The local tycoon was George B. Foley, and Foley House was a symbol of his fortune and misfortune, in equal parts. Foley, born an orphan after killing his destitute mother in childbirth, went on to possess one of those uniquely American success stories, both wildly improbable and somehow preordained by his intelligence and cunning. Starting in the 1880s with a single horse-drawn carriage, he amassed a small fortune in livery and turned that into a large fortune in lumber and construction, personally hiring urchins like himself out of local orphanages and homes like the one he'd run away from at fourteen.

They were put to work building some of the grand homes beginning to dot the Catskills and the Hudson River Valley around the turn of the century, including Foley's own. A cadre of builders was devoted solely to this project, with the ground broken in 1900 and a two-year project timeline. Foley House was situated on the highest point in Liberty—Neversink Hill—a jutting thumb of granite named after the river that wound around its base. It overlooked the town and surrounding environs, and from its apex you could see the distant Suffolk County Boy's Home, where Foley had been instructed in how to suffer and survive.

The mansion was designed to accommodate a sprawling future clan—eight, ten children, perhaps more in his grandest imaginings—with dozens of bedrooms apportioned over three stories. At the time of Foley's architectural design, he was engaged to a local girl, so these plans were not mere fancy. Shortly after their marriage, however, she contracted typhus and died. Construction was paused from 1901 to 1907, during which time Foley mourned and, for both emotional and financial reasons, moved a great deal of his business to New York City. Putting up many of the tenements in what is now the Lower East Side and Chinatown, Foley accrued a vault of lucre and built Foley Two, so-called, this time on Long Island's Gold Coast, with easements and tumbling garden walls shared with families named Vanderbilt and Gould.

That was all they shared with him, this grubby provincial who sullied their parlors and dance floors. Finding himself as lonely rich as he'd been poor, he sold Foley Two and returned to Liberty; but having grown accustomed to the scale of Gold Coast homes, Foley One now seemed paltry, unbefitting his original vision. Despite now being in his forties, he imagined himself the sire of more and more children—twenty, thirty, a biblical number! He put his team back to work, as he too went to work finding a mother for these spectral offspring. It would have been easy enough to scour the poor local towns for a girl, blank-eyed and high-foreheaded and wide-hipped, of a regional type he used to rut around with in his younger years.

But being rich, and—crucially—exposed to the snobbery of the even richer, he had in mind a woman with blood pure enough to cut his own rough sludge.

On a tour of England in 1910, he found her, a woman named Anna Katheridge, the daughter of a baron in arrears, a perplexed gentleman with a country manor coming down around his great red whiskers. These financial woes made it surprisingly easy for the baron to overlook a rich American's lack of pedigree and table manners, and on a third visit, in 1911, the baron granted Foley his daughter's hand in marriage. The wedding date was set, the house neared completion, and Anna was booked for the States in lavish style on the RMS *Titanic*, which set sail from Southampton in April of 1912.

Over the next ten years, building continued with unabated, even accelerated, vigor and urgency. Rooms were added monthly. In 1920, a fourth floor. Turrets and parapets. The building team, many of whom had worked on the house for two decades, were mostly of the opinion that Foley had lost his mind.

Whatever the case, Foley's behavior became increasingly erratic, and he sequestered himself in a large corner bedroom on the third floor, sometimes for days on end. When he emerged, it was usually with a bottle of wine in one hand and a clutch of further plans in the other, instructions to the shrugging foreman and his crew of orphan boys, most of whom now had families and houses of their own. By the 1920s, some of their teenage sons were on payroll, working beside their fathers. And while the crew felt a certain shame in the manifest pointlessness of the house's endless construction . . . well, the usual excuse went that it was Foley's money, and he had plenty of it.

And would forever, so it seemed. Like a wagon released on a slight decline, Foley's business trundled along without guidance, its speed increasing under the weight of its own inexorable success, until it hurtled off the edge of the financial cliff in October 1929. His inability to pay his workers finally brought construction on Foley House to a halt, with a final count of ninety-three individual bedrooms (most with bathrooms en suite), four floors, a fifth subterranean level, three ballrooms, two dining halls, two kitchens, an auditorium, indoor and outdoor swimming pools, an elevator, and countless nooks and crannies—spaces of no discernible use, though that could be said of the entire house, the entire property, for that matter, a craggy sprawl of shadowy pines tumbling down to the river below.

On January 1, 1931, a leap from the roof brought George Foley's dissolution to a halt. With its deceased owner's assets intestate and in massive debt, Foley's Folly, as townspeople referred to it, was put up for auction; to the dismay of many of these same townspeople, it was purchased by a local Jewish innkeeper named Asher Levem Sikorsky. Sikorsky had been looking to expand his hotel, and though the mansion far outstripped his relatively humble ambitions, as well as his available credit, he saw in the sprawling grounds an equally sprawling opportunity. Borrowing and leveraging every penny he could, Sikorsky signed the deed on Foley House in July of 1931. He renamed it after the hill on which it perched, after the river that wound by its base, and after his fondest dream of continued, continuous prosperity: *May Your Fortunes Never Sink!* read the plaque over the front door. In June of that same year, the first guests arrived at the Hotel Neversink, and finally, after three decades, its rooms were filled with children.

1. Jeanie

Yesterday, a boy disappeared from the hotel. Jonah Schoenberg, eight years old. Today, we assembled in the Great Room—dozens of local people, staff, and guests volunteered to help the police search for him. An outpouring of support for the family that eased, a little, the worry everyone in the room felt. The boy's mother and father had asked me to speak, to direct the crowd as usefully as possible. The father was in conference with the police; the mother, white and shaking. I had personally moved them into our Presidential Suite for privacy and comfort, though what, truly, could be of comfort to her at this time?

"Please," I said, "anything you need."

"Find my boy," she said, looking up at me as though I possessed some mystical power to make things right. "Find my boy."

The search party walked down the road to the base of the hill. With the hot sun rising high above us, we spread out and scaled the

hill again, slowly dragging the woods in a long, grim line. I had not
been in this region since we first bought the hotel many years ago.
But the trees bent over us as they did in my memory, thick and shadowy, swaying together as though in secret conference with each other.
After an hour, we regained the Neversink, and on the north lawn I
stopped at my father's grave—a small plot at the tree line, barely
noticeable. The headstone's marble was cool under my hand: *Asher
Levem Sikorsky, b. 1882–d. 1948.* No inscription, because none was
needed: the Neversink was inscription enough. As we pressed on into
the northern woods, calling for the boy, I felt myself somehow calling
for my father, calling for myself. I thought of the long, arduous journey he had made to wind up here. The success he had at last achieved,
and in doing so the price he—all of us—had paid.

My father was not an easy man. But why should people be easy? It is
a cherished lie of the modern world, of America, that everything
should be good and easy, as though comfort were a moral condition
rather than a historical fluke. I already see in my children an abiding,
soft sweetness, as though the country of their birth was, while they
slept, piping them with cream. They cannot know, and should not,
the feeling of true cold, true hunger—hunger so complete and total
that one's mind becomes like a dying candle cupped in a blizzard.
They do not and should not know, yet I silently resent them this
privilege they will never know they possess.

When we still lived on the farm, in Silesia, our father nearly starved
us to death. This was in the midst of the drought that came as a treble
curse so close after the Great War and the subsequent uprisings. It
was as though God, in his wisdom, had heard the prayers of our
people and answered them with a further test to prove that things,

truly, could always be worse. Three years with scarcely a single rain shower had winnowed our farm down to the four of us—my father, my mother, me, and my little brother—and a mule we'd named Zsolt. During planting season my father would trudge out in the blue morning, side by side with Zsolt, and they seemed a single creature, a two-headed beast of burden going about its senseless labor.

For we knew that, even should the rain have come again during the summer, the ground was so parched that the topsoil, and my father's seedlings, would be washed away. And so the rain came at last, and so it was. And in our barren harvest, we knew the winter would kill us at last. Anything but moving from the farm was hopeless. My mother pleaded almost daily with my father, behind the heavy closed door of their bedroom, to let us leave.

"And go where," he might have said, in a version of this conversation I must have overheard dozens of times.

"Wrocław. You know that. We have family there."

"They have a home here that is theirs. They have pride."

"Pride will not feed them."

"But loss of it will starve them." Then the sound of crying and my father's murmurings. "Tut, little chick. I will see us through this. One day, we will have everything anyone could ever want."

For my father had long carried an image in his head, a vision of himself as a figure of importance—someone who would become Someone—if fate would serve him a turn. His mother, my grandmother Perla, had spoiled him, her only son—though their family was poor, he was first to eat, and he ate well. She bought him books and sent him to school, telling him "Asher, work hard and you will bring us great honor and great fortune." How this promise must have nourished him as we bent to our empty bowls, warmed him like the small fire we huddled around after supper, thin as bundles of dry sticks.

It is difficult to explain to someone who has never gone hungry what it is like to not eat for days on end, a week; rather than simply a state of discomfort, the hunger becomes something active, the thing you fill your time with. You can think of nothing else. Joseph and I would play a game called "Restaurant," in which we would pretend it was our birthday and we could have any dinner we wanted. With my brother playing the white-shirted waiter, I would order my feast: piles of roast beef with gravy, potato pancakes, paprika cabbage in the sauce my grandmother used to make, green beans with bits of ham, and kolachkes for dessert. My brother, when it was his turn, simply wanted bread, buttered bread, endless trays of it. This was in the good times, when we had the energy to play. In the bad times, we simply lay in our beds.

I cannot remember when, but at some point, my mother began to obtain our meager sustenance. Once a week, Monday mornings, she would put on her walking boots and heaviest jacket. She disappeared down the path that led to the rutted road, her small figure moving carefully on ground covered by hoarfrost. In the afternoon, she would return with a small bag of game meat and a few vegetables—turnips and carrots, and sometimes potatoes if we were lucky. This bounty she made into the thin, watery stew we ate twice a day. I don't know where she got this food, if it was charity, or if she earned it in some way I refuse to imagine, but I came to realize it was a kind of arrangement between my father and her: if we were to cling to the side of his dusty mountain, she would bring back the sack of food. But it was never discussed. For months this went on, as though my father believed the stew was either arriving through divine providence or else somehow created from the occasional withered plant he foraged, the skeletal rabbit that collapsed in one of his traps.

One night, eating silently, I noticed our father was watching our mother through slitted lids. Hunched, scowling over his bowl, he finally put down his spoon and said, "Where did you get this food?"

To this day, I have no idea what changed that night. Perhaps he really had, in half-starved derangement, convinced himself he'd been providing the food. Perhaps he had discovered what the transaction in the village was. Perhaps he'd always known and could simply not take it any longer. In any case, he was angry, angrier than I'd ever seen him.

"What do you mean?"

"Tell me, Amshe."

"Asher."

"It is not ours," he yelled. He picked up his bowl and hurled it, half-full, across the room, where it shattered against the stone wall. Around the table he went, doing the same to our bowls. Joseph bawled, but I knew better and sat very still, feeling the white flower of hunger rooted deep in the soil of my stomach. Standing by the pile of broken earthenware, the thin gruel already seeping into the floor, he said, "We cannot eat what is not ours."

He pushed into the pantry and emerged with the paltry sack, holding it with a prosecutorial look, as though it proved something. He went out into the freezing cold and into the stable. A minute later, he emerged with Zsolt, the animal blinking past our windows, muzzle twitching as it followed the smell of the sack. The flickering candlelight played along the accordion of its ribs. My father held a gun over his shoulder, a balky musket from the Crimean War, and old Zsolt seemed resigned to whatever was coming. It was as though my father had conferred with the beast and convinced it to accept this as its due. Or perhaps, as one twinned creature, he was doing away with the other half, the part of him that had labored so long and for so little.

I put on my mother's heavy coat and went outside. The wind bit into my bare ankles, but I wanted to see what would happen, though I knew. In the field, my father scattered the bag's contents on the frozen ground. The mule worked its handsome head side to side as it bolted our week's sustenance.

My father said, "Go back inside, Jinya."

"I want to watch."

He gave me the slightest nod, a momentary flash of recognition, then returned his attention to the mule. When Zsolt finished eating, he looked up as though just noticing us, steam rising from his flared nostrils. In a single smooth motion, my father raised the gun to the mule's head and fired. Zsolt dropped to his forelegs in a polite, almost graceful curtsy, and fell sideways, dead.

For the next two months—February and March—we ate only mule. First mule tenderloin (not so very tender), then mule rib, mule sausage, mule shank, sliced mule heart. By the end, we were eating another soup prepared by my mother, this one made from boiled mule hooves. The soapy bitterness of it still sometimes rises into my throat, and I gag a little at the memory. But it took us through the winter, and it remains inside me, the long-ago version of myself that was nourished and sustained by that mule, by my father.

On a bright sunny day in April, with ice melting down the roof in rivulets, my father walked down the muddy path toward town. Two days later, he returned with a pellet-filled squab and the news that he was going to America. Until he sent for us, we were to stay with our mother's sister, in Wrocław. And so we did, living there for two drab years with my aunt Sara and her husband and family. It is strange how gray these days seem in memory—after all, we were no longer constantly hungry and cold—and in contrast, how brightly colored our desolate farm, with its sprays of larkspur, its sprinkles of hollyhock. Despite the best attempts of Sara and her family, their home was not our home, their town not our town, their life not our life. Lying in my cot in the colorless dawn, I stared at the spidery lines of cracked plaster overhead and thought how my father had been right: a proud home that is your own—a person needs this the way they need food, water, air.

I once saw my father make a salesman cry. We were now living in New York, in a Hell's Kitchen tenement filled with other immigrants, many of them Jews, shaken from their European motherlands like water off a soaked dog. No one had any money in our building. No one had any money in Hell's Kitchen. Who knew what the young salesman had done to be assigned this fallow territory? Probably just being young, a crime in itself.

I wasn't so young by then, fifteen or sixteen—barely younger than the spooked boy who stood at the door in a cheap flannel suit, clutching a black display bag.

"Yes?" said my father. I watched from the doorway behind him, fearing for the boy. We had just sat down to dinner, always a sacred time for my father after working his twelve-hour shift, no matter how lean the meals: a little fish, cabbage, a thin-sliced apple drizzled with honey if the week had been a good one.

"Is the lady of the house in?"

"We are dining."

"Sir," said the salesman, "I will make this quick."

"Please."

He launched into a rehearsed speech, barely taking a breath between words, his eyes focused on the wall behind my father's head, where an ornamental plate of my grandmother's hung from a nail. Even at fifteen, I could see the boy was not cut out for this work. "How tired are you, sir, of buying cheap vacuum cleaners for your wife that break after only a few uses? Well, be tired no more, because the Galaxi-CO 900 is here!" The boy clumsily pulled a flailing octopus of tubes out of the case, which he set at his feet. He plugged parts into other parts as he droned his script, no more thinking about the meaning of his words than the dog that barked downstairs day and night. "The Galaxi-CO 900 picks dirt up off any surface: carpet, rug, shag, tile, linoleum, wood, you name it. Its five cleaning attachments will grab particles from even the toughest-to-reach places. Plus, the Galaxi-CO 900 is guaranteed for a lifetime—that's right, a lifetime. Whose lifetime, you ask? Your lifetime. Fifty, sixty, seventy years—it will keep cleaning your carpets. The key is a patented, unbreakable polymer, from which the component pieces are molded—"

"Unbreakable, you say." My father had not moved or said a word throughout the demonstration. I'd shifted to the left, where I could see his face. He was curiously calm, looking at the rowdy machine at his feet, its sweating master bent over it smiling up at him.

"That's right, sir."

"May I?" I looked back at my mother and my brother. It occurs to me now how many of my memories of my father take this form— watching him on a kind of stage in front of me. But perhaps I am seeing him the way he felt—the golden son who'd struggled into his early middle age, forever watched by his family, who still expected him to make good and become rich; though, of course, no one expected this, only himself. And me, secretly. Despite all evidence to the contrary, I had begun by this point to believe he would do some great thing. Paradoxically—like the wide-eyed disciple of some tent revivalist promising a rapture that never came—the longer I saw him strive and fail, the heavier the bags under his eyes grew, the more I believed in his belief.

My father took the main vacuum attachment in his hands and, never taking his eyes from the poor salesman, flexed the tube. The boy stood in wonder, mouth open but lacking any words for what he was watching. My father was not a large man, but he was tough from a lifetime of brutal work, and he had the hidden strength of anger, a deep, plashing reservoir of it fed daily by the sweat he poured at the dry cleaners. His arms shook with the strain, veins popping out on the sides of his high forehead, until, with a crack like our old musket's report, the advanced polymer snapped into two pieces. He handed them back to the salesman and said, "Not unbreakable."

He walked back inside, but I remained. The boy held the pieces and sobbed lightly to himself. He would have to pay for it, I knew. I told him to stay there, and I went to my bedroom, retrieving a dollar I'd put away from my new job cleaning apartments on the Upper West Side. The money was hidden in a library book I'd borrowed, *Little Women*.

"Thank you," he said. "It's not enough, but thank you."

"It's all I have," I said, closing the door. "Go away."

My parents' third child, Abraham, was unexpected. We were still living in the city at the time, but it was in our last apartment, the sweltering basement of a Garment District tenement. My father was in his forties and my mother must have been close to that. From the start, her pregnancy was not seen as a happy development. My father's two previous failed business ventures—a restaurant featuring my mother's cooking (burst water pipes), and a neighborhood dairy (anthrax epidemic)—had sapped our savings, but Joseph and I were both finally of an age when we could contribute to the family income. Our meager earnings were beginning to accrue, and our father had just begun again to dream of an opportunity that might be seized—of something beyond our tiny apartment and the dry cleaners, of something besides wracked muscles and a spasming back and nightly chemical headaches. To start over at their ages with a new, pink baby may have been something of a miracle, but it was not a mazel.

I remember my mother pacing around the apartment, heavy with child in the summer heat, sweating and fanning herself with one of Joseph's comic books. She could not get comfortable, and so she walked an endless circle, wearing a flat tread into the already flattened carpeting. At night, I could hear her moaning through the thin partition my father had erected between our rooms.

On a humid evening, June or July, we whispered in the thick air. Where, I asked Joseph, would the baby go?

"There's a garbage chute just down the hall."

"For shame."

"I'm joking."

"Still."

"It's easier for you, Jean. You're sixteen, you can move out now if you want."

"Quit school?"

"I'm just saying, you're going to leave, and the baby will be here, and Papa will be even more tired and angry."

"I'm not leaving, don't worry."

I had thought about leaving, in fact—of quitting school and moving far away. But as it turned out, a few months after my mother delivered Abe, my father delivered us to Liberty. With his scanty savings, a loan from our Uncle Moishe, and a promissory note to the seller set at outlandish interest, he'd bought a farmhouse in Liberty, sight unseen. The city was killing him, and in desperation, he'd thought we could go back to farming, perhaps re-create that winter in Silesia when we nearly starved to death. We packed our belongings into a truck and drove north on Route 17.

As soon as we arrived, it was clear the mistake he'd made. The ground was rocky and ash dry, not farming soil. You might get some potatoes to take, but we knew it would be impossible to grow anything of substance. He was as desolate as the ground, and for three days I thought he might either commit suicide or walk off into the deep woods surrounding the barren farm, never to be seen or heard from again. What would we do? In my parents' bedroom down the long and drafty hall, Abe wailed and sobbed, giving voice to our misery.

It seems impossible, looking back, that a baby could cry without ceasing, but in my memory, he did. His cries were the soundtrack to our struggle that spring, as we sold our remaining possessions and searched high and low for any kind of employment. My mother found work cooking in a diner in Halstead, and my father did manual labor where he could. All the while, Abe bellowed relentlessly, his face a pink, contorted agony.

My mother began to worry there was something wrong with him. *Just colic,* was the terse diagnosis of a local doctor whom I talked into a charity examination (though I believe it was Abe's shrieks in the waiting room that got us into his office). Just colic, I told my mother with a hopeful smile, though I didn't believe it myself. We put him in the back room of the house, thinking he might cry it out of himself, but he kept on, undeterred.

I knew my parents considered him bad luck. Just when they'd been getting back on their feet again, along he comes, and with him the colossal, howling error of the farm. It wasn't fair, of course—our family had endured ten years of ill fortune before Abe came along—but I still knew they regarded him as a burden and a bad omen. A rabbi was summoned, and he lent credence to this belief. The boy, he said, was *tum'ah*, ritually impure. In his impurity, he'd brought our family to a state of *tumei*, as though we'd jointly contracted a fever.

"What can we do?" asked my mother.

"There is nothing to do," said the rabbi, still in his long coat and fur collar, so deftly had he diagnosed Abe's illness. "Endure it, and be flattered. After all, He does not test those He does not love."

Ironically, it was shortly after this that we had the stroke of luck that changed my family's fortune forever, though it did not seem that Abe was credited with this good turn. It was in early June. A family of five who had come up from the city found themselves in trouble when all of the local hotels were booked. Our farm was visible on a hill near the main road, and they inquired, thinking we might be a summer lodge. We had never considered such a thing, but my parents eagerly agreed, and we worked quickly to make them comfortable— Joseph and I prepared the bedrooms, putting down clean sheets and turning around family photos. My father acted as a sort of impromptu concierge, asking where they were visiting while in Liberty, suggesting the best hiking and swimming spots as though he'd lived there his entire life rather than a few months. My mother turned what must have been the last of our household provisions into a memorable feast, an act of culinary generosity borne, I knew, of utter desperation. No terms of the stay had been negotiated. No agreement had been drawn up. If they had not felt satisfied, they might have turned and left, or departed the next day without paying us a dime.

But how we ate that night!

Sauerbraten with brown gravy, lokshen kugel, borscht with sour cream, buttery rolls, stuffed peppers and mushrooms, and fried artichokes! And for dessert, apple strudel drizzled with honey! It was as though my most extravagant childhood session of Restaurant had been wished into reality. The guests sat around the main table, stunned. They had never eaten such food, the father said. They would soon return, the mother said. They would tell others of the hospitality they'd stumbled onto here. Please do, said my father, with an anxious look—I knew he was wondering if they planned on paying, and how much. In the postprandial silence, Abe's muffled cries were just audible from the root cellar, where he'd been stashed in a quilted basket. I went down and held him there in the dark. Tut, little chick, I said, perhaps our fortunes are changing.

The next morning, they did pay, and paid well. It was more money than we'd even hoped: ten dollars—enough to last us the month. Not only that, but they returned in July and brought another family with them. And three more groups came in August, curious about the Sikorsky Inn, as it was becoming known.

That was a heady year. My father brimmed with pride as we made improvements to the house, putting in an icebox and modern bathroom. My mother continued cooking and even hired a helper up from Monticello, a Polish émigré named Anja who spoke not a word of English. My brother arranged for various "entertainments," put on at eight in the large living room, or outside in the barn when the weather was nice. He was an adequate juggler, very good at telling jokes, and he also had a knack for finding strange local "talent" to perform for free, including a former college gymnast who could twist her body like challah and an older gentleman who'd trained his terriers to somersault over each other's backs. For my part, I did whatever was needed, whatever my father asked. Often this involved negotiating deals with companies, finding people who would fix things for cheap or for future payment. I came to know almost everyone in the greater Liberty area, developed friendships and trust, always paying our workers as quickly and fairly as possible. I oversaw operations of the Sikorsky Inn, and my father referred to me as the manager, although none of us had official titles. But I did know that I was the one he counted on to make things run as smoothly as possible.

As the business grew larger and larger and our time grew scarcer and scarcer, this responsibility also included looking after Abe. My father had become icy toward him, would leave the boy howling for hours in his crib without paying him the least attention. My mother seemed to lack maternal feeling—she would hold him at times, but only for a few moments before setting him down again. It seemed that to my parents, Abe had gone from being bad luck to being an emblem of our former misery, one that threatened to pull them back to misfortune from a very new and precarious prosperity. The fears had a practical source as well—after all, guests came to the inn for relaxation and pleasure, not to be confronted with a sick, screaming child.

In December, when the house was completely free of guests, I spent most of my money calling a doctor down from Albany. He removed his hat and scarf and spent an hour examining Abe, turning the child over, poking and prodding with a resolute look through the ever-mounting noise. Finally, he summoned my parents and me into the living room and said, "He has spinal stenosis. It's causing him great pain, hence the crying." He explained the condition over the next few minutes.

"But what shall we do?" said my mother, echoing her question last time.

"There are operations that can be done. But they are expensive and not guaranteed to work. I can refer you to a specialist." He wrote a name and number down on a small sheet of paper he pulled from his black leather satchel.

"How much," said my father.

The doctor looked at him with unmistakable distaste. Or perhaps it seemed unmistakable to me because I felt it as well. It would cost what it cost! The doctor said, "Well, I'm not an expert. But several hundred, certainly. Maybe more, including medication and surgical braces, that kind of thing."

"A thousand? Two?"

The doctor shrugged and closed his satchel. I thanked him at the door, and he nodded gravely, as though acknowledging what Abe was up against. After the doctor left, there was a great deal of crying and consternation, and not just on Abe's part. My mother stared darkly down at the crib. Looking at her, I became frightened. My parents believed in dybbuks, in curses and omens and hauntings. And they grew up in a time when crippled babies were often carried off into the woods. So I was not surprised the next day when my father asked me, over tea, to take the boy to the state hospital a county over and leave him.

"No," I said. I suppose, looking back, that I was—am—soft compared to my parents, just as my children are compared to me.

"Jinya, you must. I cannot, your mother will not."

"Then do not."

"The boy must go. He is a curse."

"He is not a curse," I said loudly, almost yelling. I cannot remember ever raising my voice to my father, before or after. More quietly, I added, "He is a sick little boy."

"Jean. I believe the rabbi's verdict is correct. But, okay, even if the boy is not a curse, he is beyond our helping. Perhaps he is not beyond the state's help."

"Please, Papa. We have money, we can make more. Do not give him up. It is a sin."

"Helping your family can never be a sin. We cannot let Abraham ruin us. It is what must be done."

So I went. In the car—an old Ford my father had recently acquired from a local farmer—Abe lay beside me on a blanket. Out the window, he stared with a dark and level gaze at the pine trees, the gray sky, a burst of swallows rising into the air like smoke. For the first time in weeks he was silent, and it almost seemed that, having been exiled from the family, he was finally satisfied. *At last*, I thought, *at last you shush*. I thought, too, about what my father had not said, could not say—that two thousand dollars was too much to spend on a child he hadn't wanted in the first place. That if Abraham was the price he had to pay to ensure the Sikorsky Inn continued flourishing and expanding, so be it.

I knew it was a sin, but I did as my father asked, leaving the boy in a hamper on the steps of the county hospital. I taped a note to the blanket, explaining his condition. I kissed him once and drove away.

My father bought Foley House three years later, in 1931, and renamed it the Hotel Neversink. Over the next two decades, the business thrived to a degree that I think surprised even him. Nineteen forty-two marked the first year with a million dollars in profit, and still we continued growing. Professional athletes, entertainers, heads of state have lain their heads on our pillows. The Presidential Suite was renamed as such after Mr. Truman came for a visit. He signed the guestbook, took tea in the library, ate my mother's loshen kugel with gusto. He assured us he would return.

Three years ago, my father told me he was entrusting the Neversink to me. As his health declined, I had taken over daily operations, had even begun making financial decisions with his tacit approval. For instance, I had been the one to recognize the guests' desire for a golf course, to expense the endeavor with our accountant, to determine it was in our long-term benefit, to hire the contractor and oversee the project, which continues today outside my office window. My brother Joseph moved to New York many years ago to pursue his comedy career, though we still often see him, on his tours through the Catskills. Nonetheless, it took me a little by surprise when my father made it official.

"Jinya," he said, "this is yours." We were sitting in the dayroom, an obscure little nook on the far side of the wraparound porch, his favorite place in the hotel. He wore a tartan blanket over his frail legs, which made him look a bit like General Sternwood in *The Big Sleep*, a film that had come out the year before, finally making its way to the Liberty Odeon.

"Not for a long time."

"Don't be a fool."

"I'm not a fool—"

"I know, and this is why I'm entrusting the hotel to you."

We sat in silence and I helplessly observed how the cancer, and the treatments for it, had sapped him. The great arms that had once snapped the vacuum tube were withered and spotted with bruises that did not heal, purple welts beneath the papery skin. In the cold morning light he was oddly translucent, like a jellyfish. If he'd taken off his shirt, could I have seen his heart beating in that thin chest?

"Thank you," I said, finally.

"It is nothing for thanks. You are like me, that is all." I knew I was, but it was strange to hear. "You are tough and proud. And you will do whatever it takes for this business to continue growing, for our family to prosper. Your brother has the far better deal."

"Does he?"

"Oh, yes," my father said. He coughed extensively, leaned forward to open the door, and spat out into the green, manicured expanse. "He is a fool. He is happy."

As we searched for the Schoenberg boy, I was besieged by these memories. And I could not help but wonder if this was divine punishment for giving Abraham up. Perhaps my father was right, and Abe truly was a curse from God. When I returned in last light with the distraught search party, the hotel felt vacant, abandoned. No guests checking in or checking out, no noise from the recreation or dining rooms, no sounds of distant splashing coming through the high walls of the natatorium, no old men drinking tea in the parlor—nothing. Our security man, Saul Javits, tipped his hat gravely at me as we crossed each other's path beneath the grand staircase, his face etched with the fearful sorrow I felt on my own.

I sat on a hall chair to steady myself as I thought again of my father and his dying wish to be buried beside this place he had built, where he had at last found the success that had eluded him for so long. Would it now be taken from him?

In the empty dining room, I traced a finger on the cool brass rail running its perimeter. Overhead, the enormous iron chandelier my father had salvaged from a distant estate sale hung with fantastic weight. I could see the team of men he assembled—my uncle and three others, Joseph running around their legs—hoisting it on temporary scaffolding, my father below them pointing and nodding at his own good judgment.

A faint and familiar bitter taste had filled my mouth—mule hoof, I realized, brought back by the day's remembrances. I went behind the bar, poured cherry wine into a cup, swished and spat in the sink. Another sip I took and swallowed, raising my cup to the chandelier. No, I thought—all of this will not be for nothing. As Zsolt gave his life for our family, my father gave his life to this place, willing it into existence and doing what was necessary for it to succeed. As will I. The children will grow up here. Soft as cream.

2. Leonard

1950

You'll never find me here, thinks the boy. He is hidden, could not be more hidden. Even with his eyes wide open, it is black all around, here in his perfect hiding place the man told him about.

The kid seeking him, his new friend Lenny, was supposed to count to a thousand—those were the rules they made earlier, after playing in the pool and the hot grass of the hotel's lawn. They were bored, poking an anthill with sticks, watching the tiny creatures swarm with rage. It was the boy's idea, hide-and-seek—his favorite game—on a grand scale. Lenny seemed doubtful, but the boy said it'll be fun, pointing out Lenny's advantage as the son of the hotel owners. You know every inch of the building, he said, to which Lenny proudly assented. Stay out here and I'll hide. Count to a thousand.

He hasn't gotten to play hide-and-seek for quite some time. His sister is getting older and has expressed a preference not to play "baby games," but also, the Boston apartment where the boy and his family moved two years ago is too small. He shares a room with his sister. Everyone stands in the hall waiting on the tiny bathroom, tiny even to him. Even if you wanted to, there's nowhere to wedge yourself while the other person counts, nowhere you can escape to. Their previous home, in Worcester, was a maze of rooms, including a musty basement and a storage space under the kitchen floor, accessible by attaching a small rope to the pull and yanking upward. He would sometimes stay there for hours, cozy in his small, secret place—especially when his father was angry and yelling; were it not for his mother's beseeching calls, he could have stayed there all day. Like his namesake, deep in the whale's gullet.

He roved the hotel, looking for a perfect spot. He hid first beneath the overhang of a dining room tablecloth, only to be shooed out by a peevish busboy. Upstairs were just rooms, locked doors. Back downstairs, most places seemed off-limits to children playing games: the ballroom, currently under renovation; the lobby, full of guests checking in; the riotous pool area, packed with families, his own among them. Fewer secret places than he would have thought in this vast building. He sneaked outside to spy Lenny kneeling on the hill, eyes still dutifully covered by his hands.

Around the hotel he went, casting an appraising eye at the long hedges that ran alongside the hotel walls (too obvious), a dense patch of shrubbery between buildings (too painful to climb into), and the dark woods past the green, sloping lawn (not in the spirit of the game, and a bit scary). Turning to run back inside, he was surprised to find someone standing behind him. A man. The sun floated behind his head like a halo, and the boy couldn't quite see his face. In a quiet voice, the man said, "What are you doing?"

"Nothing."

"Are you playing a game?"

The boy felt slightly embarrassed, childish, when he said, "Hide-and-seek."

"Oh, I like that game. Are you hiding or seeking?"

"Hiding."

"Hiding is the best fun," the man said, and when he smiled, the light glinted off white teeth. "I know a good place."

He whispered in the boy's ear, and the boy nodded: a good hiding place, indeed.

That was a while ago—feels like thirty minutes, though he knows it's probably just five or ten. He imagines Lenny walking through the hotel, poking into hampers, looking behind plants, peering under chairs. The thought gives him a giddy thrill, and he hopes Lenny never finds him. There is nothing like being the little thing inside the big thing—he thinks again of hiding in that small cellar, the musty guts of the beast. He would be happy to be here all day, in the cool dark, inside the inside. He would be happy to hide here forever. So he is disappointed when the door opens, a little mad that Lenny has found him so easily. But a light comes on, a yellowy light that seems to radiate from the figure in the door, and the boy sees it is not Lenny.

Leonard Sikorsky, his mother called, and he knew he was in trouble. He was "Lenny" most of the time, and "Len" when she was sad and stroking his hair, but "Leonard" was saved for when he'd done something wrong, forgotten a chore as he so often did. He'd been playing hide-and-seek, looking for the boy—Jonah—in a copse of firs near the pool area, when he heard his mother calling for him. Inside, he was sent with a smack on the butt to help his bubbe Amshe in the kitchen, peeling potatoes for two tortuous hours as the brilliant day faded through the window. After dinner he did his homework, listened to a Dodgers game crackling through on the radio, and went to bed. He'd completely forgotten about Jonah.

Now, sitting in the wooden chair, in the corner of his mother's office, Lenny fidgets with his hands as he guiltily recounts the previous day. The detective—a real police detective with the badge and hat and everything—nods at Mr. Javits, the hotel detective, who wears a gray suit and looks a little like Len's own father. Mr. Javits says, "Did you see the boy, Jonah, again?"

"No. I forgot we were playing. Do you think he's still there?"

"Where?"

"Wherever he was hiding."

Mr. Javits pats him gently on the back. "Lenny, how long would you wait if you were Jonah? Would you still be hiding the next day? Wouldn't you get hungry at some point?"

"Yeah, I guess."

The real detective shifts in his chair and clears his throat. "Had you seen him before?"

"I met him the day before yesterday. On Wednesday. He told me they're from—" Lenny thinks hard for a moment, reaching for the complicated word. "Massachusetts."

"We know," says the detective. He makes a little note in his book, with a bored expression that reminds Lenny of how he feels in class sometimes, when he wants to be on the playground.

Mr. Javits says, "That's good, though, Lenny, good memory."

They ask him a few more questions, and he's set free to join the search party. A party: it sounds fun, though he knows it's all about Jonah's disappearance, which is not fun. Still, it doesn't scare him. He thinks Jonah just left. Jonah was a strange, nervous boy, and Lenny has no problem imagining him growing bored waiting to be found, walking down the hill, down the road into town . . . Here, his imagination fails him, having never been past town: the hardware store, the five-and-dime, the soda shop where his father sometimes takes him for a treat—past that, is there a forest? Maybe a wolf got him! Rrrahwr! He scampers down the second-floor hall and lies on his belly, peering between the bars of the thick wooden banister to spy on the scene below.

In the Great Hall, so-called, a crowd has gathered and continues growing. Len's father, Henry, moves here and there, talking to cops and gesturing at the throng: hotel guests and employees, and residents of Liberty, fed for free by Amshe, having been summoned by Len's mother, who put out word of a missing boy this morning. The crowd, perhaps a hundred people extending, unseen, into the lobby, mills with the hesitating expectancy given off by large groups.

Everyone seems to be there, and Lenny makes a game of picking out the familiar faces. Uncle Joey, up from the city, always on the verge of raucous laughter, now grim and silent in the corner. Sander Levin, the young bartender, whom Lenny has only ever seen in his white tuxedo jacket, naked-looking in short sleeves. Lenny's older brother, Ezra, who winds his way quickly through the room and disappears, upset at the interruption in his summer bird-watching routine. The custodian, Michael, and even a couple of the dark-eyed maids, stand at the edge of the group, and Lenny wonders who's going to work at the hotel that day. Anyone?

The policeman who'd asked him questions exits the office and walks down the stairs to the landing, eleven stairs from the bottom, Lenny knows, having counted them all before, having made games of jumping down two, three at a time. Lenny's mother walks through the crowd and climbs the stairs to stand by the cop. She wears a dress with yellow flowers on it and a sad look, sadder than he's ever seen. The officer murmurs something to her and takes a step back, hands clasped at his waist. The man is waiting for her to take charge—everyone looks up to his mother, even the police. She raises her arm, and the crowd grows quiet.

"Hello, I'm Jeanie Sikorsky. Thank you for coming today, and for taking the time out of your weekend to assist us with this matter. I speak here for myself and also on behalf of the Schoenbergs, who are currently working with the police to provide information. Yesterday afternoon, around one thirty, their son, Jonah, went missing from the hotel grounds. He was last seen playing on the north lawn, about a hundred feet from the outdoor pool. Today, we are going to sweep the grounds, starting at the south entrance located down on Onawanda Road, head up the hill to the hotel, then move north to the river and surrounding forest. This is Officer Bates. He will be in charge of the search, so if you have any questions, he can assist you."

The officer nods, and Lenny's mother looks down at all of them, the same way she sometimes does at him—not disappointed, but conveying the sense that she knows he can do better, which usually makes him want to. She says, "Let's go find Jonah."

The crowd voices its approval in a loud, massy mumble. Lenny hurries down the stairs, and within five minutes everyone is walking down the long drive to the base of the hill on which the Neversink sits. He walks beside his mother, though it's somewhat difficult to stay by her in the crush; everyone wants to be near her, seems promoted by her presence. Even Lenny does, when she reaches down and squeezes his hand. Despite the occasion for the search, he feels happy, happy to be here with her on this strange day.

After a few minutes he asks his mother, "What do you think happened to him?"

"I don't know."

"But we'll find him."

She looks down at him, her lips knitted up tight. "I hope so."

"But where could he have gone?"

"That's what we're trying to find out."

"But," he protests, pushing a thin, sappy branch from his face as they walk between two gnarled pines, "why would he run away from the hotel?"

His mother expels a breath. "He didn't run away, Leonard. We think somebody took him."

They trudge on through the woods, up the slow, sloping hill, over a blanket of pine needles, between trees, down little dips and around fallen logs, through the humid air, nearer and nearer to the Neversink, and Lenny thinks about Jonah. He hadn't considered that the boy could have been taken. How could that be? Who would do that, and why? That the boy isn't here means he is somewhere else, taken there by someone. But who would do that? Like the sounds of insects and animals skittering close but unseen in the brush, he senses there is something about the boy's disappearance he doesn't understand. Someone bad has taken Jonah; that is enough.

As he walks, he imagines ogres and monsters, a nameless thing that steals and devours little boys. He imagines being Jonah, what he might have felt, and a wave of guilt once again overtakes him—it was his fault for not finding the boy, for not seeking! He races forward with a ragged intensity, gets too far ahead of the group and is spooked by the soft rustle of footsteps in wet leaves. What if he's next? He runs back and looks up at his mother's face, and somehow he knows they won't find Jonah. Overwhelmed with these thoughts, a hot lethargy descends on him. When they're in the vicinity of the Neversink, he asks his mother if he can please go home and rest. She nods, and he feels her watching as he crosses the north lawn to their house, what everyone calls the cottage. Now, he watches her from the kitchen window, and when his she disappears over the crest of the hill, he hurries back across the grass to the hotel. Marveling again at the emptiness and quiet, he hurries to the bar for his real prize: one of the bottles of lemonade that Sander stashes deep in the cooler, away from the pilfering fingers of children. But there are no bottles, just a condensed puddle of water in the usual spot. He leaves the bar and clomps down the service stairs to the basement, to dry goods, where the extra bottles are kept.

The room is dark and cool, a mass of shelves surrounded by the old mortar and brickwork of the building's foundations. He grabs a lemonade off the bottom shelf, but it slips from his hand and rolls onto the floor. He picks it up, and in front of him is Jonah Schoenberg.

"Hi," says Jonah.

He looks the same as he did the day before, wearing the same clothes—striped T-shirt, shorts, sneakers. His brown hair is mussed, falling over one eye. A scrape on his knee glistens black in the room's dull yellow light. Lenny says, "Everyone's looking for you."

"I know, I'm hiding."

"So you've been down here the whole time?"

"Yes," he laughs, "you finally found me!"

"I'm sorry it took so long."

"It's okay, I like it here."

"Everyone is worried."

"My father's only worried about money."

Lenny's head throbs, and he feels slightly queasy. In his vision, the room seems to swell and contract, distorting in sections the way the world outside does when you look at it through the thick, uneven glass of the hotel synagogue's windows. He knows he should be happy at finding the lost boy, but something seems wrong. "Why'd you stay down here?"

The boy shakes his head, and Lenny can't tell if he doesn't know or is keeping it a secret. "Well, anyway," Lenny says, grabbing another bottle of lemonade for Jonah, "come on. Let's go upstairs."

"This is where I live now."

"What about your parents?"

He shrugs and looks down at his feet. "They still have my sister."

"What will you do here?"

"I'm happy." The boy looks up again, smiling. "I get to watch everyone. I ride the elevator up and down, look in all the rooms. It's fun."

"I don't feel so good," says Lenny. "I have to go."

"I'll be here."

Pushing out of the room and back down the hall, shivering his way through the basement exit, a nauseating pain has encircled Lenny's head, and he feels he might throw up. To keep his gorge down, he bolts half of the foaming, sour lemonade in one greedy swallow. Outside, under the white sun, it rushes back out of his mouth in a cloying spume. The day's wet heat somehow does not abate the chills running through him, and his mind is cloudy, confused. It seems to him that this has already happened, that he's remembering the lemonade, Jonah, even the humid air through which he stumbles. Everything is shimmering and changing in size, and, again, it's like he's looking at something through heavy glass, or, perhaps, like something is looking at him.

When he wakes, he's in his mother's bed. She sits beside him, mopping his brow with a cool, damp cloth. He tells her that he found the boy. "Where?" she asks.

"In the basement. He's hiding."

"You've had a bad dream."

"It was a good dream."

Three days later, the fever breaks, and after another day, he is strong enough to get out of bed. The doctor comes that morning, pronounces him on the mend. Fit as a mildly feverish fiddle. Lenny's mother and father go to work at the hotel, and Ezra wanders off with his binoculars and notepad. Len puts on clothes, the fresh air bracing on his bare chest after days spent beneath blankets. Across the hot grass of the hill he walks, across the sloping north lawn where he last saw Jonah. Entering through the service doors, he again walks the long, cool hall of the basement. The storage room is empty, save for the dry goods it contains, and he isn't sure if he's pleased or disappointed; the thought of the boy living down here now had been both sad and a comfort. He'd been hoping it wasn't just a dream—he'd wanted to speak to Jonah more.

In the lobby, his mother stands talking to the custodian, Michael— short, shy Michael, a Gentile hire from the sticks who has always been kind to Lenny. His mother nods as she moves on, attending to other matters. Michael holds a toolbox in one hand and smiles through a soft beard of blond down. "Hey, Lenny," he says. "Heard you've been under the weather."

"I'm better now."

"Good."

"Did they ever find him?"

"The boy? No. It's a horrible thing."

"Where do you think he went?"

"I think someone took him, someone evil."

"It's my fault. I was supposed to find him, and I didn't."

"Oh, Lenny, no. Listen." Michael sighs and puts down his toolbox. He sits on it with his elbows on his legs, so that he's looking directly into Lenny's eyes, and Lenny knows that the man has something important to tell him. "This wasn't your fault. Do you know Ecclesiastes?"

"Not really." The hotel rabbi had read passages from it recently, but Lenny had paid no attention.

Michael casts his eyes down, seeming to search in his mind for the words. "It says, *As fish are caught in a cruel net, or birds are taken in a snare, so people are trapped by evil times that fall unexpectedly upon them.* What that means is that sometimes people are just unlucky. It's the way of the world. Me, I'm not so lucky, though working here is a great blessing." He gestures at the huge lobby, looking up its high, arched ceiling, the physical dimensions illustrating the enormity of his fortune.

"And I was lucky?"

"Lenny, you are a Sikorsky. You are lucky, one of the lucky ones. Never forget it."

Michael ruffles Lenny's hair and heads to the pool, and Lenny moves through the Great Hall. On aching legs, he climbs the main staircase to the second floor and lies on his belly, surveying the scene below as he had three days before.

Three days before seems like an eternity. Three days before, he'd seen the room with a child's eyes, imagining a wolf had taken the boy. Now he knows it could be anyone, perhaps even one of the guests below. The range of human experience, human destiny, is vast and mysterious. Michael's words return to him, and he thinks about himself and Jonah, two boys playing a game they didn't know they were playing: the one hiding meant for unknown sorrows, the one seeking meant for success and happiness. The lucky ones, yes. He'd always seen the Neversink as home, never understood it for what it was: a birthright.

Caught up in this moment of lordly awakening, he hardly notices the dark-eyed maid, a distant cousin, climbing the stairs behind him. At her muttered hello, he turns and registers the pressed black-and-white uniform, the pail of cleaning supplies. "Hi, Hannah." She scurries on, late, sixty rooms to clean and her day just beginning.

3. Hannah

1955

The maid stole something every day. It didn't matter what it was. It was usually something small and insignificant that would never be missed—for example, a penny from a nightstand covered in loose change, or an extra button pulled from the hem of a cardigan flung carelessly over the back of a chair. On rare occasions, it might be something big enough to be noticed; one time she'd stolen a pair of expensive yellow high heels still in their price-tagged shoe box, a brazen act of thievery that resulted in a staff meeting during which the head of housekeeping spat and swore and interrogated the entire janitoriat in pidgin Polski. It could be something she needed, but it usually wasn't. It could be anything at all: the important thing was that she stole something, and that she did so every day.

She didn't understand why it was important. At night, lying in her cot in the drafty garage apartment, listening to her son, Isaac, snore, it seemed, in fact, important to stop. She imagined being caught, fired, perhaps thrown in jail. Isaac, presently separated from her by a thin pasteboard partition, would be separated from her by prison bars and foster care. Her nightmares took the form of gray institutions, unclimb-able walls enclosing endless queues with a faceless bureaucrat at the end. During the day, too, she suffered for this habit, this vice, or what-ever it was—a low-level, febrile guilt like a persistent cold she couldn't shake. In a state of icy resolve, she sometimes managed to get through most of the day without touching or taking anything. But as the clock edged toward five, as the remaining rooms on her list dwindled to four, three, two, she would thaw and begin idling in front of wristwatches, children's yarmulkes, half-eaten lunches saved for later on the window-sill. She might run her finger up and down the length of a toothbrush angled in a glass by the sink, as though it were a lover's smooth skin; she might drop it in the front pocket of her white cleaning smock, or she might leave it and move on to some other object. Everything was up for grabs; anything was possible. If she made it to the last room, then the last room would be the scene of the crime. Not taking something was unthinkable by that point. Into her uniform's marsupial pouch the item would go—a small, suckling entity of shame and relief.

If the thing she took was the right kind of thing, she would give it to Isaac. Isaac was eight and frail from polio, convalescing at home for the last six months, and these things—a little metal soldier, a yo-yo, a piece of cherry bubblegum, a cat's-eye marble—both bright-ened his day and brought a rumor of the outside world. On these days, she told herself she was doing it for him, that he needed these things, although this was patently not the case. Isaac did not need, for example, a racy paperback book entitled *The Price of Salt*, written by someone named Claire Morgan (she'd flipped through it to a scene of such deviant filth that she slammed the book shut and glanced

shame-faced at her son, momentarily fearing he could read her mind).
He also did not need, of course, a pair of yellow high heels, size six.
Neither did she, for that matter, with her barge-like peasant feet, feet
built for being stood on all day, not for twirling across the dance floor
as she'd seen guests do on nights when she worked late, lurking in the
shadows beneath the ballroom stairwell and thrilling to the sight of
them in their evening gowns and finery, their almost inhuman ele-
gance as they danced—on one vivid and memorable occasion, a
blonde girl in sequins who spun on her axis like a top. These shoes,
and many other useless items, she kept in the small utility closet near
the front door. A purgatorial space, for while she had no use for most
of these things, she could not throw them away, either.

Why did she do it? Did she hate the guests? No. Though she envied
them sometimes, it was true—the dancing girl, for instance, or the
newly married couple at whose banquet reception she'd worked scul-
lery, whose untouched canapés, congealed on a dirty plate, nonetheless tasted better than anything she'd ever eaten—she didn't hate
them. Most of them were very nice; some were incredibly generous.
The Steinbachers, who came every fall and brought presents for the
employees' children—for Isaac, a brilliant white baseball that sat
untouched on his dresser, a promise of healthier future days. Or the
bachelor who'd stayed by himself during the week of summer mixers
that Mr. Cohen ran. She'd never met him, the bachelor, yet when he
checked out with the room in disarray, there was a lovely note thanking her for cleaning up his mess and a ten-dollar tip. From him, she'd
stolen a Polaroid picture of a young, dark-eyed woman grinning
under a white shadbush in the hotel courtyard.

That night she'd lain the photograph on her dining room table and
allowed the woman to speak up at her in judgment. You are a

monster, said the woman. There is something wrong with you. Who
does a thing like this? The woman went on with her chastisement for
a while, until the maid took her to the closet and dropped her on top
of the other stuff. Her voice came through the door but grew quieter
as the night went on, and by the following night, it had become muffled, inaudible.

And so it had gone for what seemed like forever, a circle of satisfaction and guilt so reliable that it became a hateful comfort. And it
might have continued forever had it not been for Mrs. Gerson and her
brooch.

The Gersons were a fairly unexceptional family. The maid had idly
observed them upon their arrival as she vacuumed the length of the
third-floor hallway. The father seemed like a type: late forties, slightly
stooped by the punishing mundanity of his work life, clearly some
sort of clerical job, as he was too reedy for manual labor and too timid
for management or sales. The children were unremarkable, too: an
older girl already drawing away from the family, buffered by an invisible wall of brooding solitude; a younger boy who yelled with excitement at nearly everything that happened in this new, fascinating
place.

The mother, however, was not unexceptional. For one thing, she
was enormous. Not just fat, though she was, with ankles and wrists
the size of most people's arms and legs; advancing distantly down the
hallway, her chest brought to mind a World War II newsreel clip of a
battleship's prow cutting though the mist. But she was also the tallest
woman the maid had ever seen, her low heels and blonde bouffant
putting her well over six feet. She wore a pale-yellow and somewhat
shapeless dress, to which she'd pinned a startling brooch. It was red,
a sparkling cherry that caught the light of each antique sconce the

woman passed. The flashing red light was like a signal, a code aimed at the maid's weary brain, receptive from seven hours of cleaning. She found she'd stopped vacuuming, was simply standing there in a dull trance, watching Mrs. Gerson until she turned into their room, her family in tow like little vessels caught in a crashing wake.

The maid didn't usually prize individual objects, but she knew she would steal the brooch, and two days later, when the Gersons were down at the pool, she did. She found it in a wooden jewelry box left carelessly by the TV—it was better to think it a careless act than one borne of a naïve trust she was presently violating. She lifted it out and held it in both hands, feeling the weight. It winked in the light like a living thing, a thing that somehow knew her mind and her soul, that understood and forgave her weakness, this trespass. She dropped it in her pocket and looked once more at herself in the mirror, and she felt a tremendous relief, thinking yes, this is the last time, this is the last thing. Now I can stop.

The door opened.

Mrs. Gerson entered, though it seemed to the maid as though the entire room shifted sideways and expanded to accommodate the woman's presence. With the survival instinct of a small animal, the maid froze in place, though she couldn't help glancing at the jewelry box with the foolish hope she'd closed it. She hadn't.

After a long pause, Mrs. Gerson shut the door. She said, "Do you like that?"

"What?"

"Don't be stupid—the brooch you were stealing."

"I wasn't."

"Oh no?"

"I *wasn't*." She couldn't think of anything else to say.

The room slid closer to Mrs. Gerson. The woman pulled off the terry-cloth gown she wore and dropped it on the bed. The one-piece swimsuit she wore was ruffled at the hips and crowned her chest with a an outsized, girlish bow. "It's not worth anything, that's the sad part. Just cheap costume jewelry. I wouldn't leave anything valuable out."

"I'm sorry." The maid tried to edge around her next to the TV, but a minute shift in the woman's bulk to the left blocked this path of egress.

"Could you have thought I wouldn't notice? What would happen if I reported this?"

"I would be fired."

"If not worse."

"Yes. Please don't tell."

"Why shouldn't I?" The maid registered the woman's towering anger now, and how the woman controlled it by assuming a contemplative air, a livid thoughtfulness that felt more dangerous than simple rage.

"My son, Isaac. I don't know what I'd do."

"How old is he?"

"Eight. And sick. He has polio."

"Cue the violins. So did our president, but Eleanor didn't go around stealing jewelry, at least not that I'm aware. Do you think this gives you the right to steal?"

"No, I don't." She began to cry.

Mrs. Gerson sighed. "I'm not going to tell. I don't want your being fired on my conscience." The maid stood very still, like a small child waiting for punishment to be dispensed. It seemed that if she made herself very still and very small, the enormous woman might forget her and go on with her enormous life.

"What's your name?" said Mrs. Gerson.

"Hannah," said the maid. It felt inappropriate saying it to a guest.

"Hannah what?"

"Hannah Kohl."

"Hannah Kohl. It's a pretty name. My name's Annette. Sounds like Hannah, though I like yours better. Annette Gerson."

"I know."

"Oh?"

"I asked at the desk. I was curious. I am curious about guests sometimes."

"Hmm. Do you steal things sometimes?"

"No."

"I imagine," said Mrs. Gerson, sitting on the bed, "that that isn't entirely true. I imagine items have a way of disappearing from the hotel, from rooms you clean."

It would be a simple matter now, the maid thought, to walk quickly from the room, to finish her chores and return home for the day, and wait for the phone call that she hoped would not come. And might not—after all, Mrs. Gerson had already said she didn't want to get her fired. But instead, she remained rooted to the spot in curious terror. The woman was frightening, and fascinating, and what was truly fascinating was how the woman seemed fascinated by her. "You have the look," continued Mrs. Gerson, "of a filcher. A guilty little kitten filching fish."

The maid didn't know what to say to this, so she said nothing. Mrs. Gerson patted the bed for the maid to sit beside her, and she did. "Where are you from, Hannah?"

"Poland."

"In the camps?"

"No. My father moved us before. He is Amshe Sikorsky's second cousin from Wrocław. Mr. Sikorsky helps pay our way, a little. We come in 1938, first to the city but just for two years."

"Then where?"

"Then to Monticello, to farm. A few years ago I come up here, and they give me this job."

The maid sensed that the woman wanted her to speak, so she spoke. She told how they had moved to the country, and how, in high school, she'd met a local boy who she thought was nice, but who wasn't. How he'd tricked and misused her, getting her drunk on pear cider and taking off her clothes. She couldn't believe she was telling the woman these things, but they came pouring out of her in a rush, before she had time to think about what she was sharing. She described the pregnancy and her family's shame. The wedge it had driven, made so much worse when her father had died. Death had eased her father's shame, but her mother and older sister blamed her for the series of strokes he'd suffered, said she'd killed him. Things had never been the same. She told Mrs. Gerson how things were now, that they helped here and there with Isaac and his illness, but that he was tainted to them. "I see how they look at him, how they talk to him. You know?"

"Yes," said Mrs. Gerson. "I do know."

Now that she was talking, the maid couldn't stop. She told the woman everything: their tiny home, Isaac's illness, and the constant worry she had for him—not just the polio, but the local children who had disappeared in the last few years, the helpless feeling of something being out there, a fear that sometimes rendered her shamefully glad that her boy was in bed, at home. Then she moved to the steal-ing—the sick fever that came over her, the damnable urge that over-took her innocent hands, the locked room full of other people's possessions. She told the woman everything, up to the very moment Mrs. Gerson had walked in on her.

"You poor thing," said Mrs. Gerson. "You're a kleptomaniac."

"What is this word?"

"The urge to steal. It's a condition, I have to imagine, related to your experiences, and to anxiety about your son. You must be so frightened."

"Yes," said the maid, suddenly crying again, now ashamed of how much she had told this stranger. Without warning, Mrs. Gerson reached over and thrust her hand deep into the pocket of the maid's apron. The maid stiffened, but the woman pulled out the forgotten brooch.

"Now then," said Mrs. Gerson, holding the pin in front of her as though she were speaking to it. "We leave in two days, but I want to help you. I will set up an appointment for your son to be seen by our physician. It sounds as though—what was his name?"

"Isaac."

"—Isaac has not been receiving adequate care." She put the brooch back in its box and shut the lid. "You will both stay with us in the city. I'll leave the details for you at the front desk." She put her robe back on and laid a heavy hand on the maid's shoulder. "I'll see you soon, Hannah."

The trip into Manhattan took nearly all day, though they left home in the violet cold. Simply walking to the bus stop in town took nearly an hour, with Isaac having to stop several times to rest. The maid wanted to carry him—it would have been easier—but even at eight, the child was willful and proud, and would not allow himself to be carried like a baby. They edged along on the short shoulder of the road, shrinking into themselves as the occasional truck yawned by, heedless in the waking dark.

From downtown Liberty, it was a two-hour ride to Newburgh and across the Hudson, then another hour waiting for the next train to New York. Seated on the wooden bench in the small station, they passed a bag of stale peanuts back and forth. These she'd taken from the hotel kitchen pantry in anticipation of the trip—theft, too, though not in the same spirit as her theft from guests. Peering down the long canal of bent trees from which their train was due to emerge, Isaac said, "What are they going to do to me?"

"Nothing. Give you a good checkup."

The truth was, the maid had no idea and she even suspected the trip was a bad idea. But staring at the note Mrs. Gerson had left her, in its swooping hand—a hand as outsized and lavish as its owner—she hadn't felt she'd had a choice. The woman could still turn her in if she wanted; a guest's complaint, particularly a charge of theft, knew no statute of limitations and would be investigated by the hotel detective, a young, talkative, balding man named Mr. Javits who occupied a permanent room in the maid's personal mansion of fears. Further, looking at her son's frail chest, the thin arms she could easily encircle with her hand as Mrs. Gerson had encircled her own, she knew he did need help. The doctor her mother had dug up was some elder in their country synagogue, a morose, half-blind graybeard who'd presented neither credentials nor, indeed, any evidence he knew what he was talking about. Polio, he said, would usually clear up and go away on its own. Plenty of bed rest and fluids. Now, nearly a half year of bed rest and fluids later, and having fallen behind in school, her son was still shuffling around in stained pajamas, eerily similar to her father shortly before his death. Mrs. Gerson may have been frightening, but all the same, perhaps she could help. Mitzvahs came in all forms.

The train arrived as though summoned by the coughing spell that bent Isaac double. They only just made it to their appointment at Beth Israel, and the maid sat in the waiting room for two hours picking through magazines while Isaac was being examined. She put one in her bag, a *Life* magazine with Mickey Mantle on the cover, the pages so greasy and worn it didn't even seem like stealing. Finally, she was ushered into a consultation room where her son sat slumped in a metal chair, exhausted. The doctor was a large, hale man, with a coxcomb of thinning red hair. He shook her hand and said, "Annette says you're a friend?"

"Yes."

"Well, I'm glad she got you in here. Your son needs some attention to repair the damage caused by the poliomyelitis virus. He'll be all right, I think, but we need to do more tests, and he could use some physical therapy."

"When?"

"If you could come down twice a month, that would be ideal. Probably over the next year or so."

"I don't have the money."

The doctor smiled. "It's taken care of. The Gersons are friends."

The Gersons' apartment was in a large building several blocks west of Central Park. Neither the maid, nor her son, had ever ridden in an elevator, and they watched together in minor disbelief as the lighted numbers ticked upward. Mrs. Gerson greeted them after a single knock. The woman appeared smaller in her natural habitat than she had at the hotel—still huge, but somehow diminished. The cavernous apartment was filled with books—seemed, to the maid, to be overflowing with them. The husband was as benign in person as he'd been in the hotel hallway. He accepted the maid and her son's shuffling presence with an amused tolerance that suggested his wife was forever doing mercurial things like inviting hotel staff over. He put their suitcase in the guest room, which contained a small bed and cot, then ushered them back into the large living room, where he sat reading in an armchair, his tan cardigan blending into the wallpaper. The muted sounds of the Gerson children came through the walls so softly as to almost seem imagined; in the maid's little apartment back in Liberty, such privacy was unthinkable, and even bathroom noises trumpeted with force and immediacy. Mrs. Gerson asked if Isaac wanted to meet her children. When he said no, she smiled and took him by his thin shoulder, dispatching him reluctantly into the playroom, as she called it. The sounds became even more muted, then silent.

In the playroom there was very little playing. The Gerson children seemed to regard Isaac as an annoying nuisance foisted upon them. The girl, like her father, sat reading in a slightly oversized chair. The boy was engrossed in his collection of marbles, which he pulled from a small velvet sack one by one and lined up in a floorboard crack, appraising them with the practiced eye of a Forty-Seventh Street jeweler. Isaac sat on the bed, looking at his hands, searching for something to say to them, some shared entry point.

"Your family came to the hotel."

"Yes," said the girl, without looking up.

"My mother works there."

"She's a maid," said the boy. Isaac detected no judgment in the boy's flat, factual tone.

"Yes."

"We're rich," added the boy, unnecessarily.

Isaac coughed and his chest tingled like a thousand hot pins pushed in. He said, "A boy disappeared there."

The girl looked up from her book. "What?"

"He did. From the hotel, a few years ago. And another one in town last year." Pleasingly, he had their attention now. A disappeared child was interesting; children disappearing from a place where they went every year was fascinating. In extravagant and largely secondhand, or otherwise outright imagined, detail, Isaac went into a description of the search for the latest child—the distraught mother's breakdown, the police combing the woods with bloodhounds pulling at leashes, random lie detector tests, and the warning at his school to not talk to strangers (which was true).

The boy said, "Who do you think it is?"

Isaac shrugged. An instinctive storyteller, he knew that, having grabbed their attention, it was now time to shut the flow of information down to a slow drip.

"Come on," said the girl.

"Can you keep a secret?" The Gerson children nodded. Isaac looked toward the closed door and said, "It's a ghost."

"Bull," said the girl. "Ghosts aren't real."

"I saw one, walking home last year."

"Bull," she said with less conviction, leaning forward.

So he told them about it: the time a year ago, walking to the Neversink from school, when he was still going to school, the light he'd seen in the woods near the hotel. A strange, yellow-orange light, like glimpsing something deep underwater—he'd approached to see what it was, and there, in the shadows of the trees, was a pale, unearthly figure: the ghost. His body seemed to be glowing, and in that light Isaac had seen the look in his eyes, the wave saying *join me*, the smile that was not a smile. Isaac retreated and the ghost took a step forward. Isaac stopped and the ghost stopped, as if imitating him. When he walked farther along the path, the ghost followed in the woods, keeping pace. At last, Isaac had broken into a run on his aching legs, and reached the hotel in an exhausted hobble. Panting at the top of the hill, he scanned the dark woods below and saw nothing. Had he imagined it? But then, as if in answer, a dull glow throbbed somewhere deep in the darkness—once, twice, and then it was gone.

"Whoa," said the Gerson girl. "Did you tell your mother?"

"No. I wasn't scared."

It was, of course, as the Gerson girl put it, bull. He'd been scared, but he hadn't wanted to worry her even more than she was. And anyway, it was a different, better kind of scared than usual, this ghost-story kind of scared. Most of the scary things in his life were sad and real. His polio, the feeling of walking through a swimming pool at all times. The sorrow in his mother's face, the look that told him everything was certainly not all right, no matter how many times she said it was.

"Come on, tell us more," said the boy. From the other room, Mrs. Gerson's barking laughter erupted, and the children momentarily paused. This reminder of the adult world outside the walls amplified the playroom's cozy secrecy.

"I'll tell you more," whispered Isaac. "For a marble. That one." He pointed at a big blue galaxy with sparkles in it. The Gerson boy shrugged and rolled it across the uneven floor to a crack by Isaac's knee, where it seemed to sit and listen to its new owner speak.

The Gerson woman poured them both another glass of whiskey, ignoring the maid's demurral. It hurt her throat and tasted like burning dirt, but it dampened the strangeness of the evening, so she drank it down while doing her best to explain the doctor's report. Mrs. Gerson nodded knowingly. "I was right," she said, "he did need looking at."

"Yes. The doctor says he can get back to normal with good care."

"I'm so happy to hear that." And she did seem happy. The husband had earlier excused himself to some get-together at a friend's—he was vague on the subject. When he'd left, Mrs. Gerson had relaxed, become vociferous and mastering, and seemed to expand to her previous size. The maid was sitting by the woman on a large, hard settee, and a corner lamp lit the room soft and orange, like sunlight in autumn coming through the hotel's windows as she cleaned. An opera record was playing, a little loud—*Maria Callas*, read the album cover.

"Thank you," she said, as the thick, smoky tendrils of the whiskey reached down deep into her legs, still sore from the week's work. This woman from whom she'd tried to steal had been so kind to her. No one had ever been so kind.

"Come here," said Mrs. Gerson. She took the maid's hand and drew her over next to her. She encircled the maid's small waist and pulled her down onto her lap. The maid fit comfortably there. It reminded her of before she'd become large with Isaac, reading in her father's overstuffed easy chair—a time when everything was easy, happy, and simple. The woman stroked her head. The maid became aware, after a time, that the woman was stroking other parts of her: her back, her leg, the side of her breast through the wool tunic. The combination of her feelings at this moment—shame, fear, comfort at the huge embrace, and alarm at the woman's falconing hands—created such a potent mix as to be paralytic, and so she stiffened and sat, and waited for whatever was happening to finish happening, for Mrs. Gerson to release her and make clear what would happen next.

Mrs. Gerson ran her fingers over the maid's reclined body as though she were some kind of musical instrument with an infinity of taut and twanging strings. And she did seem to sing out in musical response along with the scratched record, a quiet virtuoso aria with quick runs, basso grunts of protest ascending to shocked soprano squeals, all with her dark eyes shut tight. Mrs. Gerson put her hand on the maid's crotch and began rubbing in a circular motion. The maid cried out in revulsed pleasure for the woman to stop, ah please stop, but Mrs. Gerson did not stop.

Finally, hearing his mother's distressed moans, Isaac padded out half-asleep and stood swaying on the creaky hardwood floor. The maid twisted toward her son. Mrs. Gerson set the maid back on the couch like a piece of furniture that needed rearranging, then, with great dignity, rose and disappeared down the hallway.

Twice a month, they made the trip to New York, and twice a month, the episodes, as the maid thought of them, with Mrs. Gerson occurred. She loathed the woman's touch and afterward felt physically ill, but Isaac was improving quickly, and a few minutes of unpleasantness with Mrs. Gerson seemed a small price to pay. Also, the fact that she was submitting to this treatment in order to, in turn, facilitate her son's treatment seemed to expiate the inherent sin, as well as (she hoped) the odd and uncontrollable shivers of pleasure she sometimes felt. Early on, she managed to avoid these episodes by excusing herself to bed early, but the next day Mrs. Gerson would be hostile and distant, and she feared the disappearance of the woman's largesse.

Mrs. Gerson never mentioned the episodes, and the fact that she didn't helped cordon them off in the maid's mind—they seemed unconnected to anything else. And the fact was, despite herself, she liked Mrs. Gerson. The woman was funny and bold, said what was on her mind, and seemed genuinely interested in her and Isaac's welfare. If she was simply using the maid for deviant pleasure, holding her hostage by way of her son's health, as the maid, lying in her own small bed after a trip to the city, sometimes felt was the case, then why all the extra kindnesses? Why take them shopping at Bloomingdale's? Why send her home with a book, entitled *Mrs. Dalloway*, that Mrs. Gerson wanted to discuss the next time they came up? Was it simply guilt? It didn't seem so—the woman confided in the maid, asking for her opinion about things like a new sweater she'd bought, wallpaper she was picking out to brighten the stuffy oak of the dining room.

Mrs. Gerson's motives were irrelevant, though, considered next to Isaac's miraculous improvement. The maid watched proudly from their window as he played ball in their yard with two of the neighborhood boys, flagging a little at times, limping a bit, but keeping up. Traveling down to his April checkup, patches of weeds and blooming wildflowers pushed through the gray snow, and post-examination, the doctor said maybe one more visit over the summer. The boy was almost normal, according to benchmarks.

"How wonderful," said Mrs. Gerson, when the maid reported these developments. They were sitting at the dining room table, a bottle of wine between them. As usual, Mr. Gerson had politely excused himself after dinner. Mrs. Gerson wore a red dress with long sleeves, her blonde hair held back by a polka dot headband. She looked disconcertingly like a little girl, an impression magnified by her unusually bashful manner. "I suppose this means you won't be visiting anymore."

"Well," said the maid. "The doctor wants to see him in June."

"Yes, of course."

Mrs. Gerson drank her wine, and the maid saw she was holding back tears. "We can visit."

"No, that's okay." She put the glass down and looked around the apartment. "Have I ever told you," she said, "that everything here is Bert's?"

"No."

"Yes, everything you see. Including me, really. He's quite a wealthy man. His family owns the supermarket chain. He's rich now; when his father dies, he'll be incredibly rich. The children will never need to work, probably to their detriment."

"I always thought you had the money."

"Yes, people think that, but I don't have anything. My family is as poor as yours."

They sat in thick silence broken only by the ticking of the grandfather clock in the hall, and outside, the distant sound of traffic, the intimation of other people's lives. Mrs. Gerson said, "People wonder why me, and I used to wonder that myself, when we met. I was on scholarship at Radcliffe while he was at Harvard. He could have had anyone, and he always knew I liked girls better."

"He knows?"

"Oh yes," she said dismissively, as though the question was stupid. "It's an arrangement, like all marriages. I gave him the children. I raise them, I take care of his affairs, in all senses. Bert just wants things to be easy. He always wanted a mother more than a wife."

The maid didn't know what to say. She looked at her knee, covered in dark, worn hose, now covered by the woman's broad hand. Mrs. Gerson said, "The thing with wives is they can leave. Mothers can't."

She embraced the maid, and for the first time, kissed her full on the mouth, a deliberate and probing kiss, as though the woman were trying to extract information from some secret recess.

"I love you," she said.

The maid rose from her seat, went to the guest room and roused Isaac. He put on his clothes sleepily, but without too much resistance. The maid tossed all their clothes into their broken suitcase and fastened it shut with a piece of string tied to the handle. Mrs. Gerson remained where she'd been sitting, at the table, watching them as they left. The elevator expelled them into the lobby, the nodding doorman held the heavy oak and brass open, and the city night gathered them both into its cool embrace as they moved toward the train station. They would not be back in June, or ever.

But a month later, Mrs. Sikorsky called the maid into her office, a small room on the second floor near the cleaning supply closet. It wasn't where you would expect the owner of a thriving resort to work—a nook lit by one small window and dominated by an iron-green file cabinet that occupied half the space—but it was where she'd always worked, from the beginning, and her stubborn occupation of the room was taken by all the staff as a symbol of her humble diligence. The maid had been there only once, when she'd been hired years earlier—Mrs. Sikorsky, she remembered vividly, had shared tea with her from a silver samovar, and a plate of sugar cookies, asking after their shared relatives in Wrocław. She was a friendly woman with ash-blonde hair framing a face as habitually open as the fields that surrounded her hotel. This made her demeanor all the more frightening when she brusquely waved the maid in. It took the maid a moment to notice, beside the file cabinet, Mr. Javits. He tapped a pen against his foot and looked at the maid mildly, and she knew what was about to happen.

"You are being let go, Hannah."

"Why?"

"Why, she asks," said Mrs. Sikorsky, casting a sideways look at Mr. Javits. "A guest said you took something from their room."

"But what?" She was shaking. She hadn't stolen anything since Mrs. Gerson's brooch.

"Never mind that. It corresponds with a couple of other incidents. The shoes, for example."

Mr. Javits said, "I made some calls, Hannah. A pattern has been established. We knew someone was taking things for a while, but we didn't have corroborating proof until now."

"But my son." Jeanie looked at her, and Hannah tried one last, desperate ploy that made her ill as she spoke the words. "We are family."

Jeanie said, "And I consider everyone here family." She shook her head. "I've never fired anyone before. Even if you stole from me, I would not have fired you. But from the guests—" Here she trailed off, the thought too much to contemplate. "Come back in three days and pick up your severance check, which I hope you know you're lucky to get." And with a wave of her hand, the maid was dismissed.

On the walk home, down uneven gravel shoulders, the sun burned the top of her head like the heat of her own shame. She thought about striking out, somewhere far enough away that they wouldn't hear about this. Then she thought about Isaac at school, doing well—his teacher said he might skip a grade, even with the school he'd missed—playing with the other kids until dark every day. Outside their apartment, she picked up Isaac's baseball from the grass—the unblemished white surface now tan and tattered. She thought about seeing if her mother would take him in, but balked at the idea. She heard Mrs. Gerson's voice in her mind: *A wife can leave; a mother can't.*

Later that night, after she'd tucked Isaac in and waited for the raspy snore to issue from his side of the divider, she crept across the kitchen's complaining floorboards to the hall closet. She picked up armful after armful of stolen possessions and brought them downstairs. Half an hour of this silent labor saw everything transferred to a pile in the yard. She doused it with kerosene and watched everything burn: the shoes, the books, the socks and nylons and frillies, an Indian change purse marked with a branded symbol, a letter from someone's daughter away in college, the Polaroid photo of the young woman smiling beneath the white tree, a pack of breath mints, a miniature boomerang, several different fishing lures hand-painted in primary colors, a pair of broken glasses, a pair of unbroken glasses, an old *Life* magazine with Igor Stravinsky on the cover, three different yarmulkes, and even a Torah. Even the stolen Torah, she burned.

"Mama?" Isaac stood behind her, his face made briefly visible by a licking flame. "What are you doing?"

She looked at the flames and found she had no reply.

He stood by her. "What are you burning?"

"Things I have stolen."

"Why did you steal them?"

"Because of you, because I was afraid. But you're better now. No more stealing, ever."

The boy went back inside the house. When he returned, he threw the marbles he'd taken from the Gerson boy on the flames. Comet, sunburst, Indian blanket, galaxy: they popped and fizzed and turned black in the heat.

She went back to the Neversink for her check, though she'd vowed never to return. It had been a hollow vow; they had to eat. After three numb days of looking through newspapers for jobs and finding none, she found a message waiting for her from a Manhattan exchange. The desk clerk, Jacob, politely absented himself into the coffee shop to give her privacy.

"How horrible," the woman's voice boomed, in response to the news of her termination.

"Yes. I was reported."

"How horrible," she repeated. "Well, perhaps this is kismet. Mr. Gerson and I have just been discussing the need for a live-in nanny. I have so much to do and only so much time—" she went on, but the maid was only half listening, aware of herself as a guest watching might have been aware of her: a slight woman in her sweater and long skirt and cheap brown shoes, shoulders shaking, bent over the desk in a posture of utter submission.

And so, only a few weeks later, the maid and her son were installed in the guest room of the Eighty-Seventh Street apartment. Isaac continued thriving in his new school, devouring lessons with the hunger of a freed prisoner. Isaac's mother, for her part, liked the Gerson children, and, in a quieter way, thrived herself. Though it was her job—even more so than being the maid had been her job—she never, to herself, became the nanny—instead, remaining Hannah. Hannah, backward and forward, pointed out the Gerson girl, who was clever, like her mother.

Kismet, Mrs. Gerson sometimes exclaimed in happy wonder, emphasizing the coincidence as though Hannah didn't know she'd turned her in. Yes, very lucky said Hannah, as though Mrs. Gerson didn't know she knew. Good night all, said Mr. Gerson, stepping out for the night, as though no one knew where he was going, as though he didn't know whose bed Hannah would be sharing later.

And so they all built this strange new life together on a foundation of feigned ignorance, an arrangement that worked for all of them over the years. It was a lie so outrageous and transparent that, now and then, it seemed to Hannah almost like a kind of honesty. But she had only to unlock the little closet in her room, look at all the many things she'd stolen—chief among them the gleaming red brooch—and she knew it wasn't so.

4. Joseph

1960

Hello, Hotel Neversink! Hello, lady and gentlemens!

Hello, Henry and Jeanie, I see you hiding back there. Earlier tonight, Jeanie saw me getting into the scotch backstage, and she made me swear not to work blue. Jeanie, I don't just promise I won't swear onstage: I *fucking* promise. I swear on our father's grave. Jeanie's going to beat the shit out of me by the time I'm done, folks, just you wait. Lovely woman, my sister, but she wears the pants around here—the pants, the suit, the jockstrap. Poor old Henry there just lies back and thinks of Albany. Sometimes I think Jeanie missed her calling not being born a Soviet prison warden. Jeanie, you know I love you, and I apologize for this. To all of you, I apologize in advance.

Although, really, what am I apologizing to you for? You people have it good. No matter how it goes here tonight, you put your coats on and go home after this, maybe give the dog a kick, right?

Meanwhile, I'm on to the next gig with a damp tux and bum ticker. My name's Joey Sikorsky, I'll be here all my life. Who needs it? I'm still young. Yeah, laugh it up. I've been playing the Catskills for twenty years now, folks, and I think tonight's my last show. I think I'm done, I just can't do this shit anymore. What's the point? What's the point?

I'll be honest with you folks, I haven't been feeling too well lately. My wife left me for a dentist. A goddamned dentist. That poor guy—he'll find out soon enough that pleasing her in the sack is like pulling teeth. That life with Joyce Sikorsky is no laughing gas. Ba dum bum. But seriously, our marriage was loveless and barren.

I miss her though, that's the crazy part. Every day for the last twenty years I'm praying the woman gets hit by lightning, then she hitches up with Isaac Mengele, DDS, and here I am, crying myself to sleep, waking up with my head in the oven, sitting around in my underwear drinking scotch for breakfast. Not that I didn't do that before, but at least there was someone there to tell me what a pig I am.

But no, now she's headed up to Vermont, where the good doctor is setting up his new practice. Vermont, what's that? What kind of a self-respecting Jew moves to Vermont? Good riddance. I hope they fall off the side of a fucking mountain, get run over by goyim joy-riding in a snowmobile. Sander, can I get a little more antisuicide juice up here? Is it a problem if you think of scotch as "antisuicide juice"?

But God help me, I miss her, I really do. I just don't have it in me to meet anyone else; the fire's gone out. I meet women on the road once in a while, but it's like Groucho's line about any club that would have him, you know? So true. Last week, I met this woman after a gig in Philly. I thought maybe an elk had wandered in, mistaken the flop sweat for a salt lick. Handsome woman, old Hollywood glamour—the eyes of Vivien Leigh and the mustache of Clark Gable. She wanted to take me home, but I said no thanks. I'm looking for a nice Jewish girl, not . . . not whatever the hell you are . . . Sander, help me out, I'm dying up here.

I'll have a seat, if none of you mind. Jean, you there? Anyone? I can't see. These goddamned lights are killing me.

Hey, you're not stupid. You know she didn't leave me for a dentist. She did leave me, but it didn't happen recently. I'm going to be totally honest here. She left me two years ago. Nineteen months, two weeks, three days, but who's counting? There's not a joke in it, or maybe there is and I just don't see it. Breaking new ground tonight—hey, I know you paid for a comedy act, but tonight you're getting something different. This comedy business is no laughing matter.

I'd been in a mental hospital in Connecticut for about three months, and when I got out, Joyce had gone. Twenty-five years we were together. We met in 1935, when I'd just moved to the city, just gotten started doing comedy and was answering phones at her father's insurance business. She said I was the funniest guy she'd ever met, and I said yeah, but you grew up Orthodox in Brooklyn Heights, what do you know from funny? We got married quick and had a daughter, who's at Boston University now. Her tuition's half the reason I'm still doing this shit. I've got a son, too, but he's a dummy, thank God. The only college he's getting into is clown college. He can major in Seltzer Administration. Fitting into a Tiny Car 101. You know what he got on his SATs? Mustard. Sweet kid, but his mother's going to have to burn down the high school to get him out of ninth grade, ba dum bum.

So I came home from the hospital and she was gone, ba dum bum. She left me a really nice note; I should've brought it. I'd been in that place—it's called Rockhaven—for almost four months, because I'd tried to kill myself. I think she was afraid I'd try again. Either that or kill her father, since he's the reason I took those sleeping pills in the first place.

What happened was, I got into some gambling debt a while back that Joyce didn't know about, and the goon squad finally came after me. These guys, they don't break your arm or anything like that, they fucking bore you to death. You open the door to get the paper or the milk, there they are, two guys that look like tax attorneys saying where's the money, Joey. You go to a Dodgers game, they're in the seats behind you saying pay us our money, Joey. You go down on your wife, and one of them pokes his head out, saying the money, the money.

But after a while, this other guy shows up with the two guys, and I figure okay, here's the arm breaker. Looks like someone shaved a gorilla and fitted him for a leather jacket. One of the tax attorneys says okay, Joey, which one of these fingers do you fucking hate? Turns out he's a finger-breaker, to start, anyway. I beg and plead, but it's no good and Joyce'll be home from grocery shopping soon, so I get it over with and poke out the little finger on my left hand. They lead me into the kitchen, where the gorilla slams a drawer on it. Here, look—the doctor reset it, but it's still about ninety degrees. I told her I fell down the stairs three times in a row, and she believed me.

So I go to Joyce's father for a secret loan. Her father is the kind of old Brooklyn Heights shark that gives Rudolf Hess a good name. I know I could get Joyce to ask and he'd give her whatever she needed, but I don't want her to know, not just from guilt, but because it's not her problem. She's not the *shtik drek* who put a thousand bucks on a three-legged bag of dog food. Hat in hand go I to Hasidville.

Fathers, am I right? The absolute worst. I mean, I'm a father, I should know. Fathers are like that present you get on your birthday, a big box you're all excited to unwrap, then you open it and inside is a wool sweater. Except with fathers, it takes eighteen years to unwrap it and inside is a bunch of dog turds. This goes for me and Jean, especially. Our father was the biggest piece of shit ever to walk the planet.

What are you giving me that look for, Jean? Speaking ill of the dead—our father who aren't in heaven? It's funny, I'm the one with the drinking problem, but it's my sister who has the lousy memory. I got a name for you: Abraham.

Hey, Henry, where's she going? Oy, I've done it now, huh.

Now that my sister's gone, you want to hear a story about my father, the great man? When we lived in Poland, the crazy schmuck almost starved us to death. My mother had been going into town and begging for food, literally begging on the street, because he won't abandon this frozen hill for some reason. Then one night, he goes totally nuts and kills our only animal, this mule that we loved. Right in front of us, makes us watch him slaughter the thing. A blood ritual, he says. Some kind of ritual, scaring the shit out of your kids and wife. I thought we were going to die. Meshuggener fell asleep in front of the fire with blood all over him. Well, at least he didn't hit my mother that night.

The great Asher Sikorsky! Such bullshit. This whole joint is a palace of lies.

Anyway, where was I? Fathers. That's the whole reason I had to borrow money in the first place, why I didn't just borrow the money from Neversink, why I didn't have a trust fund. I was twenty when I

left here, and I tell my father, *gay kaken ofn yahm*, go shit in the fucking ocean, for the two non-Yids in the audience tonight. I didn't even
play here until after he died, couldn't be in the same room as that
miserable prick, even though I still feel like he's here—like the hotel
is him, this ugly golem that will never die. Well, I won't have to worry
about that after tonight, right, Henry?

I'm not asking Asher for a dime, so I go to Joyce's father. And after
about three hours of shaming me and yanking his side curls and
asking God what he'd done to deserve such a son-in-law, the old man
offers me the loan at 20 per. What can I do? I accept and pay off the
tax attorneys when they come around again, then I call my agent and
tell her to work me like a broke-dick dog. I'll play anywhere—the
Catskills, the Poconos, dinner theaters, Howard Johnson's, bar mitzvahs, bat mitzvahs, brisses, shivas. For three years I'm on the road,
grinding it out to pay down the principal to Joyce's old man. I must
have played a thousand shows. You ever think you've got it bad, try
doing an hour at the Weehawken Senior Center.

Finally I have a breakdown, just can't do it anymore. My kids
don't recognize me when I come home, and after three years I've
paid off a quarter of the debt. I know I'll never crawl out from
underneath this loan, so I tell Joyce what's going on. I beg her to
talk to her father, but she won't. Shame on you, Joey, she says, and
that's the last thing she says to me for weeks. I can hear her in the
other room, poisoning our children against me. Me in bed with my
racing forms and milk of magnesia. So one day I take a bunch of her
sleeping pills. I can't even tell you what I was thinking—not that I
wanted to die, exactly, just that I was so tired and I couldn't do it
anymore. I couldn't face Joyce or the kids, I couldn't face her father,
I couldn't pay off the debt, I couldn't work. Put on a stand-up

routine? I couldn't put on a pair of socks. I wanted to sleep for a while, like five years.

When I woke up, they were pumping my stomach, and after I got out of the hospital, Joyce signed some papers authorizing the authorities to put me in Rockhaven. *A reasonable fear I would do harm to myself,* or something. I was still so tired, I didn't even complain, just got in the taxi and checked myself in.

I did the three months, colored everything in between the lines, took my meds, admitted to my troubling ideations, went to group meetings, mopped the halls when it was my turn, played chess with the doctor, got a clean bill of health, got released, and got the news I was single at forty-five. Put myself right back out on the circuit— what else am I gonna do? Better to stay busy, I thought, and anyway I still got a three-hundred-buck-a-month vig payable to that old cocksucker in Brooklyn, plus interest accrued in the loony bin.

But I can't do it anymore, if that wasn't obvious. I'm fresh out of jokes, and a comedian out of jokes is like a whore out of fucks. Somebody have a heart and put me out of my misery. Henry, I know you'd like to kill me right now—be my guest. Take my life, please.

Even better, I'll take a header off the roof tonight, like the crazy goy who built this place. Or I could get lucky, run into the golem who keeps snatching up these little kids. Hey, at least someone is killing around here, am I right?

I'm sorry. I don't feel so good. I'm so tired. Didn't Churchill say why stand if you can sit, why sit if you can lie down? I'm going to lie down. Henry, go tell Jeanie I'm done here, the show is over, good night.

5. Henry

1963

The other day, I had the strangest feeling I was being watched. Jean had already gone over to the Neversink to eat an early breakfast before overseeing a new construction project in the north wing. I was getting dressed, putting on my tie, and all the hairs on the back of my neck stood up. I felt it before I noticed it—like realizing a drafty window has been chilling a room long after your hands have already grown cold. There was—had been—someone behind me, I was sure of it.

I turned and there was nothing, just the door and Jeanie's vanity beside it. But as I ate breakfast and read the paper, the feeling remained, like the lingering odor of the food I'd prepared, something just on the edge of detection. In my office, balancing some old ledgers, there was a scratching at the window across the room—the kind of noise I would normally, without even thinking about it, ascribe to a stray branch rubbing against the glass, perhaps caused by the movement of a chipmunk or an unseen bird. But on this day, I had a horrible vision, strange to describe even after the fact, but so powerful that it made my heart dance a double mazurka in my chest. It was this: a figure hanging beneath the window on some ledge or other, scratching his nails against the bottom of the glass.

This idea was so strong, the image so vivid, that I went outside to check, but of course there was nothing. I stood there on the sloping green, heart pounding, and my thoughts turned uncontrollably toward Jean's brother Joey—Joey Shvetz, the name he took to distance himself from the family—whom I'd watched disintegrate on the main stage, and who'd subsequently been hospitalized again. It had been a terrible thing to behold, this clever man whose faculties were failing him. To never be able to trust one's mind—worse, to regard oneself as a foe that, without constant monitoring, might do you harm—I could think of few worse things.

To steady my nerves, I strolled around the grounds, saying hello to various employees—Michael doing some landscaping, Sander Levin carrying in boxes of bar supplies—and a few young guests tossing around a football. It was a blustery fall day, the kind with the bright sun of late summer, but with a hint of winter on the breeze; the kind of day one likes to appreciate around here, before the cold really settles in and warmth exists only as a memory and promise. I found Jeanie where I'd thought she would be, talking to workmen beside the new construction. I did not tell her about my disquiet, but as I kissed her good-bye, I felt the scaffolding and its intricate hollows and shadows suspended overhead like an enormous skeleton.

The rest of the working day passed in a strange haze. I could not get the numbers to properly resolve—money was going to mysterious places, some project I hadn't been informed of, though what else was new? My mind was dull, my thoughts like peering through clouded glass. At five, I gave up and went downstairs, ready to take a glass of wine with Sander down at the bar, when from the staircase window I saw a child run across the purplish shadows of the north lawn, directly into the woods.

I ran, too, not stopping to explain myself to the wide-eyed maid, even to remove my jacket. Of course, I was thinking of the missing children around town, especially the child that had vanished here so many years before. Jonah: the months of vain questions and searching that followed, the years of sorrow—especially for Jeanie—every time his name was mentioned by a guest or newspaper article. At times, I felt—though I never would have said so—it was as if he'd never disappeared at all.

Across the grass I dashed, down the hill, feeling the way the child had looked, as though he were helplessly falling into the trees. At the tree line I snagged my foot on a grasping root and fell hard, nearly dashing out my brains on a tree stump only inches away. I rose, dirty and disheveled, my wrist in considerable pain, although I could barely feel it, so frightened I was for the child who had entered this dark realm before me, of whom there was now no trace. There were only the trees, a blanket of wet leaves, skittering animals, and the ragged feel of my voice in my throat as I stumbled forward calling hello, hello? Little boy? Hello! The farther into the forest I moved, the louder my shouts became.

In a dark copse, I stopped to catch my breath. I was surrounded by several very old, large trees, and a pervasive smell of earthy decay. As I paused, hands on knees, listening for the child, I became aware of a sickly yellow light that seemed to be coming from the trees, from the darkness, from myself. Once more I ran, though not now in pursuit but escape, escaping a presence that was just behind me, a mere fingertip away.

I don't know how long I ran through those woods, but at a certain point, I became aware of another voice calling from a distance. It was, I realized, Jeanie. The indigo sky permitted me just enough light to make my way back through the tree line, where I found three workmen and my wife, holding a lantern.

"What on earth, Henry," she said.

"Did you hear me?"

"No, one of the workers saw you go in. What were you thinking?"

I explained what I'd seen, described the little boy as best I could: small, fragile, dark hair flying behind him. But when a report was sent through the hotel, no word came back of any missing child. And the next morning, over tea, a local policeman—Chief Bates, a mere officer when he'd helped with Jonah—assured Jeanie and Mr. Javits and me that no alerts had been filed, either in Liberty or any of the surrounding towns.

When the policeman left, Javits stretched and said, "Well, I guess that's that."

"Except that I saw a boy."

"So, he sees a boy," said Javits to Jeanie. "Maybe he does, maybe he doesn't. The eye can play funny tricks that time of day. And anyway, if there was a boy, he went back home, so there's no problem in the end."

Eager, I knew, to get on with a hard day of reading the sports section and napping, Javits rose, taking his teacup with him up the stairs to his office. Jeanie sat with me after he left, looking at me strangely.

"What happened?" she said.

"I told you, I saw a child."

"There was no child."

"This we now know."

"How to explain it?"

"I don't know."

Months later, I still do not. Unbeknownst to Jeanie, I met several times with an Albany psychologist, but he offered no answers. Perhaps there are no answers. Or perhaps there are, and it is as with the man I still feel standing behind me sometimes. It is not that I sense him too late. It is that I know better than to turn around before he is gone.

6. Lenny

Leonard "Lenny" Sikorsky picked the yellow note off the front desk register: *L, please get 308 ready by four*, he managed to decipher—his father's meticulous, tortured script almost painful to look at. It was a reminder that the Fellmans were arriving that afternoon. An unnecessary reminder, as he had been anticipating the return of Rachel Fellman, and Rachel Fellman's breasts, for several months. At that very moment, the Fellman family—Dr. Fellman, and Mrs. Fellman, and Rachel Fellman and her breasts—were all riding the Hudson Line up from Manhattan and would be sheltered that night by the Neversink's new slate roof. Len had expended quite a bit of emotional and sexual energy thinking about Rachel and her breasts since the last time she'd been there, when he'd kissed her and touched them at night by the pool as it glowed a soft green, like the marquee for a porno theater he'd seen the year before on a trip down to New York with a couple of friends, local guys. They'd stayed in

a Times Square flophouse and the marquee had flashed all night
outside their window, as though to remind them of all the easy city
trim they'd talked big about scoring on the drive down and hadn't,
instead sitting in a shy little line at McSorley's, drinking their tour-
ists' steins of bitter. Birds on a wire, some joker had laughed in their
direction. The name of the movie had been *Brigitte in Paris. Brigitte
in Paris*, over and over.

He'd snuck in to see it the next evening, having spent the day
moping around midtown in a hungover funk and finally ditching the
other two in the hotel room with a twelver of Old Milwaukee. Buying
the ticket felt like a criminal act, and he'd been amazed no sirens
sounded when he pushed through the red theater door. The place was
small, dark, and smelt of bleach. The film, when it clattered and
whirred to life, told the tale of a young American woman on vacation
getting fucked by a series of Frenchmen—you could tell they were
French because they wore striped shirts and, in one case, a beret. Len
found himself bored, and realized he'd much preferred the buildup
(thinking about seeing it, peeling away from his friends, skulking
around Times Square, buying the ticket, and the four minutes of plot
before Brigitte's clothes came off) to the fucking itself, the flickering
pricks circling the juddering cunt.

Rachel's cunt—he fingered the dirty word naughtily, having only
recently been exposed to it in a bootleg Lenny Bruce album—would
also be arriving with her and her breasts. But this was too much to
expect or even contemplate while manning reception. He had to
think of other things, anything but Rachel. Oh God. A family of four
pushed through the front door and approached the front desk, but
Len remained seated—having determined it was better to seem rude
than expose the grotesque bulge in his slacks. He greeted them,

signed them into the guest registry, swiveled in his chair to grab their key (fortunately a first-floor room, hanging within reach), said if there was anything he could do to make their stay more comfortable to just call down. Hopefully by that point, he'd be able to stand again.

He ran through his standard mental list of unsexy thoughts, but each time Rachel inserted herself: standing bored in left field, there was Rachel playing third in front of him, naked; picturing his grandmother, recently deceased, wrapped in a ratty shawl, there was Rachel smiling in her place. Finally, he resorted to thinking about reports of the latest vanished child, though these abductions had simply become part of the background here over the course of his young life.

Not that young: twenty-three years, which should have been enough time to outgrow this sort of adolescent nonsense. He'd recently attended the wedding of one of the Times Square trio, and sometime, perhaps not too long from now, he would be expected to assume the daily management of the hotel. He needed to grow up.

But growing up here in Liberty, especially under the auspices of the Neversink and the great Jeanie Sikorsky, was part of the reason he hadn't grown up, hadn't seen Times Square until he was twenty-one, was capable of stirring his own member by thinking dirty words. He was not only a rube, but a pampered, sheltered rube, a provincial scion. The Hotel Neversink was its own little kingdom, quaint and wholesome and lagging some fifteen years behind the culture of an area that was itself already ten years behind. The great capitalized happenings of the decade—San Francisco and Dylan and the Beatles, and the ongoing military intervention in Vietnam—were like words you heard spoken through the hotel's walls. You could make them out but they were muffled and vague, meaningless. Apparently there was a sexual revolution under way, but not around here, not that Len could see. Here, it was matrons in one-piece swimsuits and generous portions of rich Eastern European food that put you to sleep by eight o'clock. There were lots of children, so presumably sex was being had by the guests, or had been at some point, but it was difficult, not to mention somewhat unpleasant, to imagine, not that he didn't try.

He himself was not a virgin, though that was a matter of considerable parsing, a sexual exegesis he had conducted since the event, almost two years earlier. He had been down at the Liberty Lounge, a place verboten by the Sikorsky elders and therefore irresistible, with one of the Times Square friends and two girls. The girls were from some other upstate hamlet, in for the weekend for a reason he had forgotten immediately upon hearing it. A cousin's wedding, a great-uncle's funeral. He'd lied about who he was, both to protect the family name and to avoid possible antisemitic frigidity. There had been lots of beer and poorly played pool, and then they were back at his friend's apartment, a little second-floor place off the main drag, above a consignment store. They had shared one more beer and listened to a record; then the friend had peeled off with the prettier of the two, leaving Len and the girl—the Girl, as he thought of her now, since, to his great ongoing embarrassment, he could not remember her name—alone.

She was a big girl, tall and with a look of having been attached by her big toe to an air pump and inflated. Even her hair was large—auburn curls that gathered in piles like the leaves Michael raked together on the front lawn of the hotel. She laughed a great deal at Len's lame stories and jokes, exposing a set of teeth as white and wholesome as jugs of milk in a grocery-store aisle, but there was a brittleness to her manner that made him uneasy. He sensed she was overcoming her uncertainty about this evening with a kind of forced jollity, and though he wanted desperately to lose his cherry, he also wanted to tell her hey, it's all right. We can just sit here and play records.

But then she was undressing, had her blouse off, was on him, heavy and white and soft. Dion's voice issued from the turntable, slightly warped and drunkenly under speed. *I open up my shirt and show 'em Rosie on my chest.* She smelled of yeast and chemical lemon—she had mentioned something about cleaning houses for a summer living—and had her hand down his pants, rubbing him with great zest as though assailing an especially tenacious patch of shower mold. Still, her technique was effective, and for a moment she looked down at her handiwork with something like surprise before returning to her rubbing, her buffing. A clotted heat rose up his body as she lay back, pulled her skirt up around her midsection and pulled her underwear down, far enough. That it was finally happening, and with a red-headed shiksa at that, was nearly unbelievable, as were the two words she spoke in a hoarse voice, her first sincere sentiment of the evening.

"I'm wet."

He was hard, he was ready. But his pants were wrapped around his legs like a tourniquet, and he could not seem to pull them off. With a brutal yank, they finally released their grip, but detaching them had detached him from the proceedings. For a moment, he seemed to be looking on at this messy tableau with his mother. She cast a sideways look of familiar, leveling disappointment, and it was as though a twanging wire taut inside of him had suddenly been snipped.

He felt himself soften as he plunged toward the girl with a desperation at horrible odds with desire. With his pants still garroting his calves he lowered himself, and she maneuvered him in, approximately. As she did, his thoughts turned toward the time—though, probably, it had been in his mind all night—this had happened before, with a friend from yeshiva school named Rita Meyer, a fun, friendly, somewhat naughty girl whom he probably should have married, who'd gotten naked with him one night in room 324 during a high school dance held at the Neversink. He'd lain helplessly in bed, his pale penis beached on the shore of his leg like a mollusk. Rita had feigned sleep, little reproving snores that mimicked the disgust he felt for himself, for ruining what could have been such a frolic, their young, naked bodies instead withdrawn to each side of the bed in a parody of old marriage.

The redhead bucked and sighed, and it was over. He courteously excused himself and walked home in the late autumn wind, desolate and determined not to think about what had just happened, only to spend the next eighteen months dwelling on it. He uncontrollably dwelt on the shame, an affectionate regret toward that big girl and her forgotten name. But also: Did it count? Like the old rebbe who stayed for weekend retreats, drinking tea in the sunroom, engaged in endless obscurantist debate over one minor Talmudic detail or another, what his father scornfully called pilpul—he'd settled on yes, a technical, qualified yes. A momentary breach. Though he wasn't sure. Irritating to now be unable to rid himself of an erection, to have to surreptitiously tuck it up into his waistband as he rose. He had to go prepare the Fellmans' suite as his mother had asked. He pushed the cart in front of him, feeling indecent as he passed grandmothers and children, nodding good morning, hello.

The maid had already turned down the room—one of the three biggest in the hotel—but special touches were expected. Dr. Fellman had performed emergency surgery on his mother when she'd gone down to the city with a burst appendix she'd thought was gas, and he'd also diagnosed Len's Uncle Joe's melanoma early on. As such he was treated with the same respect as a visiting sports figure or dignitary. Better than that, actually—the Dutch ambassador to the UN, visiting the Catskills a couple of months earlier, had not received such attention. For instance, a vase of fresh-cut flowers—yellow irises and spires of lilac larkspur—from his mother's personal garden. A note welcoming them to the hotel, already written by his mother. A selection of blintzes and sweet challah in a glass pastry pan set to warm in the window. A bottle of Latour on ice and a selection of library books handpicked by Henry for a perfect week of summer reading.

Taking a last look at the room, something in him rebelled at its fussiness, and at his own. A breach, not a breach! What did it matter? He went back to the writing table, pulled the ballpoint pen from his pocket, and wrote a note—one sentence, divided into two lines, like a couplet—on the hotel stationery. This he tore off and read in the light streaming in through the window.

I've been waiting so long
for you to come back and fuck me.

It was insane, of course, and he began to wad it up. But a combined sense-memory of his strivings with the redhead and Rita, and the little agonies of those failures in memory since, stopped him. He was fussy and timid and polite, had always been so, would become more so with every passing day, month, year. What about the sexual revolution, what about his own wild youth? He feared he was his father's son—poor Henry Cohen, a student librarian at Stony Brook when he met Jeanie, overmastered by his wife and her family to such an extent that he'd let the children keep the Sikorsky name. Boldness was needed, even if it backfired, even if Rachel was repulsed by his chutzpah and wanted nothing more to do with him. Better that than being a good little boy, nervous and willing but unable. He put the note under Rachel's pillow, and he knew it would be Rachel's pillow, because Mr. and Mrs. Fellman always took the master suite, leaving the smaller room, and bed, to Rachel.

As he plumped the pillow, he looked at his reflection in the window. He was just twenty-three, his head thick with woolly brown hair, his arms corded with muscle from cutting firewood, repairing leaks, doing whatever needed doing around the hotel. He had the olive complexion of his father's Sephardic line, but the blue European eyes of his mother's father, Asher. Asher, who had died when Len was five—he barely remembered him, but he did remember being led into the sickroom, standing by the deathbed and holding the great man's hand. Those still-bright eyes had struggled open, and in their pale depths he saw himself. He came from a bold line, he thought; it was his birthright. And also, there was a reasonably good chance she wouldn't even notice the note. Leave it to fate.

Outside the window, over the headboard of the small bed, the pool was an emerald square flashing in the midday sun like a movie screen. *Brigitte in Paris.* He checked the room once more and locked the door behind him, satisfied with his work.

Dinner that evening was interminable, with everyone obliged, as usual, to listen to Dr. Fellman's stories about his work—long, indecipherable tales with a vaguely moral point hovering about them, like an aimless *d'var torah* that made you feel guilty for half listening if you found other things more interesting, like, say, the leg of the girl sitting beside you. In the longest story, a young man had come to the office complaining of abdominal pains, and in the process of several examinations and an X-ray—this was slowly revealed throughout the fish course—Dr. Fellman determined that the young man had been swallowing bits of his mother's makeup. He shook his head at this thought, as if it explained something essential about the state of the current generation. Mrs. Fellman didn't say much, peering darkly over a wineglass at her prattling spouse.

After dinner that evening, Jeanie and Henry squired the Fellmans to a late comedy show, and Len's older brother, Ezra, home from grad school for a rare visit, vanished as usual, leaving Len with Rachel in what was known as the parlor. Often, in the evening, the parlor was a lively place full of guests drinking tea before bed, talking or playing cards. But the hotel was underbooked this weekend, late in August when people were getting back to work, when New York was finally beginning to release the heat it had trapped over the summer in a million-billion tons of blacktop and glass. Two old men in the corner played euchre, one puffing now and then with what was either excitement or exasperation, it was impossible to tell.

Rachel was, of course, beautiful, more beautiful than he'd remembered. Although sitting next to her at dinner, stealing glances now and then, he'd been overwhelmed not by her beauty but by her herness, her Rachelness; and something else, closer to smell than any other sensory impression, but more like a continuous vibration or ripple passing through clear water, the intimation of a large thing approaching. Her breasts, it had been reconfirmed, really were unbelievable, though her new, shorter haircut obscurely bothered him. He liked her as she'd been when he first saw her, only fifteen and with her long hair wild, tousled from an open window on the car ride over from the station. This memory of first seeing her as she'd stood in reception—he'd been running fresh towels to the natatorium—had already attained a soft golden burnish in his mind, like a daguerreotyped portrait from ye olden tymes. He lived in a state of constant yearning for the last time he saw her, whether it was five months, five days, five minutes. Even when she was there—even when she was sitting by him, laughing, taking sips from a china teacup—he felt a thick-throated sentimentality, an instant nostalgia for every passing moment.

This was, of course, ridiculous, but then he was ridiculous and he knew it. He loved her. Her: the complicated curves and contours of her throat; the mobile, intelligent eyes scanning his; the mouth gathering in a wry half smile. He didn't want to fuck her—he wanted to marry her, make her happy. Well, he wanted to fuck her, too, but that would happen as a result of the other stuff. One of the old men in the corner laid down three cards and puffed out his cheeks again—Len was like those old men, he realized; he'd always been old, though he'd tried now and then to impersonate a young person. Rachel interrupted this train of thought, saying, "I'm happy to see you."

"Me too. You have no idea."

"I have an idea. I've thought about you so much since last time. I haven't stopped."

At what should have been the best, most perfect moment of his life, Len was seized with a panic, like a cold hand reaching from the depths of his stomach up through his esophagus, squeezing his throat. *I've been waiting for you to come back and fuck me*, he remembered, in a flushed moment of panic. Jesus Christ, what had he been thinking? The note, which he'd somehow forgotten over dinner, had been a mistake, the toxic combination of stifled libido—his bored, questing prick overheated in the stale air of the hotel—and shame at the thought of previous failures. He said, "Me neither."

"What's wrong?" She brushed back a strand of tangled bangs from her left eye.

"Nothing. Just work stuff."

"I thought you were off."

"I'm never off." He stood and said, "I'm sorry, it's just that I remembered something I told my mother I'd do tonight. Will you meet me at the pool later?"

Her complicit smile, a flicker of pink tongue between bared lips, hummed his blood. "Sure. But hurry, I might get tired."

He smiled back with as much naughtiness as he could muster, then dashed down the hall and up two flights of stairs, rubbing the set of master keys in his pocket like a magical totem that might keep the Fellmans out of the room for the next minute or so. When he ran into Mr. Javits straightening a supply closet across from the Fellmans' suite, he found the smile had lingered stupidly on his face. Mr. Javits was a fidgety man, the kind who always had to have a project; since his actual job often required very little of him, he liked to "pitch in," as he called it, relaxing by way of roving the grounds and setting himself to unnecessary tasks with relentless good cheer. He was also a chattering gossip and a meddlesome snoop, apt traits, maybe, given his duties at the hotel—monitoring employee behavior and the moral probity of guests—but nonetheless, Len had never liked him.

"What are you so happy about?" said Mr. Javits.

"Nothing."

"Where are you going?"

"308. The Fellmans are out, and I remembered that I forgot to grab something from their room."

"You remembered you forgot, huh?"

"Yes, I did."

"Well, it's a good thing you didn't forget to remember you forgot, and it's a good thing you ran into me, because I ran into Mrs. Fellman a little while ago, before she went in."

"She's in there?"

"She seemed a little schnockered, said she was going to sleep, and I'd be willing to bet she wouldn't be so wild about getting woken up, even by such a young, strong, handsome buck such as yourself."

"Crap."

Mr. Javits tilted his head. "This thing can't wait until morning?"

"Not really. Maybe if she's asleep, I can just duck in."

"Probably not such a good idea, what with the—you know."

"The children?" There had been another a few weeks ago, one town over. Another fruitless search party. Len had read about it in the paper.

"Yes."

Mr. Javits was unusually silent and Len found himself wanting, perversely, to press. "You have any theories on it? I was thinking, what if it was someone here? Like a deliveryman or something, someone who moves around the area a lot?"

"No!" Anger flashed across Mr. Javits's face, and Len was afraid—he'd never seen the man close to upset, or in any mode other than rambling and fussing. "I'm tired of the talk around here. This kind of speculation is poisonous to the hotel, to the good people who work here. We cannot begin doubting each other, looking over our shoulders, thinking maybe this coworker is a murderer, this friend a monster. Do you understand?"

"Sure, yeah. Sorry."

"Good." The usual look of benign inanity reassembled itself on his face. "Okay, Lenny, I have to pitch in with setup for tonight's show. I'll see you."

Mr. Javits walked away, and Len waited, then moved in front of the door, wavering. He knocked lightly, to no response. After a third knock went unanswered, he put the master key in the lock and turned it. "Hello?" he said.

The door sighed open, releasing musty trapped air. He closed the door behind him, pressing his towels—his alibi, however lame—to his chest, and peeked to the left, into the master. Seeing no one, he relaxed—nosy Mr. Javits had probably gone to scrub a toilet when Mrs. Fellman reemerged and went back down to the show. He walked into the guest room, retrieved the note from under the pillow with a sigh of relief, and was turning with it in his hand when someone walked in.

It was a woman. It was Mrs. Fellman. It was Mrs. Fellman naked. Not entirely naked—she still wore her eyeglasses, fogged over from the shower. He expected her to scream, but she just stood there.

"Lenny?" she said. Almost as an afterthought, she raised a forearm over her pendulous breasts and dropped a hand to fig-leaf her crotch, though it was already obscured by a thicket of dark hair. The effect of her nakedness was odd—she looked enough like Rachel to be easily superimposed over the image Len carried of her daughter in his head. She was Rachel accelerated and enlarged—Rachel plus twenty-five years and pounds.

"I was—" Len tried and failed to think what it was he was doing. *Cleaning the room? Removing a dirty note some insane person had left behind?* "—delivering towels." He handed one to her from the stack and she wrapped it around herself.

"What is that?"

"What?" They looked together at the rectangle of paper in his hand. Mrs. Fellman walked unsteadily across the room, backing Len against the bed. Len held the note to his side, and Mrs. Fellman snatched at it.

"Leonard." She pressed forward, mashing herself against him, forcing him half-backward onto the mattress. Len held the note behind him, the way he did when playing keepaway with some young visiting cousin. She grabbed again, two, three times, practically lying on top of him. He felt himself stiffen, God help him, and he surrendered the note. She backed away, primly adjusting her glasses to read.

As she did, the pool light outside came on. Under one of the new halogen lamps that Len had bought at great expense for Michael to install sat Rachel in a deck chair. Rachel, and Yogi, the young lifeguard he had instructed to leave her alone, to let her stay past the usual nine o'clock all clear. Watching her, he felt calm, detached from the situation. Ah, Rachel! She brushed her hair back and peered down at a book, probably a preparatory reading for one of her upcoming freshman classes at Vassar. A Vassar girl and him!

But no, it wouldn't be now, it couldn't be. Mrs. Fellman lowered the note and said, "Sit down," though Len was sitting. She perched on the corner of the bed, still looking down at the filthy sentences.

"Do you want to maybe put on some clothes?" said Len.

"I assume this was meant for Rachel?" He couldn't bring himself to answer, and Mrs. Fellman said, bitterly, "I'll have to assume, if not, that it was meant for me."

"Yes," said Len.

"Yes, what?"

"Yes, it's to Rachel."

Mrs. Fellman looked at him with her usual expression, as though she were frozen midkvetch. She did complain a lot—about New York in the winter, Israel in the summer, the state of city schools (though Rachel and her older brother had both gone to private yeshivas), an underheated dish in the restaurant, an overfirm cushion, or really anything that crossed her mind—but, despite this, Len had always liked her. He sensed a kindness under the crossness, and found the kvetching playful, somehow girlish, a transparent ploy for attention with the implicit understanding that she wasn't really upset—unlike his own mother, who, on the rare occasions she complained about something, was to be taken seriously, with the source of displeasure dealt with pronto, in his father's words.

Mrs. Fellman began to cry.

"I'm sorry," he said. "I'm so sorry. It was just a dumb note. A joke. I didn't mean anything by it, I really like your daughter, and—"

"No, you don't understand," she said between sobs, then sobbed harder.

With a sense of great trepidation overwhelmed only by his regret at having upset her like this, he scooted beside her and gingerly patted her back. "What is it?"

She untucked the edge of the towel from over her left breast and moved it up to her eyes, and it came away with a smudge of mascara that had survived the shower. She took a deep breath and said, "Leaving the note for Rachel was foolish, but I don't mind, Lenny. I'm not stupid, you know. You're young, you have desires. It's more that—I'm sorry, you don't want to hear about this. Why don't you go?"

"No, you can talk to me."

"Ach. Harry hasn't touched me in so long, I couldn't even tell you.

Two years, has it been? And only then when he'd had a little too much wine during Seder, and he went right to sleep afterward. He's very busy, you know, the big doctor." On the last word, her voice caught, and she took a few deep breaths. "So I look at this note," she still held the damn thing in her hand, Len realized, "and it doesn't make me angry. It makes me jealous. Not of you, Len, but of being wanted like that. And I wonder if I ever will be again."

"Mrs. Fellman," he said.

"Diane."

"Okay," he began. The familiar was like an unpleasant bite of food in his mouth, hard to chew, hard to swallow. Still, he managed it: "Diane—"

"Wait. And I know my daughter—I know Rachel is beautiful. But I was too, once. I was a great beauty, do you believe that?"

"Yes."

"Do you? I was prom queen at my high school. I was the envy of them all. My neck used to be long—like a swan's is the cliché, but it's true. Not this fireplug I have now. I had to literally fight the boys off, Lenny. It seems so recent, and now. Now! Harry going on at the table like that, boring everyone. Oh, we have a nice life, I know I'm lucky, but still."

Her back heaved twice more under his hand, and she shook her head. "Jealous of my daughter, what could be more ridiculous?"

"Diane, you have no reason to be jealous."

"The old are always jealous of the young."

"You shouldn't be—it's not that great." She laughed, spurring him on. "And you're still beautiful."

She looked at him, checking, he saw, for sincerity, and finding it, he hoped. Because, at that moment, he meant it. Though he'd never seen her that way—had seen her only as a mother, a figure to be circumvented and appeased, a dark presence behind the bright light of her daughter—he did see it now. He saw her as a woman, a desirable woman, with dark hair and dark eyes that held forty-something years of a life's secrets, erotic and otherwise. He felt the warm body beneath his hand, beneath the thin, damp fabric of the towel, and he felt the rushing blood of his heart. And in the same instant he saw Rachel, as she would be after twenty years of marriage, a vision of present and future merged into the person of the woman who had given birth to her, Rachel before Rachel, *Brigitte in Paris.*

If the look on his face had not confirmed his sincerity, the tent in his pants did. Mrs. Fellman looked at it, and he hunched over, mock-casual, with his arms crossed. She briskly pulled his arm away, and as though addressing a very good dog, she patted his crotch fondly—once, twice, three times. "You're a sweet boy, Lenny. I'm going to sleep."

She got into the master bed and reached for the bedside light, but Len had already grabbed the note and stuffed it into his back pocket, already fled the room, already moved into the bright hall, the clean, blameless hall still smelling of lemon bleach from the day's cleaning, already clamored down the stairs, already moved outside, past the locked gate and onto the wet concrete of the pool, where Rachel was just getting up from her chair. Yogi had left; there was no one around.

"I didn't think you were coming," she said.

"I wanted to come earlier; I just got stuck on that job."

"No rest, huh?"

"No."

They embraced, were kissing, and she felt him against her, and he felt her feel him. He had brought the erection downstairs with him, like a family heirloom being handed down from one generation to the next.

"Come on," he said, his voice thick with urgency, and led her into the thatched shadows of the newly re-roofed cabana bar.

Afterward, pants rolled to the knee, he sat beside her on the lip of the pool, lightly kicking his bare legs in the cool water. A leaf floated past, tilting up and down on the ripples. She put her hand on his, and he sighed in amazed contentment. There was no question now, no parsing needed. He was a man, finally, his bar mitzvah notwithstanding. He'd performed admirably, and he indulged himself in looking, a little magisterially, at Rachel and the Neversink, the Neversink and Rachel.

How strange, he thought, to have everything you wanted by twenty-three. In a way, perhaps, disappointing. And yet, how great—how great to know this would be your life, to have only to live it. As though in emulation of his soaring spirit, a summer wind blew through, bothering the water, tossing Rachel's hair, stirring the dark trees that surrounded them, witnesses to their love and to what he would later know to be the happiest moment of his life.

7. Alice

1973

It was the most boring moment of Alice's life. She couldn't remember ever being so bored. Sitting with her parents and the older couple who had joined them for dinner, the boredom was so intense that it manifested as physical discomfort, a feeling of such overwhelming restlessness that she rubbed her hands on the itchy cloth arms of the chair and repeatedly kicked the table leg. Her mother put her arm on Alice's to tell her to stop, and she knew she was annoying the adults, but this knowledge did not help; in fact, it made her angry—they should try being her and listening to them, to whatever it was they were talking about, dreadful nonsubjects from the distant, gray, obscure world of adulthood: annuities, commutes, the pros and cons of tile roofing versus shingles.

She knew she was being childish, and she hated being childish, though she was a child and, at nine years old, would continue being one for at least another two or three years. Even before your bat mitzvah, by eleven or twelve, you were nearly a teenager, which was something different. She'd recently watched her older sister, Elise—installed for the week at a cousin's house in White Plains after a pitched family battle, during which she'd expressed the sentiment that the Catskills were stupid and tried out a new word that Alice knew, given her father's guffaw, Elise must have read and never spoken out loud: *borjeeoyce*—pass into this realm.

Alice wished she could have stayed home too. They came twice a year, July and December, and would keep coming for the rest of time. The Neversink was, after all, in the family, as her father liked to say, though it wasn't his family. His name was Fred Emmenthaler. Her mother, Rose, was Joey Sikorsky's daughter—the infamous Joey Shvetz, who, as Catskills lore went, had suffered a breakdown on the Neversink main stage. Joey was the family's black sheep, and, Alice dimly understood, her parents' tireless allegiance to the Neversink was partly an attempt to ingratiate their line back into the fold. Even at nine, she sensed it would never work—Great-Aunt Jeanie reserved them the same nice room and greeted them warmly upon arrival, but she never lingered long, and soon they were alone again, sitting with other boring people from New Jersey.

She kicked the table again, harder. Her mother leaned over and whispered, "Stop being a child." Her mother's favorite tactic for controlling her daughter's childishness was to point it out, which usually resulted in Alice at least being quiet—a behavior that was nonchildish, if not especially grown-up. But now, sitting at this table, she did not care, she needed to break free and run, shake off the dullness that had settled on her like the dust in their unfinished basement back home. She felt like she might actually die if she had to sit here another minute.

Mr. Schenkman tilted a bald head that reflected light from the dining room's large chandelier toward her and said, "Is it past your bedtime?"

"No," said Alice. "Is it past yours?"

Her father said, "Alice! What has gotten into you?"

"Can I go?"

Mrs. Schenkman said, "There's still dessert and coffee."

Alice's mother said, "I don't think she needs any coffee."

"Can I go, please?"

"No," her mother said.

Her father said, "Where do you want to go?"

"Just back to the room. To read."

"Fred, it's not a good idea."

"Why?" Her father turned to her mother, and Alice saw that the discussion was now past her, again in the adult realm.

"You know why." Her mother looked at her father, then said, "The ildren-chay."

"I understand pig Latin," said Alice, although she wasn't sure what her mother meant.

"Oh," said Mrs. Schenkman, "it's so horrible. Two decades and no one caught. How can it just go on and on?"

"I have my theories," said Mr. Schenkman. "I think it must be a hotel guest, someone who takes little hunting trips to the country, if you catch my meaning. In the city, you have cops everywhere. Here, there's probably five police in the entire county."

"Can we not discuss this right now?" said Alice's mother.

"Discuss what?" said Alice.

Her mother sighed. "Do you know the way to the room?"

"Yes, definitely. Yes yes yes."

"Straight back, then, and we'll check on you in an hour. You'd better be ready for bed."

Or what, Alice thought, but knew better than to say it. She walked slowly out of the dining room, her legs stiff from tensing them in sullen protest under the table, but as soon as the dining room disappeared behind her, she was running down the carpeted hallway with a feeling of joy in her heart so immense she felt like she might explode. Had she ever been this happy? An elderly couple gave her a reproving look as she flew by them down the hall, aimless in her revel. She jogged first past the pool, brightly lit in the early evening, overseen by a young lifeguard who stared dully over the rippling green water, then through the lobby and back, past the dining room, to the closed door of the auditorium. A sign warned, "Show in Progress, Do Not Enter," so she did not, instead turning heel again and racing up the main staircase, past a family of five and a put-upon porter pushing the luggage cart behind them; past a sitting area with empty gilt-backed chairs, herself streaking by in the mirror; past doors and doors and doors and doors and doors and doors and doors.

The closed doors fired her imagination. She had decided she wanted to be an author, though she hadn't written anything yet, besides some "creative free-writes," as her teacher called them, in her fourth-grade class. But she loved books, and she loved picturing what might be happening just behind all those doors. Other people's lives seemed so incredibly interesting, in contrast with her own life and the lives of her parents, which were dull, though very nice. That would be the great thing about being an author, she thought—you could have your dull, nice life while simultaneously occupying the lives of anyone you wanted. Cleopatra, for example. They had learned a little about Cleopatra in her class, and she had looked up more about her in the *Encyclopedia Britannica* during recess. Why had no one written about Cleopatra, she wondered? She would, when she got older.

She kept moving, charged with a sense of adventure, certain she was on the verge of discovering something she hadn't seen yet. The hotel was massive, an unknowably huge labyrinth of rooms, corridors, passages, floors, and compartments—a world unto itself. She'd always loved secret places, perhaps because of the lack of secrets or privacy in her own life, a lack of which she had lately become aware. Her life contained no private spaces and no secrets she could immediately think of, besides getting in trouble earlier in the year for throwing a rock at a mean boy during recess, but that wasn't the same kind of secret. Elise, for example, had real secrets—her body, on its own, constituted a mystery. Her sister's entire life, for the last year or two, had become entirely, annoyingly private, a succession of whispered phone calls, shut doors, long bathroom ministrations, rendezvous. Alice's existence, suddenly, felt immature and slightly ridiculous in its unadorned simplicity. She got up and ate her breakfast, went to school, came home, had a snack, maybe rode bikes with her friend across the street, watched TV and petted Banjo, ate dinner, described her tedious day in even more tedious detail, did her homework, watched more TV, went to bed. Lying there, the Plainview crickets sawing their nighttime plainsong, she felt the unspecial suburban landscape outside like a personal indictment.

Having climbed to the fourth floor, she was disappointed. On her way up, she'd imagined a secret tunnel leading out to a rooftop esplanade, a hidden garden on the roof, with a bright fireman's pole plunged back down through the heart of the hotel. Instead, it was all just more guest rooms. There was an interesting closet near the stairwell, but it proved to be full of towels and cleaning supplies. Poisoned cleaning supplies, perhaps? No, she thought, don't be stupid, just the dumb stuff your mother keeps under the kitchen sink. Poisonous, yes, but boringly poisonous, not skull-and-crossbones poisonous. She walked back downstairs in a growing mood of discontent. What if there really wasn't anything to see; what if there were no secrets? This was a terrible thought. If the adult world was just what it seemed, that is, a series of boring transactions and conversations, then there wasn't any point in getting older. The only thing that made it seem palatable was the intimation she got now and then that there was a vast, interlocking web of things beneath the surface, as if a blanket had been thrown over an unspeakable, writhing tumult. But maybe the hotel was just a hotel, New Jersey was just New Jersey, her sister was just an unhappy teenager.

On the second floor, she decided to play a game, make a bet of sorts: she would knock on one of the doors at random, and if an old woman came to the door, it would be a good witch in disguise. She would tell Alice where she should go next, in code, and this would lead her to something interesting. At the first door, she knocked and stood with her heart pounding, but no one answered. At the second, no one did, either. But at the third, she thrilled as the door opened to reveal an older woman. Maybe not old-old, exactly—not her grandmother's age—but old enough. Wrinkly.

"Yes," the woman said.

"My name's Alice."

The woman smiled the smile of a good witch. "Hello, Alice."

"Hi." She stood there, waiting for the information.

"Can I help you with something? Are you lost?"

"Do you have something to tell me?"

The woman leaned out of the door and looked up and down the hall. "Where are your parents, little girl?"

"They're still at dinner."

"Do they know where you are?"

"I'm supposed to be back in our room at eight thirty."

"I see. Why don't you go there now?"

"I'm bored," she admitted.

The woman paused, thinking. "I have an idea. Why don't you go down to the coffee shop and put a lemonade on our tab? Mrs. Moskowitz, room 208."

"Will I find the next clue there?"

The woman looked at her with irritation and mild concern. "Clue? No, just lemonade, I believe. Go on down there now."

Walking away, Alice tried to convince herself that the good witch was being sneaky, had secretly given her a clue, but it didn't feel that way. It felt like an annoyed woman had told her to go away. As she padded back down the carpet, she ran her fingers on the walls and felt her mood deflate further. The walls were the same cream color as their house—as her school, now that she thought about it. Everywhere was that color; the only exception, the only place where fun things really happened, was in books. At the end of the hall she went into their room, but felt too antsy for bed, so she grabbed her novel—*A Wrinkle in Time*—and went obediently down to the coffee shop.

There was only one other person there, an older man with a newspaper. No one behind the counter. She climbed onto one of the high vinyl stools, pinioned the book on the hard linoleum, and had just found her page when a man's voice said, "Alice?"

She looked up, surprised to see Len, the hotel manager, on whom she'd had a crush since she could remember. He had curly hair, and big arms, and a gentle way about him that put her at ease, like a big, friendly dog. "Hi."

"Where are your parents?"

Why did everyone always ask this? "Dinner. Can I have a lemonade? Put it on Mrs. Moskowitz's tab, room 208."

"Sure," he said, with a look of amusement, as he pulled a pitcher from the fridge behind him. He filled a glass with ice, poured the lemonade, and set it in front of her. "On the house. What are you reading there?"

"*A Wrinkle in Time.*"

"Never heard of it. Good stuff?"

"It's great."

"I don't get much time to read these days, unfortunately."

Len busied himself cleaning something, and Alice addressed herself to the book once more. Then, with all the force of a good narrative turn, it struck her: Len was the clue. The good witch had known he'd be down here.

"Do you have a clue for me?" she said.

He turned. "Excuse me?"

"A clue. For where I should go next." She suddenly felt childish and stupid, but continued. "I'm on a search."

"For what?"

"I don't know. Something interesting."

He looked at her, at her book, then another smile creased his handsome face. "Yes, I do." He cast a quick glance at the man at the end of the counter, making sure he wasn't eavesdropping, then he leaned in. She strained up to hear his words, and felt goosebumps sprout on her neck when he whispered, "There's a door."

"A door?"

"A magic door."

"Where is it?"

"I can't tell you, that's the thing. It moves around. You have to find it." She stared up at him, and he wagged his head at her solemnly. Then, breaking the spell, he straightened and said, "What time are your parents done with dinner?"

"Twenty minutes."

"Make sure you're done with the search by then, okay?"

"Okay." She drained her lemonade and rose, the sugar amplifying her excitement as she exited the coffee shop. How could she have doubted there was more than meets the eye? You just had to be receptive, open to the world, and it would bestow these discoveries on you, these adventures. She walked slowly back across what her parents reverently called the Great Hall, scanning the enormous room. Sofas, paintings, shelves with books and knickknacks, lots of people moving to and from the ballroom and lounge, up and down the big stairs that curved up to the floors above. A gilt-edged clock ticking on the wall in a nearby alcove told her she had only fifteen minutes before her hour of freedom was up, fifteen minutes to find the magic door. For a moment, she despaired: the Neversink was so big, it would be impossible.

Then she saw it. A small metal door below the grand staircase. It was half-hidden in the shadows and set obliquely to the main sitting room, so that you had to be walking toward the stairs and looking carefully to see it. Her heart quickened—this was the door, without question. But did she dare enter? There were so many guests around, plus bellhops and maids scurrying this way and that. She stopped and opened her book, pretending to read as she stood—just a strange, bookish girl, nothing to see there, pay her no mind, as she edged into the darkness under the stairs.

Still, she paused. She didn't want to get into trouble, and she was about to give up the pretense of following the clue, when she thought about the book in her hands. What would the story be like if Meg and Charles Wallace and Calvin didn't enter the tesseract? If they were too afraid? They would never have had any adventures, never have rescued Mr. Murry from IT. There wouldn't have been a story at all. With a sharp intake of breath, as though to clear any sensible argument from her mind, Alice pulled the handle and ducked in, shutting the door quickly behind her.

A small wooden staircase led downward. The lights were on, but they were low and yellow, and she had a feeling of being underwater. The basement hall's floor was tile, and the walls were stone, the foundation of the building. She had the feeling of being privy to an enormous secret—the thing below the surface she'd sensed and sought after. It was here, down here.

But now that she'd followed the witch's clue, what next? There was no more *down*. What there was was more doors, a line of them down the hall, terminating with a large exit at the very end, a hundred or so yards away. The lights flickered overhead, seemingly responsive to her thoughts. Which door should she pick? The first ones, to her left and right, were locked. The third, to her left, was also locked. A tiny shard of disappointment lanced the fun of the moment, and she saw herself as she probably was—a bored little girl playing make-believe.

But the lights above her flashed, and the door on the right opened. She stood before it, peering into the darkness as her eyes made sense of the shapes. Shelves piled with all manner of cans and bottles, though she couldn't see what they contained. Dozens, hundreds of them, all filled with magic potions, she thought, poisons and serums and elixirs. She entered, and the door, heavier than she'd realized, closed behind her. The small square window let in a little light, but not enough, and she reached around on the wall, trying and failing to find a light switch.

Did something move in the corner of the room? Surely not. She pulled on the door handle, but it seemed to have locked behind her. She steeled herself and looked again at the corner, resolving to wait for her eyes to adjust, refusing the trick of fear and darkness that was making her see a man. A gray, faceless man, looking at her. Then there was a clicking sound, and light. A light radiating from the man who couldn't be there, who was there in the corner smiling at her. As hard as she'd wished before for the hidden to be real, she now wished it was all make-believe, wished the man away, but instead he drew nearer, and at last she screamed.

A custodian in search of an errant mop handle discovered her in the morning, sixteen hours later. A pair of paramedics carried her upstairs, emerging into the almost intolerable aboveground light, to the sound of her mother's sobs. She'd been examined by a doctor called to the hotel, who touched the necklace of purple bruises around her throat and said it was a miracle she'd survived. *Groys nes*, he'd repeated, over and over. She'd overheard him talking to the police. There had been another body down there—the remains of a child who'd been less lucky than she had. Her attacker must have thought she was dead, she overheard one policeman say to another. They asked her a few questions about the man, took down what she could remember, thanked her, and gave her father a business card. The hotel detective, Mr. Javits, didn't ask her anything, just seemed relieved she was okay— over and over he said what a brave little girl she was.

She'd been driven home in a car filled with terrified gratitude, as though her parents were afraid she'd be taken away again if they opened their mouths. They'd installed her in her bedroom, put a stack of books by the bed, and there she'd stayed, reading and writing, and eating food when her father brought it in on a tray. It was kind of great, actually—she could miss school if she wanted, the entire semester. Elise seemed a little jealous, even. You owe me, she told her sister with a laugh—no more trips to the Neversink!

But at night there were the stairs, the room, and the man in the corner. The queer light he cast all around him. His kind smile as he approached, the arms encircling her, and a darkness so consuming and total that even when she regained consciousness it was like she was dead. This she could not think about, could not talk about, even when her parents brought a therapist in to see her. This she would bury so deep it could never be unearthed. Each morning, the sun streamed in through her blinds to tell her she was safe, and she would finally sleep, knowing as she drowsed away that she would never go down, would remain above, always.

8. Mr. Javits

1975

When the redheaded lady showed up, Mr. Javits thought she was just another weirdo. There had been plenty already—weirdos—ever since that hot August in 1973, when little Alice Emmenthaler's abduction had led police to the boy's body. Jonah Schoenberg: stashed in a burlap sack, at first covered in vinegar to mask the smell, his bones hidden behind the shelves of dry storage for twenty-five years. At this lurid news, like morning steam rising off the sloping lawn on the north side of the hotel, people seemed to rise out of the ground, materialize. Mr. Javits didn't mind the regular guests and their natural curiosity, or the journalists and writers who came from the city to write a story. They were just doing a job, even if Mr. Javits happened to think it was a lousy job, although who was he to talk, being a hotel detective—a job his wife, Hedda, still could not entirely believe he held, and this after nearly thirty years of doing it. She'd always thought it was a stopgap, and frankly so had he, with his associate's degree in journalism from CUNY Queens. In 1946, they'd moved to the valley for a year after college, a return-to-the-land kind of thing some people their age were doing after the war, and he'd become friendly with Henry Cohen, Jeanie's husband. So when Henry had said the Neversink, in its boom period of fame and expansion, was hiring a hotel detective to handle all the stuff that came with it—drunken misbehavior and petty theft, mostly—Mr. Javits had said sure. Sounds like a lark, thinking of those old MGM comedies, screwball pictures with a hotel dick searching for, who was it, Bob Hope or somebody in drag hiding under a dessert cart. He fell into the job and thought he would fall right back out after that year, but then Hedda had gotten pregnant, and they'd bought a little house, and then she'd gotten pregnant again, and, and, and. At some point she'd wanted to move back to the city, but he was making seventy bucks a week by then, his salary steadily raised by good old Jeanie. What could he do to make seventy bucks a week, starting out, in the city, knocking on doors with his six-year-old journalism degree and his cheap tweed suit, leaving aside the fact that the money also went four times as far out here? Maybe some local rag would take him on for fifty, which would land them in some downtown hellhole they'd barely be able to afford the privilege of being murdered in. Was that what she wanted, for them and their babies to get murdered? To be raped by some randy beatnik out for a night of jazz and mayhem? In this manner, he browbeat and frightened Hedda into letting them stay in Liberty, into letting them live all these years in the very same house up on its quiet hill, with windows looking out on a land he unabashedly loved—the rivers! the glades! the fishing! the friendly souls! the sun slanting off a grass embankment like the ground itself was winking at your good fortune and your good sense in staying!—and it was ironic when the kid disappeared in 1950 and tawdry whispers of abduction and death blew through the hotel, a locale and business that seemed as wholesome and safe as a glass of milk squeezed directly from the cow's teat. Having grown up during the twenties in an overstuffed tenement in Weehawken, with an immigrant mother making money however she could in the louche gin joint downstairs, their living room a de facto after-hours gentleman's club with reeking patrons tilting through at all hours, Mr. Javits had developed a constitutional aversion to vice and a corresponding love of anything that spoke of nature, hard work, health, goodness. So these morbid curiosity-seekers, these weirdos, of whom he took the redheaded lady to be one more, who showed up at the Neversink, rankled him deeply. What did they want? To be close to the aura of scandal or death? Or just something eventful— that was the charitable view. As a resident of this valley for nearly thirty years, Mr. Javits could grant there was not much going on, but still, there had to be something better to do than hang around a place where long ago a little boy was killed. Going blackberry picking, for example. The very thought of their succulent sweetness, especially baked into a pie or turned into jam, was enough to make Mr. Javits salivate like their basset hound, Alberta (Schweitzer), who, to be honest, was lately not doing so good, seemed to have something wrong with her eye and the lip that drooped beneath it, loosing a constant stream of gummy spit that pooled on the floor or ground, wherever she'd gotten tired and stopped moving. It had occurred to him recently that he was going to have to put Alberta out of her misery—take her behind the farmhouse, in the discreet local phrase—and so perhaps death, and resentment of death, was on his mind anyway, was concentrating his natural aversion. (Jeanie, for that matter, had gone a bit downhill since ceding daily control of the hotel to Len two years prior, and had declined on a steeper slope in the wake of the body's exhumation, spending most of her time now in the cottage behind the hotel, sequestered and swaddled like a holy penitent, though the prospect of Jeanie's death was so horrible that Mr. Javits couldn't consider it for one conscious second.) But he hated these people because, whatever their motivations, their very presence brought an aura of seediness to a place he loved. They skulked about like hungry ravens, entering and pretending to be guests, jangling ersatz room keys, hoping to find their way into the basement, to look at the "secret room" the newspapers had already reported on ad nauseam. One man, a little weasel in a Yankees cap, Mr. Javits had to hustle out when he personally caught him sneaking down the stairs. *You can't go down there*! he shouted at the man, and the man shouted back that he was going to his room, and Mr. Javits shouted back, your room is in the basement? Shame on you! Shame on you! He removed his navy coat with the hotel insignia on the breast and advanced on the man, and the man fled back through the lobby, casting a worried look over his shoulder. Though Mr. Javits was not by any means a hulking brute—was in fact on the shortish side, five feet seven as he told people, though really closer to five five and some very loose change—he was fit as a fiddle, the product of a lifelong fitness regime of his own devising. Every day, he did two hundred push-ups, one hundred sit-ups, and, most importantly, he ran eight miles at five o'clock in the morning. In the dark, he laced up his running shoes, put on his battery-powered head lamp, and jogged down their gravel driveway out onto old Route 117, a moribund logging road creased with ankle-breaking ruts and sudden, precipitous edges. Animals scuttered in the darkness at his downhill approach, the occasional owl hooting as he passed. Route 117 took him in a broad loop down the hill or small mountain where they lived—he'd never really been sure which it was—in a corkscrewing approach that bottomed out in the poorest stretch of Liberty. Here, the houses sat, wet and disheveled, like abandoned children left to play in the dirt, and he always shivered internally, brought to mind of his own childhood and a particular memory that often arose, of a man's work shoes caked with mud beside the curled edge of the carpet on which Mr. Javits sat reading. Reading, but really letting his mind wander, something it seemed to do with increasing frequency as he'd become older and more aware of his surroundings. As he sat there, his thoughts moving from the book, to the teacher who'd lent it to him, to the classroom at school with its chalky blackboard and wainscoting of cursive letters, he became aware of a man's feet standing before him. The man said something, but it was like Mr. Javits was underwater—although when he thought about it now, he couldn't say whether that was how it had sounded at the time or how it sounded in his memory. And was there a difference? But he knew he never looked up at the man, embarrassed, even at his tender age—for himself, his sister, his mother down the dark hall, the man that stood before him, everyone. The man was putting on his work boots, and Mr. Javits saw how the socks were dirty, too, and wrinkled, with a hole on one ankle where the black hair peeped through, reminding Mr. Javits of the stitches his friend Reuben had gotten after catching an errant baseball with his right eyebrow. The ends of Reuben's stitches were like the hair of a fly, something that had burrowed repulsively beneath the skin. Was fly hair even hair?

Curiously, at that moment, a fly had alighted on the east-facing window, the window that looked out on the Orthodox church, with its golden turrets and blue dome like the abandoned egg of a giant robin, an egg incubated by resentment and loneliness that had grown monstrous. The fly writhed, and the man, he noticed, had stopped talking, and then Mr. Javits was dealt a colossal blow that upended the room. There, among the furniture hanging from the walls and ceiling, was the man's face—a blond boy, hardly older than his cousin David, with thin whiskers and a native, rueful look hued red with anger. The man left and there the memory faded, a sepia shot of sagging chairs and cracked plaster. He supposed that was why he ran in this direction, through town—to remind himself of where he came from, and that he was not there any longer. Even at fifty, making a comfortable living at the Neversink—still working for Jeanie, doing security and whatever other little odd jobs popped up that needed doing around the place, the important thing being to always stay busy—he still feared, and sometimes he imagined he felt, disorder and poverty exerting a gravitational pull on him and his family. And there was a perverse satisfaction, a sick thrill, in running by these houses daily, similar to picking off a painful scab. Passing out of the poor side of town, he jogged through the small park where, in the summer, the homeless lay with rusted hibachis hovering over them like sentinels of sleep in the stillness of near-morning, then around the town center—the gas station, the lending library, the post office, the dentist's with the white colonnades in front made to look like toothbrushes, which always made Mr. Javits chuckle. What kind of a person would make their front porch up to look like toothbrushes? Well, a dentist, obviously. What kind of person becomes a dentist? What kind of person becomes a hotel detective, for that matter? (Head of hotel security, a title change conferred long ago, but still.) Why do people do anything? Why did that boy get killed so long ago, and why the other children in the area, and why had the girl been attacked, why? It would have been better if the boy's body had never been found. Well, it would have been even better if the boy had never been killed, obviously, and especially never killed on Mr. Javits's watch, so to speak. He didn't exactly feel responsible or guilty, because, after all, he was one man, and it was an enormously busy hotel by 1950, with hundreds of guests coming in and out daily, and you couldn't expect him to keep an eye on every single one of them. This, anyway, was what Jeanie had told him the second day after the boy had disappeared, when he'd collapsed, weeping, in a chair in the corner of her small office, grief- and guilt-stricken in equal measure, imagining his own boy, Charlie, being abducted, and worse. Little, blameless Charlie— the fear felt by a child who was loved and cared for would be worse for its fresh horror, a new thing with no precursor; the dawning of this fear would be worse, it seemed to Mr. Javits, than whatever real pain could be inflicted. The night before, he'd lain in bed sweating through a series of night terrors in which he was intermittently Jonah, Charlie, the murderer, or just himself looking on, helpless, and he hadn't been able to tell whether he'd been asleep or just thinking. Then he'd gone to work to be interviewed by the police, and to be screamed at by the mother of the boy, who had called him incompetent and worse. He wept against the wall in Jeanie's office, having tendered his resignation. But Jeanie, he would never forget, leaned over him and put her hands on his shoulders, and told him, Saul, you're one man. The parents couldn't stop it, the police couldn't stop it—neither could I, and neither could you. God, she said, could have stopped it, but He didn't stop it either, and we must believe there is a purpose. She hadn't hired him to prevent robberies or anticipate abductions, just to keep a kind of order and morality to the place, and he'd done a fine job in that so far. Her face, at that moment, had looked holy to him, cherubic and red-cheeked, a countenance of elemental goodness, the sun shining down on him. He'd continued weeping, but the reason had changed, though he didn't say so at the time, from guilt to a bottomless gratitude that he worked for someone so pure of heart, a woman he would have killed for. A woman he had come to think of as his real mother, though he knew he had a real mother already, an old drunken *nafka*. But life, he felt, had led him down this mysterious path, led a city boy into the woods and far country to a job he had no particular interest in or aptitude at, all so he could, among these dense groves of pine and alder, these thickets of stinging nettles, find his mother, who held him there to her large chest, rocking him, telling him to put it out of his head. And he had, more or less, for twenty years, until the little girl was assaulted, and the cops found the little boy's body, and the weirdos started showing up, among them the redheaded woman whose name was Lucy.

She appeared outside his office one morning at ten, knocked on his door with its plaque reading *Head of Hotel Security*, which implied there were other security officers for him to be the head of, an untrue but handy suggestion at times when he was trying to impress upon someone—a budding young thief earlier in the week, for example— the ubiquity of people like him, those who guard against malfeasance and immorality. But the redheaded lady didn't seem impressed. Watching her settle into the chair across from his desk, Mr. Javits put his detective skills, such as they were, to use on her, trying to place who she was and where she was coming from. She was around his age, fiftyish, with hair like copper filament. She wore sandals, shapeless jeans, and a floral blouse with the top button open, exposing an expanse of flat, freckled clavicle. She was neither attractive nor unattractive, though she had a pleasant demeanor—had been nothing but pleasant when she'd set up this meeting with him the day before, catching him down in the dining hall just as he stupidly held a hunk of sopping bread over his bowl of matzoh ball soup—but from the second she'd opened her mouth, Mr. Javits had hated her, and he continued to hate her as she balanced a legal notepad on her knee like a journalist ready to take notes on a hot story. Was she a journalist? A writer? No. She seemed like a local housewife with too much time on her hands. So why had he agreed to this? Because whoever she was, she claimed to have information about the boy's disappearance, not to mention a subtle natural facility at making him feel somehow culpable, a feeling that unpleasantly recalled the meeting with the boy's mother all those years earlier. She sat smiling across from him, judging him, he felt, and he produced a hideous smile in return, like the skin of his face was being pulled taut by invisible hands behind him. What can I do for you, Lucy, he said, and she said, well Saul—if you don't mind me calling you Saul (he did)—I think I have some information that might be useful about the Schoenberg boy, and the girl. Okay, he said. Well, she said, I think I might know who it is. Who *who* is, he said. The killer, she said, and he looked at her. She seemed to have been expecting him to get up, dance a little jig, vault over the table in his excitement, and he could see his reaction disappointed her. I'm sorry, he said, but I don't understand why you're telling me; this seems like a police matter. And she said, oh, I've tried, believe me,

I've tried. They aren't interested. They think I'm a nut! Really, said Mr. Javits, leaning back in his chair with some pleasure. Yes, she said, I told them I could lead them right to the killer—to his house!—and they said they'd get in touch if they needed the information. I didn't know who else to come to, so I came here, hoping you would listen. He adopted a posture that suggested listening, and Lucy proceeded to tell him her story, how she'd grown up around here, heard about the abductions like everyone else, lived in a kind of fear, under a shadow like everyone else. Worried about her boy every day like everyone else around here, but he was fine, thank God, up in college at Geneseo. Then, two years ago, her husband died suddenly—Mr. Javits said he was sorry, and she said thank you—and she'd had to move into a smaller house. In her new neighborhood, she began noticing a man who lived a few doors down the street. Tall, very thin, black hair and eyes. Moved like he was always worried about someone sneaking up behind him. *Furtive* is the word, she said. I didn't think much of it, just a weird person (yes, a weirdo like you, thought Mr. Javits), but then I started to really pick up on his movements. Maybe it was just because I stayed up nights, having no husband and no job, but I could see him walking down the street, sometimes very, very late—two, three, four in the morning. I would watch from my window in the middle of the night, and sometimes I would see him coming, like a shadow, almost darker than the real shadows. And I saw that not only would he be out late—which I know is not a crime, maybe a little strange, but again, I'm a night owl myself—but he would look in windows. He would sometimes stop and look back to make sure no one was behind him, then walk through a yard and appear on the other side. Once he went behind mine. Your house, said Mr. Javits. Yes, the woman said, he came through my yard to the side, and I grabbed the shotgun from the cabinet where I keep it. I went downstairs and peeked into the bedroom, and he was standing out there, as sure as I'm sitting here. He was looking for something, for someone, I could feel it. I don't mind telling you it chilled my blood, Saul. I can imagine that would, yes, he said. Yes, and so I called the police and they said they'd send someone out, only they never did. I didn't sleep that night or the next. And I became a little, I admit, obsessed. I asked my neighbors about him, and they shrugged, saying, oh, Mr. Andrews, he keeps to himself, been a fine neighbor as long as they could remember, though a little odd, big on his nighttime rambles. So one time I followed Mr. Andrews. I saw him going out earlier in the night, and went out behind him, wearing black. I'd planned it. He went down the street, me about two blocks behind. I thought he was headed into town, but when he got to the park he cut through it, and from there into the woods. Well, needless to say, that was as far as I followed. I stood behind the jungle gym, shivering. Into the woods at ten at night! Who does that? So I started doing research, and I discovered some very interesting things. I have a theory— But Mr. Javits had tuned out, thinking how much she reminded him of his mother. They looked nothing alike, but there was something similar in their manner, a brittleness that put him on edge. She would be insulted if he didn't take her seriously, act on her theory, as though he'd asked her to speak with him in the first place. He was so tired of theories. Everyone with a theory! he thought, everyone suspicious, going around worrying about everyone else—this was the true shame of these disappearances, how they turned neighbors and coworkers against each other. He leaned back in his chair, nodding while she spoke, looking out his window at the tree next to it. A large bird sat on the nearest branch, and as Mr. Javits nodded and hmmmed, he tried to figure out what kind it was. Black and orange—an oriole? It was more yellow than orange, though, and speckled, and anyway, he'd never heard of an oriole coming up this far north, not that he was an expert, by any means. A goldfinch? He'd never been too much for birds—Hedda was much more of a birder than he was—but as he'd gotten a little older and started to slow down a little, he'd found himself increasingly drawn to them. Lucy herself looked like a bird to him, an awkward, skinny bird with fiery plumage muted by age, the color washed out in its final molting. She was saying something to him, he realized, asking a question, and he said, sorry, what? And she said, I was just wondering if you had a list of who you or the police had questioned. Questioned, he said. About this Alice girl or the Schoenberg boy way back when—you would have conducted interviews presumably, she said, and he tried to remember if he had. He'd certainly talked to people. Asked around, certainly he had. And he'd cooperated with the police investigation, although he couldn't certainly say who they'd spoken with or brought in, if they had. Certainly—certainly!—he'd lost sleep for weeks over the missing boy, had prayed for his safe return, for all the good it did: none, clearly. He'd never really prayed for anything before, but he remembered one overcast night when he'd wandered out onto the new golf course—the fourteenth hole, with the sloping green—and he'd spoken out loud, saying *Ha Shem*, please make the boy safe, and when he said it, he hadn't been sure whether he was talking about the Schoenberg boy, or Charlie, or himself. But interviews? He wasn't sure if he'd done anything as formal as that. And then he'd missed something else, and she said, oh sorry, I was just asking if you'd mind coming over and having a look? At some of the information I've put together. Since the police won't look at it. Mr. Javits said honestly,

Lucy, if the police aren't interested, I'm not sure what I can do. She stiffened in her chair and he felt, for a moment, that he was being interviewed, interrogated. Counting on her fingers, she said, Saul, you're someone who's lived in the area for a long time, you're familiar with investigative techniques, you work where two of the crimes have occurred, and you have a relationship with the police. I need your help. She wrote her address on a yellow legal sheet, tore it off and handed it to him across the desk. And he said, sure, okay, he'd be happy to come talk, and was she available mornings?

Thursday morning at five, Mr. Javits kissed sleeping Hedda and set out on his run, through the rutted marshland the most recent rains had left behind. Monsoon season, Hedda said, but it was always monsoon season around here. Where did all this water go? he wondered, picturing the swollen cascade behind their house and the shimmering gray stones. The road's wet soil sucked at his shoes, and he thought, great, is this how it's going to be all day today? It was raining now, he realized, little misting drops visible in the triangle of light his head lamp cast. Cold, too, and he swore to himself—goddamn this place. Goddamn it. The curse reverberated in his head, and when, a little farther down the hill, a muddy rut caught his left ankle and pitched him forward onto the ground, it felt like payback, blatant *nekome*. He got up and tried to keep running, but he'd twisted his ankle—sharp pain stabbed him with every step. He paused, unsure. He'd planned on doing his usual run, stopping at Lucy's house around seven in the morning, then running back so he could make it to work by nine. He should, he knew, limp home and clean up and drive down to meet her instead, but something in him—punitive or plain stubborn or he didn't know what—insisted on continuing, pushing forward. Perhaps she would drive him if he couldn't make it back. He slowed his pace, in no special hurry to get to her house—content to walk through what felt like a corridor of singing, sawing insects, a twisting hole in the dark created by the beam coming from the lamp on his head—though get there he eventually did, just as gray dawn was breaking and the air was rising with a mineral musk from the new concrete sidewalk where town began. Her address was 200 Elmira Road: he checked three times on the damp piece of legal paper, and three times it assured him that yes, this was the place, one of the bedraggled homes in the poor part of town, a narrow, faded yellow thing, beside a house with a sagging trampoline. It was surprising, since Lucy had seemed fairly prosperous, and Mr. Javits felt somehow tricked, conned into coming down the hill before work, interrupting his run and hurting his ankle. It further occurred to him now that he may not even be able to run for several weeks, a dismal and infuriating prospect. Why the hell had he agreed to this? To meet with this weirdo? This weirdo with her crackpot theory and information the police had no interest in? Ridiculous. Seeing clearly how ridiculous the whole thing was, he turned on his good heel to start right back up the road, but a voice stalled his progress. "Good morning!" She had come onto the porch and was already greeting him with a cup of coffee, already thanking him for making it down, already asking about his ankle, already helping him up the stairs and into the house, already apologizing for the bedraggled state of the house, which had been brought about by her widowhood (cancer, she reminded him) and subsequent depression, though she found she was pulling out of it lately and that committing herself to the case (as she called it) had been a huge help mentally, already leading him through a cluttered living room, already showing him a broad oak desk on which sat the cumulative fruit of what she said was two years of investigation. The centerpiece was a large corkboard with a map of the Catskills pinned to it, and various thumbtacks planted here and there. She was pointing at it, and he was thinking how grief could drive people to do almost anything, just look at his own mother, whom he hadn't seen for, God, how long was it? Five years now? In her old age she'd become a fanatic, a zealous Lubavitcher who obsessed over obscurantist Talmudic concerns and volunteered with a Mitzvah tank once a week. On his last visit he'd seen her working in it, distributing pamphlets to bemused Bergenites. He'd been incapable of squaring the gray, bobbing, beshawled head of the woman smiling hopefully at potential converts with the mother of his childhood, the housecoat that had smelled of perfumed booze as she walked him and his sister in a penitent silence to their elementary school. In the school bathroom, he would wash his hands over and over where she'd touched him, certain the other kids would smell it on him, looking at his own face in the warped mirror, hangdog and middle-aged at ten years old.

Mr. Javits! Lucy was yelling at him. I have spent the last two years working on this. The least you could do is pay attention for a few minutes. Listen to me.

He listened. Over the next few minutes, she detailed her findings. Since 1950, when Jonah Schoenberg disappeared, there had been seven others, represented by the pushpins—yellow, red, green, blue, purple, orange, and white—clustered around Liberty and the hotel, itself represented by a red Monopoly hotel glued to the map. She described these disappearances, some of which Mr. Javits had heard of, some not. There was the local girl a few years back, who'd worked as a cashier at the grocery store. He remembered her, a small girl with ash-blonde hair parted directly down the middle, kept out of her face by a braided buckskin headband. But she'd been a hippie, and the town consensus had seemed to be that she'd taken a secret pilgrimage to the West Coast, or wherever things were happening. Anywhere but Liberty. Lucy went on for quite a while. She was fiercely animated, red with righteous energy, saying, Do you see? She pointed at a green Monopoly house in the middle of the pushpins. They're all in a circle around where we are. It's the same person! With the flourish of a stage magician saving their best trick for last, she tore the room's curtains open, saying look, that white house way down the road, you see it? He saw it—a distant tumbledown hovel like all the other hovels around here, nothing special. Did you know, she said, that in 1947, a local girl was attacked at a Monticello train station? Guess when Mr. Andrews moved in? Guess! Mr. Javits couldn't guess. 1947! And the cops won't lift a finger, even though I've told them all of this. Well, said Mr. Javits, Are you sure they haven't looked into it? Investigations take time. She said, They haven't investigated anything for the last twenty years, why would they start now? She looked out the window as though gathering herself, then sighed and turned, saying, Mr. Javits, again, will you help me? And Mr. Javits said, Well now, look, I'm pretty sure the police have it well in hand, but he was stopped by Lucy's bitter, accusing laugh as she drew the curtains. The worst part, she said—I mean besides the killer being allowed to walk the streets— was how the forces that be could make you doubt yourself, your own sanity. How it made you feel like the world was arrayed against you and how it put you in a state of constant paranoia, wondering whether the oversights of people in charge were due to incompetence or malice. Malice? said Mr. Javits. Or some combination thereof, she said, and she proceeded to say lots of other things, during which time he looked at the map. Rather than representing the places where children had vanished, the map seemed to him like it represented some sort of assault schematic, the plastic hotel piece surrounded by the ominous pins, like a small rank of invading armies on a general's battle plan. A little spit collected on the right side of Lucy's mouth as her voice crescendoed, but it was difficult to hear her. It was like she was underwater, or he was, just like when he'd been a boy in Weehawken, the furniture flying. And so he could hardly hear her at all when, after thanking her for the information and telling her he was going to talk to people and get back to her, he walked out with her still making sounds at the back of his head. The day outside was absolutely gorgeous—birds chirping and the sun stupidly placid over the eastern rim of the valley's ridge. He waved back at Lucy, who was silent now, staring at him, and walked carefully through the yard to the road, his ankle yelping in protest with every step. But he really did have to leave, and he couldn't have asked her for a ride, not after leaving so abruptly, but gosh it was such a nice day, and it would have been a shame not to walk anyway, but man did his ankle hurt, and that was okay because into every life doth a little rain fall, but was that the Bible or a pop song, and what did it matter if it was true? Truth: he thought of the map and the accusing pins, and he thought of her accusing look, and he said to himself, Now Saul, look, be reasonable, do you really think this woman, this weirdo, cracked the code after two decades of yourself and the police not turning anything up? I know you're upset about the boy and all the weirdos he brought out, but is the answer to start listening to every kook who comes by the office with a theory? Do you really want to increase the strain on Len and everyone, Jeanie especially? Jeanie who was presently lying ill in the cottage, too weak on some days to get up and even say hello to a single guest, a tradition of hospitality begun by her father, Asher, and continued by her until a few months ago? He did not. A serendipitous branch on the side of the road served as a walking stick that eased his passage up the hill, and he made it to work only a few minutes late, full of good feeling and esprit de corps, ready to keep the place clean and suitable for healthy family fun.

Nonetheless, he found himself, at four the next morning, limping around the grounds outside the cottage, girding himself to meet with Jeanie in a few hours, when the sun rose and the day began, although his day had begun hours earlier, had never really stopped since he'd met with Lucy. The meeting hovered in his mind like a bad smell that would not go away, a persistent stench indicating something unseen and rotten. The map and the pins, and her following him out yelling *Children don't just disappear* and *Why won't you do your goddamned job?* Mr. Javits had tried his best to let the day's demands and the flow of his attention lead him away from those words, but, like a stray, starving dog, they seemed to follow him wherever he went, nipping at his heels, constantly reminding him of their presence. His lunch—which he always took early and lingered over and never failed to appreciate, tasted bland, even slightly rancid. Perhaps the sour cream had turned. He secretly dumped the plate in his office trash, where Natalya, the head cook, would not see and take offense. Outside his window, the branch was bobbing as though a large bird had just been there and taken flight at the sight of him. He peered up into the sky, but there was nothing, just a few wispy clouds in the air, again looking like the trace of something that had recently fled without his detection. His detection, ha! If the redheaded woman, if Lucy, was correct, he'd thought, sitting at his old oak desk, worn smooth by decades of agreeable contact with his elbows (as he read the sports column, ate a midday snack, snoozed), he was responsible for the deaths of several children. She hadn't said this, of course. Maybe she hadn't even thought it. But the implication was clear to him. If he'd failed to do his job—worse, if, on some level, he hadn't wanted to do his job—he was culpable. *Culpable*: one of those odd words you've seen and heard a thousand times without really noticing or thinking about, then suddenly they become strange to you, implausible. That night, at home, he'd looked up the word *culpable* in their dictionary, which he couldn't remember ever cracking, and saw that it shared a root with *culprit*, which he'd never noticed. Capable of being—as good as—the culprit. He was culpable, able to culp. As they'd eaten dinner (alone—their daughter, Samara, was out with friends, a sickening thought with the culprit, the real culprit, out there in the night), Hedda had asked what was wrong, and he'd said nothing, nothing. She'd prattled on, as she did, talking about Charlie's upcoming visit, about the shiksa girlfriend he might bring. Could Saul imagine? He couldn't imagine. He couldn't imagine anything, it seemed. Had he ever imagined anything, ever looked past what was there in front of him at any moment, ever looked for what wasn't there? Ever detected anything? It didn't seem so. He was the tabletop dulled by unseen elbows, the branch quivering seconds after that invisible bird took flight. He plead an upset stomach, which was not hard to do since he had one, and went upstairs to bed, hearing the faint sound of the music Hedda was listening to as she cleaned up, the new Carole King record already played to scratchy bits. *It's too late baby, now it's too late. Something inside has died. I feel like a fool.* He swallowed one of his wife's sleeping tablets, which she'd been prescribed during a bad spell of the flu two years ago. Not expecting it to have any effect, he woke in the middle of the night, shaking from a dream he couldn't remember, one more unseen thing. He found he'd been crying, and he got up to wash his face. The clock in the hall read 1:45, and he knew he wouldn't be able to sleep again—if you could call what he'd gotten sleep—and so he put his shoes and work clothes in a bag and went for a drive. It was the kind of night you can tell is cloudy even though it's perfectly dark—even without gazing up and seeing no stars, there was something about the texture and the coolness of the air, like a shroud hung over the sky up there, the perfect, secret sky that is always there whether you can see it or not. He thought of his mother and he was crying again, and, Jesus, how long had it been since he'd cried? A long time, maybe since that day when he'd cried in Jeanie's office. His thoughts seemed to spiral like the car, the old Plymouth, as it went around and around the hill or mountain, down to the bottom where the poor people lived—Lucy, goddamn her and her Mr. Andrews—past the post office and the park and the dentist's with the toothbrush portico. He drove past the entrance to the Neversink and past the Liberty Lounge—its door was open, just releasing its babbling rabble into the night, like a mouth disgorging the contents of its guts into the gutter, where they belonged. A boy stood out front who could have been the blond boy from his childhood, black hair peeping through his dirty socks, presently lighting a cigarette with a perplexed look that seemed to ask how it was possible that he'd been transported from the home of Sara Javits in Weehawken, New Jersey, in 1933, to outside a bar in upstate New York in 1975, and Mr. Javits wondered the same thing as he juddered along the old logging road that went up the back way to the Hotel Neversink. It seemed he'd never made any decisions, never really thought anything through, had just allowed himself to be swept along by the ceaseless flow of life. He parked the car atop a small ridge with a gully on one side and on the other an expanse of trees that the distant hotel loomed over. The moon broke momentarily through a thin spot in the cloud cover, casting dull gray plates on the grass at Mr. Javits's feet—they floated around him like the ghosts people said haunted the Neversink, like the strange, fuzzed memories that Lucy had jarred free and that had been haunting him all day. The tall man: Mr. Javits kept returning to a time when—it must have been around 1960, a sunny day in the fall with the wind blowing leaves around in little calico whirlwinds—he had gone outside for some air. He'd walked out one of the rear exits, and there, shadowed by the hotel's western eave, a man in a hat had stood watching the lawn. Had he been tall? Yes, Mr. Javits thought, he had. The lawn was brightly lit by the late sun, and Mr. Javits could see children playing there. Maybe, he'd thought, it was a father fondly watching his son or daughter, but something had been strange about it, something off, and Mr. Javits had watched the dark figure for a few seconds, possibly half a minute. Nothing incriminating there, but then he'd approached to get a good look at the man, and in doing so had snapped a fallen branch on the ground, blown down in a recent rainstorm. The man had fled. *Wait*, he'd cried, but he'd turned the corner and there had been no one. Had Mr. Javits gone to Jeanie? He couldn't remember now; it was as though a black curtain had been lowered over the whole affair, or maybe it was just that it had carried so little real significance at the time. But thinking back on it now, Mr. Javits had the unshakable feeling he'd seen the tall man at other times throughout the years—standing in the library, sitting in the dining room, coming down the stairs, strolling the grounds. Once, when he'd gone to visit Henry in the cottage, this same foggy figure had walked right past him without a word, not even a nod at Mr. Javits's polite hello.

Strange, he'd probably thought at the time, but then, people were strange. Like everything else, he'd paid it little attention. The gray plates at his feet shifted, the ghosts danced around him as he considered what he had to do. He would have to tell Jeanie what that Lucy woman had said, and he would have to finally do the job she'd hired him for: ask questions, go through employee records, dig things up, detect. He would stand before this woman he loved, and he would tell her there may have been an ongoing connection between the Neversink and the children. And they would both know the implication: if he discovered something damning, it would mean the end of the hotel. He drove to the Neversink, parked, and walked to the cottage and paced for a very long time, waiting for the sun to rise, for Jeanie to wake up and take her morning tea. But the sun, it seemed, would never rise again. And as he paced, his bad ankle twanging every now and again, he was reminded of another time, back in Weehawken, when he was twelve or thirteen, out late doing something or other, playing inept baseball with some local kids or fruitlessly courting a girl from his school, maybe, someone even poorer and lowlier than he was, and he'd come back to the apartment only to find he'd lost his key. There was no call box on their building. He'd stood outside the doors, looking up, locating their window, his mother's room, the bright wedge of light that burned out into the eternal city dusk, and he'd imagined her up there—a different her: one making dinner for them, one who had a normal job, one he could be proud of, one he could love. He'd stood there imagining this version of her until it almost seemed real, like he would go inside for a hot meal and help with his homework and a kiss on his forehead when he lay down to sleep, and this reverie had lasted until a drunk staggered out and Mr. Javits had slipped in behind. It seemed to him now that he'd wished that woman into existence—that she lay sleeping in the house he now lurked outside of like a burglar, a thief of happiness. This, thought Mr. Javits—Jeanie, the Neversink, his love for this place—this was real. Lucy's story? Another theory. Everyone had one, and, like he'd always said, the paranoia it caused was the really dangerous thing. The fact that it could have made him worry Jeanie in her sickroom, fill her head with his sick fears, this was the real shame of it all. But the tall man. Ach, he needed to clear his head. And so he sat in the front seat and thumbed on his running shoes, double-knotting the left one tight. He put on his head lamp and jogged down the hill, slick with night dew, past the hotel and down to the gravel access road, ignoring the shrill note of pain in his ankle that sang out with every step, running faster and faster, ignoring what was behind him and what was in front of him, ignoring it all, knowing that right now, as always, the important thing was simply to run, to keep running, to keep running, on and on and on.

9. Rachel

1979

On the last weekend of the month, Rachel Sikorsky went to the city. It was a long-standing tradition, a marital agreement based originally on Len's tacit understanding that, in order for her to live in the boondocks, she needed to still feel connected to her family and her past. As the years had gone on, it had become more simply an escape: from the endless demands of the foundering hotel; from the provincial dullness of Liberty, a place enlivened only by the ambient dread of a killer lurking somewhere in its gray midst; from the love of her wonderful husband, multiply exhausting in its relentlessness and the guilt it produced when she felt drained rather than nurtured by it; and, most of all, from herself. And indeed, from the moment she arrived at Liberty station, black overnight bag by her side, until she stepped off the train two days later, she did feel like someone else—a tourist.

She felt this way in two senses. First, in terms of how dramatically New York—crystallized in her mind at eighteen—had changed during the decade she'd spent in the hinterlands. Her old neighborhood, previously a stronghold of quaint continental bohemianism, had become overrun by homosexuals, supplanting the wispy-cheeked boys of her youth who'd strummed guitars on the steps of the Gaslight or Café Wha? On one visit, she saw two men holding hands and kissing in front of a bar, an unthinkable sight even five years before. The whole city had become more crime-ridden, darker, seedier, and sexier as well, and she felt old at times, as out of touch as any gawking Midwesterner.

But in a deeper and more elusive sense, it also seemed on these visits that she was touring her potential lives, all the former possible versions of herself that had been preempted by the choices she'd made ten years earlier: Len, motherhood, the Neversink. For these thirty-six hours once a month, it was as though all of these different, dead versions of her came to life, doing away with the real one.

She felt it from the moment she set foot on the train, a shiver of potentiality, and as the scenic monotony of the valley gave way to suburbs and the first concrete encroachments of the city—as they passed beneath the North Bronx bridge graffitied with the words *GALAXY KREW*—she felt increasingly like a person returning to, not visiting the city: the prodigal daughter. Sitting on her stool at Sabatini's, stirring her drink, looking out the window, with its backward-stenciled name, at the hectic crush of Forty-Second Street, tracing with her toe the hexagonal black-and-white tiles of the old-fashioned floor, making conversation with the courtly barman in his heavy knight's vest of gold-black brocade, she wondered who he thought she was. A lawyer with a drinking problem? A Park Avenue mother taking a break from her shopping? Or just another tourist?

While she was hailing a cab on Park Avenue, the electric feeling entered her—like a charge released into her tensed calves by the coursing energy of the street—that she wasn't herself any longer. Sliding over onto the cool leather, speaking the familiar address to the cab driver, his slight nod and the meter flag saying here is another someone going somewhere. The flashing eyes of pedestrians that momentarily held then released her, the disembodiment they conferred as, for a second, she became the thing being seen and vanishing, making room for the next thing. In the city, she became everyone, anyone, no one.

At her parents' apartment, she became the dutiful daughter, perhaps the child who had never left. Ten minutes spent there brought on a drugged feeling, a sense-memory of adolescence, of being clogged with hormones and wracked by a restlessness that turned to lethargy at a moment's notice. It was not actually unpleasant. Unpacking in the guest room—her old room, with its antique wainscoting and crown molding like the edges of a birthday cake—this lassitude would creep over her, and she would wonder why she'd bothered doing anything. She could still be living there, eating her mother's brisket twice a week, reading Le Carré or Cruz Smith in the study with her father while Dvořák wheezed from the enormous stainless-steel record player, petting their immortal tabby, Frisco, and taking evening walks over to Washington Square.

On these walks, she became the single woman, the self-sufficient seeker, a person who, at thirty, might still be finishing her PhD. This woman would have made more of her time at Vassar, would have spent nights in the cozy old library with its creeping ivy and fathomless stacks, would have sought out mentorship and guidance, and would have graduated with honors and an eye toward advanced study; this woman would not have spent four years preoccupied by romance, smuggling in her illicit lover and fiancé-to-be, talking on the dormitory phone until two most mornings, mooning her way toward a C average.

At the Plaza, on Saturday nights, she became a married woman again, but a different married woman in a different marriage. This woman, sipping a glass of white wine in the corner of the lounge, seated like Marie Antoinette in an ornate gilt-backed chair, was married to one of the men who passed by. That one: the older graybeard in a sleek suit—a financial analyst and expert squash player who gave head with the desperate greed of a starving dog thrown prime rib-eye. No, that one—the younger man checking in at the front desk—an unassuming tax lawyer of great secret ambition, the kind of cautious man who just needs an intelligent, bold partner to help him inherit the earth. Or someone else, any of these men, Jewish or not, old or young, married, unmarried, fat, thin, vigorous, lame, handsome, harelipped, hairy as a mountain ape or bald as a newborn babe, she married them all. Whoever they were, and whatever their faults may have been, they all shared the same vital virtue: they were not her actual husband.

And yet she didn't want to cheat on Len. She had, in fact, been afforded that opportunity a few months before and had turned it down. One of these men, one of her phantom husbands, had brought a dewy glass of scotch over and stood beside her. He was handsome at a glance, very handsome, though he became less handsome with sustained inspection. His features were exaggerated and overripe, like fruit gone just past sweet to cloying. He said his name was Daniel.

"I'm Rebecca." It was a name she'd prepared on the off chance anything like this happened. She'd thought it was to protect the sanctity of her real life, though, saying it, she wasn't so sure it wasn't the other way around.

"Do you mind if I join you for a minute?"

"It's a free country."

"So they say."

He sat in a chair diagonal to hers. On the glass table between them, facedown, lay the book she'd been reading, *Tinker, Tailor, Soldier, Spy*. He picked up the edge and laughed. "Not what I expected."

"Oh? What did you expect?"

"A pretty woman by herself in the hotel lounge? Probably *Cosmo* or *Vogue*? Kidding." He held his hands up and she found herself charmed by him in spite of the corniness, or perhaps because of his willingness to put on a corny show for her benefit.

"Funny stuff."

"But really, Soviet spy novels at eight thirty on a Saturday?"

"What can I say? I'm into political intrigue."

He asked her about herself, and she told him: English professor at Brown (Princeton seemed too brazen) in the city for a conference; traveler, this year to Buenos Aires (how she longed to go there, poring over travel brochures in her few unoccupied moments); dog lover (Len had been denying her a retriever puppy for ages, saying it was wasteful buying purebreds, saying they were too busy right now to train a dog, but they were always too busy for that and lots of other things, besides); and last, unmarried (the ring sat in her room, but this was due to a heat rash encircling her finger, the boiling city in July).

"Never marry," he said. "Take it from me."

"You're divorced?"

"Twice. Never again." He sipped his drink and his big lips glistened, obscene and fascinating.

"Even if you met the perfect woman?"

"Even so. I'd still be an imperfect man."

"So the divorces were your fault?"

"Oh, yeah. Not entirely, of course, but yeah. I'm an army brat, there's this sense of impermanence with everything. I want something permanent until I have it, then I get spooked. So I keep the door cracked. Just a little, but it's enough."

"Sounds terrible."

"Well, you know, I'm not sorry I got married to them."

"I thought you said never marry."

"Did I? This isn't my first drink tonight."

He bought them another round, and then it was nearly one in the morning. Their conversation had felt conspiratorial from the outset, and they sat close to each other, as though trading secrets, though mostly it was talk about his business here (boring money stuff, he said) and his life in Miami, where he'd moved seven years earlier. He came up to the city about once a month to keep an eye on things, otherwise he worked with a phone to his ear and his eye on the blue sliver of ocean he could see from his office window.

With a childish fist over his mouth, he yawned and said, "Listen, I have a meeting at ten in the morning, and I've got to hit the sack. I'm going to be very forward here, because I like you and I think you like me. I hope you don't find this kind of thing insulting; I don't get the feeling you're the kind of person who would. I'm in room 485. If you want, come and knock, I'll be up for a little while; I have half a bottle of some pretty good whiskey up there. But I'm not waiting up, either—I'll be asleep inside of twenty minutes. So, no pressure, but it would be fun. And either way, it was really good to meet you, Rebecca."

She sat there those twenty minutes, watching the ormolu clock behind the bar as though it were an official countdown, finishing her drink, frightened by how easily this alternate person had emerged. It was as though the details of this life had nested in her for years, waiting for the perfect moment to fly from her mouth and soar to and fro in the air around her disbelieving ears, stunning her with a barnstorm ballet of deceit. After thirty minutes had passed, she took the elevator up to the fourth floor and walked to her room. She got undressed, thinking of the stretch of hallway—thirty feet or so—separating the two of them. Lying in bed, she vowed never to lie about who she was ever again.

The summer faded, and with it, Daniel. The memory soon felt like a story someone had told her once, perhaps after a few drinks, while she'd half listened. There was just too much to do at the hotel. Business slowed in autumn—business had slowed in general, especially with what had happened to Alice, and the discovery of the boy's body—but as it did, the hotel entered a hectic annual phase of repair and renewal. Walls were repainted where children's fingers had smudged them with chocolate or jelly; the pools, inside and out, had their expensive yearly servicing, including a retiling of the lip (especially odious this year was the drain cleaning, a chore that had always fallen to Michael, the long-time maintenance man who'd recently left—Rachel found herself bent over the pool's edge, fighting off nausea as she tugged on a stubborn hank of hair); the golf course was reseeded and landscaped; the kitchen appliances required deep-cleaning and parts replacement; the staff received their performance reviews and a couple would probably have to be let go (always with the accompanying talk of Jeanie and her loyalty, though this, like so many things about the old woman, who continued her decade-long decline in the cottage's guest room, was mythological—Rachel knew for a fact she'd sacked a light-fingered maid in the fifties). October through December, the hotel was like a patient on bed rest, requiring constant care and attention, to be disturbed as little as possible.

She continued making her trips every month but no longer felt she was exploring alternate identities. She was who she was: a mother and wife taking a monthly break with her husband's blessing. On a brisk March day, she emerged from Grand Central, her face stung by a whipping wind. Sabatini's was empty, save for a large woman at the end of the bar picking ice from a glass and chewing it a cube at a time. Rachel ordered her gin and tonic and relaxed as the liquor spread through her veins. Looking out the front window of the restaurant, she complacently thought about what she might buy on Saturday—an antique chamfer-edged mirror she'd had her eye on at a West Broadway furniture store. A man passed by, his hat down, and a strange shiver went through her. She worried, not for the first time, that she might be getting sick with whatever it was the children had been passing back and forth the last three months.

Her parents were well, the brisket was good, Frisco was old but hanging in there. She slept soundly. The next day, reading with her father, she finished *Smiley's People*. Sighing with pleasure, as though she'd completed a difficult and important project, she closed the book. She scanned the nearby shelves and picked out a worn annotated copy of *The Brothers Karamazov*. This, she thought, this is the next thing, this is good. The room was warm and snug. She yawned virtuously, read the first page twice, and woke up three hours later.

After a little light shopping with her mother, they parted ways and she installed herself at the Plaza. She ate dinner and considered having a drink at the bar, but the look of it—brightly lit, lined with four men in nearly identical gray business tweed—depressed her, and she returned to her room. She called Len and was apprised of the day's non-events (burst pipe, Javits out sick with the flu). As always, his deep voice reassured her; as always, he missed her. She read a bit more of the borrowed book, then turned off the lights.

Then she was at the Neversink, and it was empty, except for her. Room to room she went, calling for Len, but there was no one there. Passing a wall mirror, she saw that she was a young girl again, and she was suddenly afraid, certain she'd been abandoned. Then she heard voices coming from the floor below, and so she went down there, into the Great Hall, where a crowd was milling around. Some kind of celebration, though no one looked especially happy—they wore black and had expressions of grim forbearance. She heard Len's voice and pushed through the crowd, toward the middle. A woman stepped aside and she could see Len, but it wasn't Len. Another man she'd seen before. She saw his face. It was—

—a nightmare of some sort. She sat up in bed with the distinct feeling someone had been in the room with her, though that was impossible. She tried to remember the dream, but its wispy contours were already fleeing like a tattered ghost, escaping under the edge of the door, where a yellow band of light came from the hall. She checked the time: 1:15. Without thinking much about it, she got dressed in the clothes she'd laid out hours before on the suitcase and brushed her hair. Feeling a chill, she put on her coat and took the elevator to the ground floor.

The bar was empty now, as was the lounge, save for a couple seated at the far end. She ordered a martini and watched the bored bartender make it. The smooth, learned, repetitive motions were soothing, almost as soothing as the drink was when she took the first cold sip. She felt the dream recede like a bad smell just on the verge of clearing.

It was strange to be up at this hour, but she'd known she couldn't possibly go back to sleep. After a drink, she'd read more and try again.

The couple laughed at some joke, and Rachel glanced over; as she did, the man turned. It was Daniel. He turned away again. It had been only a second, but it was him. The exaggerated and slightly moist features were unmistakable. He'd looked at her, but no recognition had crossed his mobile face. He hunched toward the woman—some anonymous bottle blonde in her forties—with the same conspiratorial attitude that Rachel remembered from their evening together. The woman said something, and he threw back his head to laugh wolfishly; he'd reacted the same way, she remembered, when she told him how she'd once been stuck naked in an outdoor shower at Manhasset Beach because someone had taken her swimsuit. It had been, maybe, the one true thing she'd told him that night.

She watched Daniel and his prey in the angled mirror behind the bar. Eventually he stood, presumably having made his offer. He walked away, to the elevator bank, without looking back. The woman brushed a wisp of hair away from her face, lost in thought, and Rachel remembered that feeling as well, luxuriating in the long minute after he'd left, considering his offer. Unlike her, however, the woman smoothed her dress—spaghetti-strapped black with a ruffled gilt hem—and made her way to the elevators.

The thought of going back up to her room and trying to sleep was now unthinkable, so Rachel ordered another drink. As she sipped it, she looked at herself in the bar mirror across from her—the mass of dark hair, the long nose and wayward gray eyes looked unfamiliar. This version of her had slept with Daniel and would do so again. This version would not be taking the Hudson Valley Line tomorrow, would not be on her hands and knees fixing the pilot light under the kitchen stove, would not be adding up the dismal winter numbers in the office and steeling herself for an argument with her mulish husband, would not be settling in next to him in their drafty bedroom with the wind knocking wet black trees around outside the window.

"About to close up. Get you anything else?" asked the bartender, Windexing the glass shelves.

"No, thanks." The ormolu clock behind the bar said forty-five minutes had passed. The martini was gone, leaving only the oily dregs of vermouth and olive juice at the bottom. She walked down the fleur-de-lis-printed runner to the elevators. As she neared, the doors opened, and Daniel emerged. Again he glanced at her, and again he did not recognize her. She moved past, heart pounding, into the elevator, rode it to her floor and then back down. He was just pushing through the large double doors at the end of the cavernous lobby. She trailed after him, low heels ticking on the marble floor, dimly aware of being watched by the bartender but not caring. The two martinis, the lingering grasp of thwarted sleep at this late hour, and Daniel's inability to notice her had all combined to make her feel untouchable and disembodied. A ghost in her long coat, she swept through the doors and out onto the street.

She followed him right onto Fifty-Eighth Street, along the parquet sidewalk in front of the hotel and its shops, then right again up Sixth Avenue. She saw herself in the windows she passed, furtive in her fur coat, large collar turned up against the wind. With sunglasses, she might have been a Russian spy on assignment in one of the books she'd been reading; a double agent trailing her man through the maze of the city, a mole among moles. *A double agent*—the words echoed in her head as she measured her steps, pausing half a block behind as he paused at the crosswalk to Central Park—was that what she was? It seemed so. He moved across the street and she thought about the evening she'd spent months ago with the small figure sauntering ahead of her in the darkness, how easily she'd forgiven herself for it and forgotten about the deception. She was a counterintelligence agent in her own life, plainly traitorous to her husband, and, it seemed, to herself—though here the mechanism of the deceit became murkier. Who was she, and who was she really working for? And whoever's employ she was in, how much did she know?

More pressingly, why—why was she doing this? It seemed to her that rather than following Daniel, she was somehow following the other version of herself, the one who had slept with him. What would it have meant to become intertwined with this man? This strange man who now whistled something, strolling along, literally whistling in the dark. She strained to hear what it was, some merry little number that repeated after two or three phrases, something from a musical she'd heard long ago. *Pirates of Penzance*, maybe. Yes. *He is the very model of a modern major general.*

The buildings of Central Park West were visible over the left edge of trees, windows burning in the night; it reassured her to be so close to other people, though for the moment it was just her and Daniel. It occurred to her that he was exactly the kind of guy who would walk through Central Park late at night—that he might be a bona fide hedge-lurking rapist. He cut into the foliage off the main walk, momentarily confirming these fears. Instead, it was a cobblestone path leading out of the park. She was briefly camouflaged by the presence of other people: drunks, late-night dog walkers, other unclassifiables of the city night. But two blocks north, he cut left on Sixty-Fourth Street, and they were alone again. His steps echoed ahead of her, and she hesitated—if he turned now, he would surely see her, recognize her from the hotel, know he was being followed. He crossed the street, already melting into shadows cast by the carefully manicured trees that lined the block.

He entered a nondescript brownstone with a striped awning. Rachel stood outside, shivering, then moved across the street and sat on the dark stoop of an adjacent restaurant. After a minute, a second-floor light dutifully flicked on. Through half-closed blinds, she could see his figure moving around the apartment. Another figure emerged, a woman. There was some further movement, then they both disappeared and the light went off. She sat there for quite some time before getting up and beginning the long walk back.

The next morning, Len answered the phone with a froggy hitch in his voice. "Hello."

"Hi, it's me."

"Hi. What time is it?"

"Eight thirty. You were sleeping?"

"My dirty little secret. We sleep in on Sundays."

"What does Suse eat?"

"Honestly? I let her stay up watching TV with me, eating ice cream. She's usually crashed until nine or ten."

"Len."

"It's just so nice to sleep in once a month. I know, I'm a horrible father."

"No," she said and looked around the room, the Queen Anne bed beneath her and heavy curtains drawn against the prying eyes of the city. "You're not. Sorry to wake you up, I was just wondering if you'd mind me staying one more day this time."

"No. Why?"

"Well, I ran into an old friend last night. From college. She invited me to dinner with her and her husband, and I just thought it would be nice. But I understand if you think no. We shouldn't really pay for another night here."

"No, you should. I could come down."

"What?"

"Sure, Javits could watch things for the night." She paused, making a contemplative sound while ordering her thoughts, but he'd already understood her reaction. "Never mind, it's fine."

"Are you mad?" she said.

"Me? I totally understand, an old friend. I was just offering to be nice, honestly."

"You sure?"

"I'm sure."

Feet still sore from last night's walk, she took a cab the twenty-odd blocks to West Sixty-Fourth. The restaurant, she had noted the night before, opened at eight. She requested the table in the window and ordered coffee to start, saying someone was meeting her. No one would rush a woman being stood up—she knew that from working in the hotel restaurant. You treated a woman being stood up like a terrorist wearing a vest made of dynamite. She could take two or three hours, bravely ordering breakfast after a long while, dabbing her eyes now and then.

But as it turned out, she'd sipped only half the coffee when Daniel emerged, holding the hand of a small girl. They were followed by a woman carrying a baby. He wore a conservative blue suit and overcoat, and the little girl a bright-red jacket with wooden buttons. His wife wore a long fur coat with a high collar, which, combined with her sunglasses, conferred a regal, even imperious, look. They walked east and disappeared north at the next block.

Rachel put down three dollars and pushed back out into the street. It was a bright, cold winter day, and the rising sun, rather than warming the air, clarified and sharpened the chill. Daniel's family had crossed the road and was walking two blocks ahead, slowly. She drew nearer. The wife held the baby over her left shoulder, and it seemed as though the child had identified Rachel as an enemy agent, tracking her behind them with an unhappy watchfulness.

The clan stopped on Sixty-Ninth Street, at a small Episcopal church named St. Stephen's, a picturesque brick building set back from the road in a tranquil yard and further obscured by a rank of holly bushes. The building's red-tile roof and angular dormers gave it an oriental look. They entered next to an area of scaffolding where it appeared a new section was being built. Christ, she thought, seriously? She'd known they must be going to church, but the almost Dickensian hypocrisy had seemed implausible until that moment. She stood in the cold, hesitating, then moved down the concrete walkway, under the scaffolding, to a heavy wooden door.

Inside the long, narrow building, prefatory organ music softly piped. The Daniels sat confidently near the front on the left, with an air of assuming their normal spot. Rachel sat in the back row, twenty or so pews behind, on the right-hand side. Daniel leaned over and said something to his wife, who shook her head. The conspiratorial air was gone. In the light of day—in a church—his face was less grotesquely sensual; it conveyed a stoic mournfulness. There was a posture of unhappiness between the two, though Rachel supposed she might be inferring that from the night before—it didn't take a genius to guess their marriage wasn't in the best possible shape. The preacher, or priest, or whatever he was—she'd never been to an Episcopal church, had gone to temple infrequently in her life, though more than she liked since marrying Len—came out and began speaking in a soft Boston accent, and her mind instantly wandered back to the central question: What the hell was she doing?

It was, of course, crazy, as was the night before. Following him had begun as a half-drunken lark, a curious tour of the unknown. But when she'd seen the woman through the window, when she'd understood the level of deceit he was engaged in, a different kind of curiosity had taken hold. All the way back to the hotel, she'd thought about it, what it would be like, leading two lives. How did he do it?

In a sense, she knew: it was what she'd been doing on these trips to New York, living a shadow existence or existences. Yet wasn't it all make-believe? Didn't she know that when Sunday came, it was over and her real life would once again resume? But maybe that was how Daniel felt—maybe the occasional room at the Plaza was his little vacation, maybe he told himself the same thing: This is not your real life, and come Sunday morning it's all over. How much of our phantom selves, she wondered, as she stood and sat and kneeled in automatic imitation of the assembled, did we take back home from these excursions into make-believe?

After five hours of fitful dreams, she'd awakened wanting to see Daniel's real life being lived. How did he do it? So here she was, and she realized as she stood and sat, and stood and sat, that it was not edifying. Maybe it was the milieu—the painted hanging lamps, the two-dimensional stained-glass saints frozen in prayer—but it all seemed simple and clear. He was a liar, a cheat. A man who screwed other women at the Plaza, not a mile from his sleeping wife and children. What had she possibly thought there was to learn about it, or about herself? She rose, excused herself past an elderly woman, and pushed on the door, but it did not open.

Something was blocking the way, and when she pushed again there was a loud scraping sound. The priest paused midsentence. She hurriedly walked down the side aisle to the front exit and outside, where she saw the edge of the scaffolding that had caught the door frame. She looked behind her, but no one was there, just the homely little church, its dormers like raised eyebrows. She clutched her coat around her and walked back to the hotel.

Having the whole day to kill, she sat with coffee in the lounge, trying her best to get a toehold in Dostoevsky. Why were good books so much harder to read than bad ones? It seemed like it should be the other way around.

The white-coated waiter returned with coffee, refilling her cup and asking if she wanted lunch. No, she said, just bill it to her room. Like a magic trick, as the waiter left, Daniel seemed to appear in his place. Without asking, he sat down next to her. "Rebecca, right?"

She looked at him, unable to speak.

"Were you following me?" He paused and went on. "I saw you at St. Stephen's earlier, and when I did, I got the strangest feeling I saw you here last night. Is that so?"

She nodded.

"Well, I don't know what you're doing, but you should stop."

"How do you do it?"

"What?" he said.

"Whatever it is you do here. Have affairs, lie about who you are."

"You don't know anything about me."

"I know a little. That woman last night, the blonde." He stood to leave. "Wait," she said. "I really want to know. How do you make it work in your head? Going to church the next day with your children and wife."

"Has it occurred to you that she might know?"

It hadn't, and the realization that it hadn't was more startling than Daniel's appearance had been. He ran a hand through his thick brown hair, seemed to think about just walking away, then, with a nearly imperceptible shrug, he said, "I don't know why I'm bothering to tell you this, but we have an arrangement."

"You sleep with other women at the Plaza?"

"I try. I don't always succeed, obviously."

"How does that work?"

"Marriages are strange." Pursing his big wet lips with contempt, he looked down at her wedding ring and said, "But then, you know that already, don't you?"

She didn't know why, but she felt the need to win this argument, whatever argument it was they were having. "So I guess if I went back to your apartment and knocked on the door, and I told your wife we'd slept together, she wouldn't mind?"

"Don't talk about my wife," he began in a quick hiss, then stopped himself. He looked around the lobby to make sure no one was listening—the nearest person was a porter loafing at the concierge station, thirty feet away. He leaned over the chair's back and whispered, "Listen, I love her and my kids more than you could ever know. And if you come near us again, I'll fucking kill you, got that?"

"Yes."

"Good. Have a nice life."

She called Len and told him her friend was sick, canceled the room, and caught the train home that afternoon. Seated backward, she watched the city, then the outskirts, then the suburbs, then whatever was outside the suburbs vanish continually to the south as the country reappeared: shambolic houses with sagging fences you could see over; a dog trotting through the small ravine that ran beside the track choked with gray February sludge; an abandoned factory sitting in the middle of the river, with its brick stanchions like a fisherman in waders. Earlier, she'd canceled her standing reservation at the Plaza. There would be no more of that—no more of these trips, no more alternate selves, no more pretending.

Thinking of Daniel's face, her hands still shook. The scariest part was not the threat he'd made. Even if he was serious, she wouldn't be back. It was the intensity of his words and feeling, the fervency of his allegiance to his wife and his children. Had he been telling the truth about the cheating, the arrangement? It didn't really matter. What mattered was that he claimed his life with utter certainty. She'd never cheated on Len, but had she ever felt that strongly about him, about their life? And was it so inviolable that she'd threaten a stranger? The answer to both questions, she knew, was no. Some part of her had never completely accepted her own life, and so she now understood that there was one more version of herself she had yet to inhabit.

As the train rumbled toward Liberty, it seemed to her she was coming here for the first time. Looking out the window, the familiar procession of small towns (even the names: Scott's Ferry, Newburgh, Monticello) seemed strange, as did the landscape's landmarks. The used car dealership, the distant ski lodge, the bending river, the last rickety bridge before Liberty station—she saw all of them with new eyes. It was nearly dark when the taxi climbed the long hill and pulled to a stop in front of the Hotel Neversink. She paid the driver and got out, and the cab pulled away, leaving her on the drive with her suitcase. In the purplish light, the hotel was ablaze, filled (half filled, anyway) with people, all those different lives. How incredible that this was hers. At that moment she felt she'd never been here before, like a stranger to her own life: a tourist. And anyone watching, as she picked up her suitcase and moved hesitantly toward the front door, would have thought that was exactly what she was.

10. Alice

The man sitting next to Alice at the bar had a face like the map of the storm on the TV wedged in the corner, a huge, violent system plowing through the Midwest. His features shifted constantly as he talked, aswirl with expression and varicolored—red nose, blue-red eyes, grayish teeth. Or maybe it was all the drugs in her system: cocaine, Quaaludes, Benzedrine, Valium, marijuana, alcohol, and Benadryl, if you restricted the list to things she'd taken in the last twenty-four hours. Now that she noticed it, everything around her seemed to pulse, not just the man's face.

"What brings you to Iowa?" That she was not from Iowa he had apparently sussed out from their previous exchange, which she'd already forgotten.

"A book tour." It seemed like a lie, but it was true, and she could hardly believe it herself. She'd been on a bender that began with her New York release party and continued until nowish. It wasn't like this was an enormous deviation from her usual behavior, but it was nice to have a real excuse. The man didn't seem to register what she'd said, so she tried again. "A tour for a book?"

"That you wrote?"

"Yes."

"What about?"

Even at her sober friendliest she found this question difficult to answer, and she was far from her sober friendliest. "I don't know," she said, "some stuff happens at a college. People want different things and make hard decisions."

It would have been easier, she thought, if she'd written a novel about vampires or nuclear war. Then she could respond to that question with "vampires" or "nuclear war." But instead—for her undergraduate senior honors thesis—she'd written a big, unwieldy campus novel, something of a roman à clef, about a cult of personality that springs up around a professor, mainly for the purpose of irritating the real-life professor in question. That the professor had, in fact, been flattered; that he had shown it to his agent; that she had signed Alice on; that a publishing company had bought the book; and that it had come out to quite a bit of fanfare—all seemed inexplicable to her, let alone a strange man whose face was twirling around like a pinwheel.

She was internally braced for more questions, but a flash of lightning and an immediate thunderclap forestalled her interlocutor. The lights flickered off momentarily, and a couple of sillier people screamed. Alice took the opportunity to get up and push her way through a horde of bargoers, past rows of tattered vinyl booths, to the front of the room, where one of her hosts, a young assistant professor named Don, stood with bourbon in a plastic cup. He and her other university hosts had dragged her out after the reading to this place, a dive bar housed in a large Victorian near campus. She'd wanted to go back to her hotel and sleep for two days, though she had to be in St. Louis tomorrow. Or Chicago.

"You brought the weather," he said. Through the front windows, rain lashed the brick street and the other large Victorians in the immediate area. It had been sprinkling when they got there, twenty minutes before. As they watched now, the rain seemed to double in force every ten seconds or so. It seemed that in another five minutes they would be underwater, inside a filled-up bowl.

"Don't blame me."

"No? I bet a black cloud follows you everywhere."

Don was not unattractive, though married, judging by the ring on his finger, and she wondered what it would be like to sleep with him. Probably boring and anyway not worth it; he seemed like the type who would write agonized letters, tell his wife, compose a poetry chapbook about his divorce called *Nuclear Fission* or something. She took his cup from his hand, raised it in a mock cheers, and downed the whole thing. He smiled at her, not unpleasantly, just quizzically and with a bit of earnest concern. "You okay?"

"Yep."

"Well, I'm going to see about getting a drink," he laughed, moving back toward the bar. "You need something?"

"No, I'm fine."

Did she need something? Yes, always, but what? There was a general aimless movement around the room, a purposeless churn of professors and grad students soundtracked by the classic rock pumping from the jukebox. *Angie, Ah-hayn-jeh,* Jagger ludicrously crooned. She'd been introduced to dozens of people over the last day, but could not remember any of their names. They all ran together, earnest grad-student types who radiated admiration, envy, hostility. The girls tended to dress in flowing garb, the guys tended to dress like blue-collar laborers. One of them, a gaunt, bearded kid, noticed her standing by herself and came over. "Hey."

"Hey."

She looked at him, and he said, "Mitch."

"Right, Mitch." With his pale skin and hollow eyes and the whiff of whiskey on his breath, she'd picked him out earlier as a type. He reminded her of a couple of the more adventurous boys she'd gone to school with, a type discontented with merely reading about dissolution, compelled to experience it themselves—the real thing, or a convincing simulacrum of it anyway. "Hey, I have a question."

"Shoot."

"You know anywhere to get drugs around here?"

"Sure," he said, "we can just duck out back for a smoke."

"I was thinking about something harder than that."

"Oh." In that moment, she became aware she'd never actually been smirked at before. "Well, yeah, I know a guy. But we'd have to get out of here."

"Happily."

He shrugged. "Okay, I'll pull my car up, wait here."

He exited the front door and ran down the wooden steps, large feet slapping against the wet pavement, disappearing quickly into the rain. She stood by the door watching. Don approached from behind, fresh drink in hand, and said, "You leaving already?"

For a moment, she felt an immense sadness and guilt. Why wasn't this enough? Why couldn't she ever be happy where she was, satisfied in the moment, here at an outing thrown on her behalf, talking to a nice man who might have wanted to flirt with her a little?

"Yeah, I guess so."

"Be careful." He looked at her for a long second, and in that moment she felt utterly transparent as the drug-addled fraud she was. She'd acquitted herself decently at the reading, the product of prefatory drinks at the hotel bar beforehand and two buoying Bennies, but she'd thought she caught Don looking sideways at her a few times. Now she was sure, when he seemed to say, "Twisted."

"What?"

"Twisters. Tornadoes." He gestured at the TV in the corner. "They're saying on the weather report. Be careful out there."

They drove south through town and across a bridge that looked out over a railroad hitching yard. Then through a suburban area, past a supermarket, and into the country. Mitch had popped a cassette into the tape deck and *Highway 61 Revisited* came on, a choice that, were this one of her creative writing workshops, the professor might have called a little on the nose.

He tapped his fingers on the wheel nervously—she'd flattered herself thinking his fidgety reticence was nerves caused by being with her, the big visiting author, but now she saw that he was scared. Distant lightning forked in the sky and the wind shook his little Datsun, in which they crawled down a country road everyone else was too smart to be out on. Cornstalks whipped in a mad dance, a dark, dense frenzy to her right, and it fully occurred to her what a terrible idea this was. Had she really wanted to get high this bad? She guessed she had.

"It's here, I think," said Mitch. "Right around here."

A few moments later, Mitch stopped and reversed with his arm behind her headrest. He turned left down a long gravel drive. The

white house at the end had a hunched, reticent look, almost seeming
to back away at their approach. When they parked in front, the water
ran down the windows in gelatinous sheets.

Mitch said, "His name's Jimmy. I get stuff from him now and
then."

"Okay."

"I don't know if he's here. Probably is, considering this weather. He
might be a little weird about me bringing a new person, but it'll be
fine." He talked as though she didn't live in New York, didn't do
drugs, didn't ever deal with the weirdnesses of drug dealers. Putting
up with weirdness—and creepiness, boringness, stupidness, laziness,
rudeness, etcetera—was like the tax you paid for the enormous privilege of buying illegal substances for a 500 percent markup.

Shooting the fifteen-foot curl between car and porch thoroughly
soaked them, and they shivered like dogs on the porch after Mitch
rang the doorbell. A light came on inside, and after what seemed like
a very long time, the door cracked a little. "Yeah," the voice said.

"It's Mitch."

"Who's that?"

"A friend."

"I meet her before?"

"No, she's traveling through town. Come on, man."

The door fully opened and they were admitted into a dimly lit hall.
The man in the shadows to her left wore a baseball cap and dark
glasses, as though he were in disguise. He led them into a living room
that was pretty much as she'd expected: ratty couches that looked like
they'd been rescued off a sidewalk, junk and boxes piled up against
the wall, curtains drawn, guitar akimbo in the corner, pervasive smell
of cat shit in the air. The guy, Jimmy, was older than she'd initially

thought, maybe forties, with acne scars so deeply pitted you could have pressed Tic Tacs into the largest of them. "What's your name?" he said.

"Alice."

"Why are you here?" The conversation felt like a weird double of the one she'd had an hour ago at the party.

"Here at your house, or in town?"

"Town."

"Just visiting."

"Nice time to visit." As if in response, a gust of rain hit the window, sounding like someone had tossed it from a bucket. Jimmy turned to Mitch and said, "So, what brings you out?"

"Thought you might be holding."

"Got some Dilaudid yesterday, how's that work?"

"Works for us, I think."

"That works," said Alice.

Jimmy went into an adjacent room even darker than the one they were in, and returned with a pill bottle. He shook a few out on an oblong metal plate on the coffee table, which was dusted with drug residue. "Ten per," he said. "How many?"

"Ten," said Alice, and he looked at her. She said, "I'm taking some with."

He counted out ten and she counted out five twenties from her wallet, money she'd withdrawn from the bank in advance for just such a hopeful, happy occasion. She handed him the money, and with an extra bill and one of her credit cards, she crushed four of the little white pills on the plate, grinding them beneath the bill with the edge of the card. Once the lump of crushed drugs felt smooth, she lifted the bill, scraped off the lingering residue, and chopped the pile into two lines. While she was doing this, Jimmy got up and fooled with a record player in the corner. A country song she didn't recognize came on, cued by the corny one-two of the fiddle's scrape. She rolled the bill up, inserted it into her right nostril, and vacuumed up the pile, then handed the bill to Mitch, who did the same.

Reclining on the sofa, she realized she should have asked what the milligramage was, but it was too late. Jimmy was telling Mitch about a car he had an eye on, lovingly describing the old yellow Stingray with its eight-stroke engine, and the rain was falling outside, and the woman on the record was singing something about how her love was like a rose, and a black-and-white tuxedo cat wandered in, and Alice wondered if she'd ever been part of a more peaceable scene. If you forgot the narcotics on the table, there was something even wholesome about it, something homey and Midwestern. Mitch gave her a cigarette and lit it, and she gulped in the smoke, which filled her lungs like something solid and in turn made her feel more corporeal.

Then she expelled the smoke, and likewise her attention diffused into the thick air and she was only intermittently aware of various things: Mitch talking about the book he was writing, the cat rubbing against her ankles, Jimmy getting up again and looking out the window. She became increasingly aware that there was another person in the room with them—she counted over and over: one, two, three, four. One, her. Two, Mitch. Three, Jimmy. Who was four?

She knew. It was the man from the Neversink—he'd entered the room unseen. He'd been visiting more and more lately. Her eyes were closed but she could tell it was him, could feel him bathing her in his glow as he sat beside her on the couch, looked at her with a kindly stare, and encircled her with his long, dark arms.

She jolted awake to Mitch shaking her. "Come on," he said.

"What?" He was waking her, she felt certain, because of the gray man.

"You hear that?" said Jimmy.

It was a mournful sound, a keening that seemed to be coming from the record player. "What is it?"

"You really aren't from here, are you?" said Jimmy. "Tornado sirens. Let's go."

"Where?" But she saw he was opening a door in the hall, pulling the chain on an overhead lightbulb.

"Come on," said Mitch again. "Down to the basement for a little bit."

"No," she said.

"Those sirens mean there are tornados on the ground, let's go."

At some point while she'd been on the nod, the house had apparently begun vibrating a little—it notched up a bit more, and, like a group of animals on the savannah registering a sudden predator, they all seemed to notice it as one. Mitch had a pleading look, and she relented a little, allowing him to shepherd her toward the door. Jimmy stood at the top of the stairs, arms full of the squirming cat. Thunder cracked, and the thing jumped away, knocking his glasses off in the process. When he crouched to grab them, he momentarily squinted up at Mitch and Alice with the eyes of a blind creature, something used to being in the dark, and again there was the feeling of aluminum between her teeth.

"No," she said.

"Come on," Mitch said.

"No."

Mitch pulled her arm, wrenching her toward the basement, and it provided extra momentum for her to slap his face. He stepped back, holding his beard, as if he feared she might have knocked it askew. "What the fuck?"

"I'm not going down there," she said.

Without looking back, Mitch pushed past her, and the two men disappeared behind the closed door. With a shuddering whump, the lights went out, and the woman's voice on the turntable slowed to an eerie moan, then nothing. The house's vibration was beginning to buck the uneven floorboards. A welter of knickknacks and magazines fell from the top shelf of a cabinet in the corner, its doors flying open like arms trying to catch the falling junk. Alice found she was not afraid, simply curious about what would happen. She drew back the curtain.

Weirdly, the rain had almost stopped, revealing a sky underlit by greenish aquarium lights. In the cornfield across the road they'd driven in on, she saw it: a thicker blackness against the black horizon, a funnel moving slowly this way and that. There it was. At the same time she noticed it, it seemed to notice her. It came across the field and ripped up the road, bearing closer in a blurry havoc. She looked back at the basement door and relaxed a little, secure in the knowledge that whatever else might be true, she would not go down there.

She scooped the remaining pills into her wallet and returned to the sofa, waiting for whatever would happen to happen. The house was shaking and shaking, with a mounting violence similar to the earlier rain—every moment simultaneously as intense as it could get and less intense than the next moment, which was already happening. The beams of the house scraped out a rising, rosiny whine; the air inside seemed to condense as though the house itself were taking a breath; then it screamed, and all the windows exploded. She couldn't breathe, couldn't think, was lifted from the sofa, was going to die, then she was on the floor.

It had passed, she somehow knew.

She was sitting in the heart of the sudden stillness. The wetness on her hands was blood. She'd landed on glass. She was alive. Some amount of time later, the men emerged from the basement. Jesus Christ, they both were saying unimaginatively, at different tempos and with different inflections, Jesus-fucking-Christ.

"Jesus Christ," said Mitch to Alice, "are you okay?"

"Yeah."

"That was close," said Jimmy. "That was really fucking close."

Mitch said, "It sounded like the house was lifted on its foundation."

Jimmy said, "It might have been for a second."

"Jesus-fucking-Christ," they both said.

Later, after the TV had given the all clear, Mitch drove Alice back to her hotel. She sat primly with her hands together on her lap, the wounded left one wrapped in an old T-shirt. It was still out, the cool stillness after a great storm has passed that is like nothing else in the world. The eerie quiet was ruined by other cars now passing on the street, people already getting back to their lives, distant sirens, a team of power company workers fixing a downed line.

He dropped her off in front of her hotel and drove away without saying a word. She walked through the lobby, ignoring the stares of the front-desk clerks, down the hall to her room. It was cool in there, sepulchral, and though she turned on all the lights it retained the memory of the darkness it had been in before she entered. In the bathroom she washed her hands again, then swallowed another of the little white pills. She turned on the TV to David Letterman, a segment with Super Dave shot from a cannon into a brick wall. Through the narcotic haze she felt—what? Well, mainly, disappointment. To be forever in that moment with the storm bearing down, with life narrowed down to the wind and the walls, that would be happiness; that would be just fine with her.

11. Len

The noise coming through the wall had, in approximately ten minutes, graduated from a low rumble of voices, to loud talking, to louder squabbling, to singing and chanting, to what was now intolerably loud chaos. For the third day in a row, the Polish Policemen's League was making a racket. Len pushed back from his desk, the desk on which his head had been resting for the last twenty minutes, as the sound culminated. Standing, he briefly considered the utility shed down the lawn and the .22 locked inside it. He could take the gun, go in there firing at the ceiling, and go out in a blaze of—if not glory, something. A blaze, at least. And it might satisfy some obscure codicil or subaddendum of the hotel's insurance if his face was shot away by a drunken Polack.

He'd idly thumbed through the insurance policy in bed the night before, momentarily seized with the appeal of burning the place to the ground. But it wasn't clear what constituted arson in their opinion, or acts of God—force majeure, in the strangely poetic insurance argot. Another wave of yelling from the next room propelled Len up from his desk and out into the hall, a resigned smile gathering on his face. He wasn't going to commit arson or, for that matter, any other act of felonious pluck. It was all a distraction and a fantasy—of being able to wrest some control away from fate, being able to dictate the terms of the hotel's demise as it went through its inevitable and seemingly endless death throes.

He pushed open the heavy latticed oak doors of the banquet hall, a space that in several senses exemplified the current terminal state of the hotel. First, and most obviously, it was completely run-down. The yellow wallpaper seemed to be actively detaching itself from the wall; it puffed in brown sections like the flesh of a rotten banana. In the corner, water collected in a small discolored pool under the mirror image of a discolored spot on the ceiling. It smelled bad everywhere, a pungent blend of mildew, dry rot, and insufficiently applied bleach.

Second, the clientele—i.e., the fifty or so men in this room—blearing at him. Len had no issue with authority, was a law-abiding citizen in every important respect, even had the little policeman's friend sticker on his car. But this bunch was the worst, the goddamned worst. They'd been coming since the late seventies, since the period following little Alice's assault and the discovery of the boy's body, unfortunate events that had made the hotel's declining fortunes official. With the Neversink's old clientele quickly disappearing and anonymous hotel chains springing up everywhere, Len had been forced to try various tactics to drum up new business. One idea, a stroke of seeming genius at the time, had been to offer special rates to police unions. It was an untapped reservoir of bookings that would provide a reassuring presence to other guests: two birds, one stone. He'd made some calls to connections they had in the city, and in, like a herd of drunken bulls, had stampeded the Polish Policemen's League.

With their shorn heads, muscular necks, and broad torsos covered by carapaces of beer fat, they looked like bulls, too. Snorting and bucking, pawing at the keg by the untouched buffet table, outrageously drunk at eleven in the morning. They'd be pissing in the halls by three. A week they came, every April, as though to formally usher in another miserable year. Their spokesman and de facto chief, Sergeant Mikulsky, called red-faced from a nearby table: "Len!"

"Sergeant."

"What brings you?"

"I was wondering if you might keep it down a little?"

"Down?" Mikulsky surveyed the room with an incredulous face, mirth clouding his already clouded little black eyes.

"Well, it's sort of loud. There are other guests, you know?"

"Are there," he said. The two men beside Mikulsky leered at him expectantly as he stood and addressed the room. "Boys," he called. "Boys! Mr. Sikorsky here has informed me that we're being a little loud." Several officers booed and Mikulsky waved them down. "None of that. We're here as guests, civilized guests, so let's behave like that. From now on," his voice dropped into a dramatic stage whisper, "from now on, I want you talk like this. Real quiet. Real, real quiet. Shhh!" They all laughed as he tiptoed around the room, shushing them individually, fat red index finger pressed to fat red lips in a prissy pantomime.

Len walked back to his office and closed the door against the raucous explosion of laughter to come. When it did, it rang in his ears like the world—like the entire goddamned miserable world—was laughing, just at him.

"Why don't we close up," said Rachel, for what must have been the ten-millionth time that young year, "and be done with it." They were in the hotel kitchen, a huge tiled space built for a staff of thirty, now manned by three full-time cooks and two part-timers, local kids they paid in cash. Len was upside down, his head in a nonfunctional oven, trying to find the pilot.

"And do what?"

"Anything. Literally anything else."

"For money, I mean."

"Are we making money here? We could do nothing and make more money. Not making any money would be a vast improvement."

"I don't want to have this discussion." He heard her sigh. The pilot flickered on, but he stayed in the oven, avoiding his wife's face. It was nice here. "My grandparents built this place, Rach. I can't just walk away from it."

"Yes, you can. That's exactly what you can do. Your grandparents would not want you destroying our lives, our children's lives."

"How do you know that? You didn't know them, maybe that's exactly what they would have wanted."

"We're still young."

"I'm forty-five."

"That's young. We have time to start over."

"I don't want to start over." The pilot light flickered back out. Everything hated him. He pulled his head out and looked at his wife standing over him in a posture of exasperated complaint, as he'd known she would be, the only way he could imagine her these days.

"This place is my birthright, okay? I want to turn things around. I want to save it."

"Oh my God." With a sweep of her thin, freckled arm and a bustle of her black hair, still full and girlishly long, with only a bit of gray at the temple—and oh, how he'd loved that hair when they met! How he still did!—she gestured at the kitchen, decaying like everything else. The Salvadoran dishwasher in the corner scrubbing a banquet pan didn't hear or understand, or graciously pretended not to. "There's no turning it around. There's nothing to save. Wake up, Leonard. People are frightened of coming here, to Liberty. And even if they weren't, the Catskills are done. The dream is dead."

"Look," he said, hugging his knees to his chest. "Here's how it is, okay? This place is like life. However bad it gets, you just keep going. It gets worse and worse, and you keep going until you can't anymore, until it ends. That's how it's going to be. We just keep going with this thing until it ends."

She walked away, not even needing to respond with the obvious—that she had no intention of going until the end. And she was probably right; there was no turning it around. What did he hope would happen? Force majeure, he supposed, sticking his head back in the oven.

The restaurant that night—and most nights—was dead, depressing. Len sat at the bar with his ritual postwork drink prepared by Sander Levin, the longtime bartender. There was a table of policemen in one corner of the large room, whom Len had seated as far away as possible from a young couple who stared down at their menus in mild bewilderment, as if wondering how they'd wound up in this place. It was possible they were the only other guests in the hotel at this point; Len hadn't checked the registry. Sander, encased in a frayed tux, eyes clouded behind thick glasses, leaned over the bar. "Mr. Sikorsky," he said. "We need to talk."

"So talk."

"I gotta give you my notice."

"What?"

"I'm leaving."

Len stared at Sander, who straightened with defensive dignity. Sander had been there since time immemorial. As long as Len could remember, he had been behind the bar in his white tux and steel-rim glasses, iron hair plastered back, a living monument to constancy through the decades, a tenure during which, to Len's knowledge, Sander had not missed one day of work. This was like one of the structural pillars in the lobby calling it quits.

"Come on," said Len.

Sander shook his great head, trembling very slightly—more emotion than Len had ever seen him display. "You have to know this kills me, Mr. Sikorsky. But I just can't make a living anymore. I even picked up a couple of shifts over at that new TGI Fridays in Bellhaven, trying to supplement. But I make more there than I do here."

"TGI Fridays."

"I'm sorry."

"But what are you going to do?"

"Well, I was thinking Florida. My daughter and son-in-law are down there, in Fort Myers. I wouldn't mind some nice weather for a change. If I sell the house, I'll have a little money to move with. Louisa's starting a plant nursery; I could be a help."

"Listen, we can work something out. You should have told me sooner." A roar issued from the policeman's table, and in the nearly empty room, Len found himself having to yell to speak over them. "I can give you a raise. Or some kind of profit sharing."

Sander looked at him with an expression so full of pity that Len had to look down into his drink at the two little olives impaled on their plastic spear. Sander said, "Mr. Sikorsky, come on now, let's not make a big tzimmes over this. It's been a good run, I've loved my time here. I loved your father and mother, it's just time, is all."

Len got the idea the next morning, reading the paper with his coffee, a small thing about an easement dispute at Yasgur's Farm, site of Woodstock nineteen years before. Len had been a little too old for it at the time, already running the hotel's day-to-day operations, unable to take three days off to eat acid and roll around in the mud with naked girls named after horoscope symbols, not that that sounded unpleasant. By 1969, he and Rachel were almost through their extended courtship—the four years she spent at Vassar, the four years he spent visiting her there. He'd logged enough time in Vassar's dorms to deserve an honorary degree.

Rachel did go to Woodstock with some friends and said it was far out, though he sensed a hesitation on her part. Deep down, he thought, beneath the intellectual hippie routine, lurked a good upper-class Jewish girl, too well-brought up and smart to buy into all this free-love stuff. Though afterward, she did bring back a powerful joint, get him high on the roof of the hotel, and proceed to make love to him there all night. He did have Woodstock and its ethos to thank for that.

Maybe, he thought, old Yasgur could help him out again. He put the paper down and called Saul Javits. It was Javits's day off, and he let the phone ring a dozen times, knowing the man would be puttering around his mountaintop cabin, doing twenty things and nothing at once. Finally, in the manner of an old-style detective, he answered: "Javits."

"I had an idea."

"He has an idea. It can't wait until tomorrow, this idea?"

"I was thinking—the twenty-year anniversary of Woodstock is coming up, right?"

"Next summer. August."

"There's gonna be a thing, I heard. A tribute, some of the old people playing."

"Well, drop a dime, someone picks it up."

"My thinking, exactly. What if we throw an event, get a big name to come and perform in the ballroom, make a whole thing out of it. Position ourselves as the Woodstock hotel."

"Why?"

"What do you mean, why? Because we need to drum up business, that's why."

There was a long silence as Javits thought about it. He said, "I don't know. Seems desperate."

"It seems desperate because we're desperate. Drowning men look desperate, they can't help it. They're too worried about drowning."

"You want we should bring in Jimi Hendrix to play the national anthem? Maybe Richie Havens can sing 'Freedom' for three hours?"

"Yeah, exactly."

"I was joking, Lenny, come on. This isn't the Neversink, we run a nice place here, for families. You know the kind of people that would attract?"

"People with money? And what kind of people are we attracting now?"

Javits sighed and said, "It's a downturn. Things'll pick up."

"Not on their own, they won't. I'm going to talk to Mickey, see what she thinks." Mickey Shulman was a talent agent who had booked the main stage at the Neversink and other hotels for decades. She was a longtime friend and business associate, a contemporary of Len's father and former agent of his Uncle Joey. At seventy-something, she still worked nine-to-five and represented a stable of working entertainers. There was another long silence, and Len finally said, "I'm not asking for your opinion, Saul. We've got to do something."

"Hey, if you didn't want to know, why call? Tell Mickey hi. Mazel tov."

Mickey was more enthusiastic than Javits. Not a bad idea, she said, which quelled Len's doubts, a little. Later that day, having made some calls, she faxed over a list of possible performers and their guarantees. Len went down the list. Among them was, indeed, Richie Havens, although his fifteen-thousand-dollar ask seemed a little steep. But some others were more affordable—for instance, John Sebastian, whose name Len dimly recognized. From the Mamas and the Papas, he thought: "California Dreamin'."

He found his daughter, Susannah, working on homework by the outdoor pool, on which floated a scrim of dead leaves. He made a mental note to clean it, though the weather was still too cold for anyone to want to swim, if there had been anyone there in the first place. The girl was wrapped in a blanket and writing on a sheet of loose-leaf paper with an edge bothered by the wind.

Len said, "Why are you out here?"

She shrugged. She was thirteen, and had last willingly engaged in a conversation with him maybe two years earlier. "Mom said watch

Noah." Noah was eight and nowhere to be seen, and Len's heart pounded a little as he walked to the edge of the pool. Down the adjacent sloping field, his son sprawled on a small hummock, engaged in incomprehensible, operatic war play with plastic toys that turned into other things.

"Noah!" he yelled, and the boy turned. "Come back up here! Stay where your sister can see you."

The boy moved reluctantly into the pool area, settling with his toys near the cabana. Len returned to his daughter and said, "Hey, do you know who John Sebastian is?"

"No."

"He's a musician."

"Okay, great."

"Mamas and Papas, I think. You know who they are?"

"Old-fart stuff?"

"Right, that's who we want."

She looked up. "What are you talking about?"

"Nothing. What are you working on?"

"Algebra. It's complicated." She looked back down.

You have no idea, he thought, walking back inside to the front lobby where Rachel was meant to be working—you have no idea how complicated. As usual, walking through the Great Hall, he was assaulted by the number of things that needed repairing, replacing, soldering, mending, patching, and painting. It would take a team of repairmen a year, on the outside, to get the place back into good condition, and that would be if the hotel was closed the whole time. Somehow it had all gotten away from him.

As he turned the corner into the lobby, Rachel was nowhere to be seen. The front desk sat vacant, and for a horrible moment he was struck by the sense that the hotel had already shuttered without his knowledge. In the same moment, he seemed to see into the future, see the lobby and the adjoining natatorium in a state of utter dilapidation, covered in garbage, carpet torn away, walls dripping with graffiti, industrious weeds pushing through cracks in the riven cement. He shivered and cried, "Rachel!"

"What?" Her voice issued from the café, and like a child lost in the supermarket, he moved toward it with grateful desperation.

She sat at the counter, eating rugelach and drinking a cup of coffee, the edge of the saucer holding down the page of her book. Some paperback mystery—she was always in the middle of one, reading with steady inexorability over the last decade. Len Deighton and Carl Hiaasen had replaced Woolf and Foucault. He gestured to the entryway, said, "The desk?"

"Oh," she craned her neck around him. "I didn't hear the tour bus arrive. One moment."

"Is the sarcasm really necessary?"

"I don't know, is scolding me really necessary?"

"It just looks bad."

"To whom? To whom does it look bad?"

He slumped on the stool next to her and pulled out the fax sheet from his pocket, which he unfolded on the Formica countertop. "Fine," he said. "On that note, take a look at this."

"What is it?"

He explained, glancing at her now and then, though less often as he went on and her face remained frozen in an expression of mute incredulity. "You're serious," she said, finally.

"Yeah, I think I am."

"I don't know what to say."

"Mickey thought it was a good idea."

"Mickey gets a 5 percent commission, of course she thinks it's a good idea."

"It's not all business—she'd tell me if she thought it was bad."

Rachel looked at the sheet for another few seconds. "You want to pay Abbie Hoffman ten grand?"

"Abbie's a natural for this. People will love it."

"And John Sebastian? From the Lovin' Spoonful?"

Len took the sheet. "I thought he was the Mamas and the Papas. One of the Papas."

"Are you out of your fucking mind?"

"Desperate times, Rach."

She stood. She wore a pair of jeans under her hotel smock, and as he saw the heavy curve of her hip, he again felt the press of the future, like something physical, already real and simply waiting for him, for them both. "Spend money to make money, right?"

"As the saying goes, yeah."

"I want you to listen to me and understand what I'm saying, Len. If you take twenty thousand dollars out of our savings, out of Suse and Noah's college money, for this harebrained scheme, I swear to God I'm going to leave you. You can ruin our lives if you want, but not our children's lives. Is that clear?"

"What you're saying is clear, yes."

"Good. Reporting back to post, captain." She left for the front desk, and he remained in the café, washing up her cup and plate. That night, lying beside her, the three inches of mattress between them might as well have been the desert of Midian. His eyes weren't open—who lies in bed with their eyes open?—but he couldn't sleep and knew he wouldn't all night. Rachel appeared before him as she had one night shortly after they'd gotten married, shortly before she'd become pregnant with Susannah, on a walk they'd taken in the nearby woods, the Neversink River babbling somewhere in the invisible nearness. She was wearing one of his flannel shirts, open off the collarbone, dark hair massed like the storm clouds hanging above the nearby flame-streaked trees. She'd walked ahead of him on the trail and turned, looking at him as if there were no one else in the entire world, and said something. What had she said? It hadn't been *I love you*—nothing that obvious or common; it had been one of those funny little beginning things that form the strange bedrock of a relationship, eventually obscured by the elaborate and sprawling mansion built on top. She stared at him now, in the vision, and very clearly said, *Do it for us. Please, Lenny, do this thing for us.*

The policeman was young, twenty-five at most, brush-cut and apple-cheeked from a raucous lunchtime bender, and passed out dead in the hall. In an unlikely coincidence, he'd happened to fall over directly in front of one of the five occupied rooms—Len had checked the register—and was blocking the guest's door. Len managed to roll the cop out of the way, freeing Mr. Teitelbaum, who'd been coming up for an early springtime golf getaway practically since the course had been built, forty years ago. He was a thin man, with a thick wedge of white hair pointing down like an arrow at the lumpy, prone form beneath his feet.

"If your mother was alive to see this," he said, the white V shaking back and forth.

"Thank God she's gone, huh?"

"You know I would never suggest such a thing. Your mother was a great woman, and I loved her very much."

"I know, sorry."

"But yes, perhaps it is a small blessing she isn't here for this."

"Yes, perhaps."

Mr. Teitelbaum moved slowly away and Len dragged the policeman a few feet in the opposite direction before realizing he had no idea where he was taking him. He unlocked a room and pulled him inside, just to get him out of the hall. He got the man's feet free of the door and it shut behind him. There was no possibility of getting him onto the bed, and for a moment, standing astride Officer Lasky—according to the lanyard twisted around his neck—Len was struck by the knowledge that he could do anything he wanted to the man: pour water on his face, beat him with a shoe, stick his fingers up his nose, anything. It didn't lack a certain appeal. Mr. Teitelbaum was right—his mother, had she still been alive, would have been instantly felled by the spectacle of these drunken lunatics crawling around, of the current state of things. Of course, his mother would never have let things get like this, would have done something to save the hotel, as she had, in fact, done several times during her four-decade tenure at its helm.

He shook his head and left the room, jogging down the stairs to the first floor with a mounting anger that constricted his throat. Beating on the door yielded Sergeant Mikulsky, bathrobe-clad and similarly red-faced with drink, although ambulatory and sentient, more or less.

"What?" The TV blared in the room behind him, the floor of which was littered with refuse and bottles.

"Officer Lasky, you know him?"

"Yeh, Teddy."

"He passed out upstairs in the hall."

"Oh boy. Ted got into it at lunch, huh?" Mikulsky chuckled and shook his head with evident pleasure—boys will be boys, after all—then wiped his face with his sleeve, replacing the mirth with a mock-serious frown. "I mean, how horrible. What can I do to help matters?"

"You can help me move him, for one thing. And for another, in the future, you can supervise your men and keep them from behaving like a pack of animals." Len felt a slight satisfaction, a very minor victory, in seeing Mikulsky's habitually facetious look dissolve.

"Okay, hold on," he said, closing the door, not gently. He reemerged a minute later, in slacks and a half-buttoned shirt, barefoot. Having regained his sarcastic mien, he gestured lavishly toward the stairwell, saying, "After you."

They hauled Officer Lasky to his room, also located on the third floor, a minor fortune, and lifted him into bed. With surprising tenderness, Mikulsky rested Lasky's head on the pillow and turned it to the side, saying, "So he doesn't throw up."

"Great. Thank you."

Len started to walk out, but felt Mikulsky following him. The man walked a pace or two behind him down the hall, and when he spoke, there was a jaunty note of menace in his voice. "I gotta say, you got some nerve talking to me like that."

"Is that right?"

"I'm the steadiest business you got right now. Every year, me and my 'pack of animals' put what—eight, nine grand in your pocket? I'm looking around, thinking, who else is booking this dump?"

"Feel free to stop coming," said Len. "Actually, I insist."

Mikulsky slurred on, apparently not having heard. "And besides that, I protect and serve the people of New York City—the fuck do you do?" Len moved into the stairwell and the wooden stairs creaked hollowly under his feet, with Mikulsky's creaking right behind him.

He wasn't entirely surprised when, on the landing, his arm was
yanked up behind his back, his face pushed into the floral wallpaper.
The words were spat carefully into his ear. "You just run a goddamn
hotel. Some lousy Jew innkeeper wants to talk to me like that?"

"Let me go."

"Don't worry, we won't be back next year." Mikulsky pushed him
away, as though dispensing with a particularly odious piece of refuse,
and Len half fell in the corner, taking a knee against a cobwebbed
sprinkler valve. Mikulsky said, "I didn't want to tell you, but we'd
already decided to hold next year's thing in Atlantic City. This fucking place has really gone downhill."

In accordance with Rachel's wishes, Len didn't take twenty thousand out of savings. As it turned out, it cost only thirteen. Mickey
was able to negotiate Abbie Hoffman—"Ab," as she called him—
down to eight thousand, and John Sebastian down to five. And the
money didn't come from their savings account, technically, but
rather from cashing out one of the several mutual funds his mother
had randomly placed money in during profitable years, the banking
equivalent of stashing cash in mattresses. He didn't tell Rachel,
trying to figure out how best to put it, or maybe just putting it off.
But he didn't feel guilty about it, either. Standing by and watching
as his inheritance, spiritual and otherwise, slowly crumbled into a
pile of dust simply wasn't an option. And, he thought, given time
and a chance to think about it, she might soften, though she showed
no signs of softening yet—spade in hand, bent over the flower bed
encircling the welcome sign out front, the muscle in her jaw under
her ear pulsing as though she were chewing an especially tough
piece of gristle.

Javits put his ancient journalism chops to use and wrote out a press release for publication in the *Sikorsky Times*, a mailing circular started by Len's father that still went out to over twenty thousand guests: "Woodstock Twenty-Year Gala Announced!" Javits used a couple of stock photos he'd found of Hoffman waving a book and Sebastian in tie-dye and glasses, strumming an acoustic with a pacific grin. The article copy was somewhat vague, since besides the presence of the two musicians (and other luminaries, the article insinuated), no real events had yet been planned—but it made reference to concert performances, speaking engagements, and a variety of "workshops," a word that, Javits said, could refer to virtually anything: ceramics how-tos, ecological powwows, responsible investment seminars for aging hippies. A version of the press release was sent to the *Hudson Valley Leader*, and a small buy was slated for the *Times* at the end of the year.

After conferencing with Javits and looking over the materials, Len walked the halls with a rare sense of ownership, rather than his usual feeling, which was closer to that of default overseer. Of course, he had chosen this—he had grown up at the hotel, had learned to do everything there with an expectation of taking it over, had done so when his father passed away and his mother became ill. This, as opposed to his brother, Ezra—a diffident, fey child who'd gone to Columbia and never returned for more than three days in a row. Ezra had gladly surrendered his ownership stake and received a modest trust income that supplemented his modest income teaching something Len could never remember—aquatic medieval semiology or a similar field, something so abstrusely academic as to seem like a parody of abstruse academia.

No, he thought, grabbing a rag and bottle of Brasso from beneath the bar and polishing the railing that encircled the perimeter of the empty dining room—you chose this. But time and inertia have a way of blurring the clear-minded decisions you've made, obscuring cause behind years of effect, until it seems your life has always been this way and you never had a choice to begin with. So what, he thought, running the rag up and down the length of the long, cloudy pole, seeing his face warp in the reflection, so what if this was a cockamamie scheme? Was that the word she'd used? Something like that, but anyway, so what? It was something, at least. If nothing else, thirteen thousand was a bargain to feel the way he did now: like a man. The way his grandfather, Asher, must have felt when, after several ill-fated business ventures in the city, he'd bought a parcel of land in the Catskills and finally made his way—first as a farmer, then a small-time innkeeper, then as an entrepreneur, risking it all once more to purchase the hotel. At every step of the way, including immigrating to America, Asher had taken risks the family felt were foolhardy—what if he had listened to them? The railing glowed with Len's labors, affirming his own decision, a worthy risk taken to preserve his grandfather's legacy.

Later, Rachel glowed as well, lit by an inner flame or simply the rare conjugal exertion. Len had surprised her in bed with a forcefulness she clearly found appealing, or at least surprising. When they made love she half smiled up at him, and he saw in a gasping instant how easy the whole thing could be: you did what you had to do, you worked and provided, you made your wife and family happy as best you could. She lay against him in their dark room, the northern wind outside rattling the shutters as though they were in a remote outpost, utterly alone in the world but for each other.

"What got into you," she said.

"I don't know. It had been too long."

"Yes, it had."

"I love you." In the dim lamplight of the room, her face, though tired and lined with worry and perhaps now almost old, contained all of her, every moment over the past fifteen years—from coltish know-it-all college girl, to mother-to-be and bride, to young and proud then young and exhausted mother, to fully grown co-proprietor of a storied business, to a depleted woman in her middle years. She was still beautiful. But to Len, who had known her so long, her face was beyond beauty, beyond evaluating in those terms—it was beautiful in the same way water is beautiful. The beauty was inextricable from what it was, its value inextricable from its necessity.

"I know you do."

"And you love me."

"Of course," she responded after a very slight pause.

"But?"

"No, no but. I do love you."

"But."

"But I don't love how things have gotten. I don't love living here, stagnating."

"Stagnating."

She turned off her side and onto her back. "I don't love seeing you drive yourself crazy. I don't love Suse and Noah going to that hick school. Did she tell you her science teacher didn't know Uranus had rings?"

"I didn't know that, either."

"You're not a science teacher."

"Neither are you."

She sighed. "No. I'm not. Who am I?"

"Rachel Sikorsky."

"Who is that?"

"A mother, a wife. A businesswoman."

She turned to her side of the bed and was crying, he knew, but he could not bring himself to comfort her. Because what would he be comforting her for? For the life they'd built together? For their marriage and children? For these things he could not apologize. Neither could he stand her sobbing, so he rose to get a glass of water from the kitchen. In the hall, he first heard his daughter's rock music mutely thudding in her unknowable, hostile lair. Then he stopped at Noah's door and was relieved to hear soft snoring. Lately, the boy had been having night terrors, kept saying a man was entering his room and watching him. The therapist said it was sleep paralysis caused by stress and informed by the stories of children being snatched from their rooms, the park, the grocery store. Living here seemed to be taking its toll on everyone.

The moon shone through the kitchen window in a soft pool at his feet. Although he'd been raised by devout parents and was observant, Len had never before felt God observing him. God had always struck him as less omnipotent than omnipresent, less a sentient force than an essential fabric. But now, looking at the white, liquid light, he was struck by the sense, perhaps wishful, of God as an intelligence out there, watching him. Here I am, God, he thought, here I am in my moment of need. Deliver something unto me, or failing that, me unto something.

On Sunday, after a large breakfast with a subdued tone owing to the dual regrets of vacation's end and the unspeakable revelries of the night before, the Polish Policemen's League began checking out. Len thanked them at the front desk as they dropped off their keys; some returned the greeting and shook his hand, but many didn't meet his eye. Word had clearly spread about the Mikulsky imbroglio.

Sergeant Mikulsky himself appeared, bag in hand, around ten thirty, brow beetled beneath a flattened flattop. He handed Len the room key and said, "Len, I'm sorry about the other day. I was out of line."

"It's okay, Sergeant."

"It's not. I was a little tight, and I got defensive about my men. You know how it is. You keep with your own."

"I do."

"We've always enjoyed coming here."

"Please come again."

"We will, we will." The handshake felt authentic, even if the words didn't.

At eleven, Len got Peter, the young bellhop, to man the front desk, and went around to check the three remaining unchecked-out rooms for late risers, among them Officer Lasky. As he passed the kitchen, Rachel stepped in front of him, wielding a piece of paper. "What," she said in a soft tone, barely louder than a whisper, "is this?"

He took it. It was the *Sikorsky Times* ad copy for the Woodstock festival. Javits must have left the materials lying around in his chaotic office, and Rachel must have found it on one of her penitent straightening jags. He said, "I have to get the rest of the policemen checked out, can we talk after?"

"About what?"

"What do you mean?" He nodded at the paper. "About the thing."

"If you went ahead with this, there's nothing to discuss."

"Of course there is."

She stuck out an arm and held the frame of the doorway in which she stood. It looked less like she was steadying herself and more like she was single-handedly holding up the entire building. "Oh God," she said. "You just don't get it." She pulled off her work smock, folded it neatly in two, and handed it to him.

"That's it? You're quitting?"

"Yes."

"No notice?"

She laughed. "Would you rather fire me?"

"You know Mama never fired anyone? Even the maid they caught stealing."

"So the legend has it."

"Where will you go? Where will Noah and Suse go?"

"I've made arrangements. My parents' place. It's a little small, but it'll work for a few months."

"You've been planning for this?"

She stared at him with such penetrating pity that he had to turn away. Out the hall window, a young girl dipped her foot in the pool. How recently it seemed they had sat there, and yet how irretrievable it was. As she spoke, Rachel's voice seemed to come from that girl. "This has been happening for years. Surely you saw it coming."

"No. I wanted to make it work. I wanted to make all of this work."

"Oh, Lenny."

She shook her head, wadded the smock up, and deposited it on the steel kitchen counter just inside the door. "I'll call you soon," she said, and kissed him. He watched her walk away, down the corridor and out the side exit, presumably toward the cottage, to explain things to the kids and pack whatever was going with them to Manhattan. But then, she'd probably already done those things. All that remained was the leaving.

Completely at a loss for what to do next, he defaulted to the task he'd been in the middle of, moving up the stairs to the second floor.

He knocked on Lasky's room, 324. No one answered, so he turned the skeleton key in the lock and entered.

The room was in shambles. Not the usual shambles the more slovenly guests occasionally left behind: food wrappers on the floor, clothes left under the bed, perhaps a forlorn condom dangling off the side of a wastebasket. The place was actually destroyed. The mirror had been pulled off the wall and shards of glass twinkled in the carpet. The wall to the right of the door had been gouged several times, as though the room's occupant had been looking for something behind the floral wallpaper. The pillow lay ripped obscenely open, and a single small feather floated serenely past Len's face.

The image of that feather stayed in his mind as he wound his way downstairs, through the main hall, and past the lobby, where Peter stood in smiling conversation with another guest checking out. He felt like the feather, borne on unseeable currents, the strange winds of his life. In the parking lot, Lasky—red-faced, brush cut, clad in civvies— leaned against a car, talking to two other men.

"Hey," said Len, approaching.

Lasky turned. "What?"

"The room. Your room."

Lasky shrugged. "Boys played poker last night, got a little rowdy."

"It's destroyed. You're paying for it."

Lasky looked at his compatriots and grinned. "Fuck you. Place is already destroyed."

He threw his head back in a long, ragged laugh that lasted the length of time it took Len to cross the remaining distance between them and punch him in the mouth. Lasky dropped to the ground, and Len had just enough time to get in one more punch before the blows began landing on him. A sledgehammer fist on Len's back dropped him beside the prone cop. The policemen surrounded his felled body, and two more quickly crossed the lot to join the fun, a migration witnessed only by the hotel itself. As it witnessed Rachel packing a toiletry bag in the cottage and crying softly to herself. As it witnessed Susannah and Noah in private conference by the station wagon, the elder explaining once again to the younger, with a touch of irritation, where they were going, and that, no, they wouldn't be back for a while. As it witnessed Peter the bellhop looking in on Officer Lasky's ruined room and regretting it for the sake of the new maid, whom he loved and who he knew would be spending the better part of the morning cleaning it up. As it witnessed Saul Javits napping in his office. As it witnessed Sander Levin driving up the long hotel road in his old Nova, parking, and pulling on his white jacket, specially dry-cleaned for his final shift.

"Stop!" Sander yelled.

The cops turned to see him, this anachronistic figure in white tuxedo and steel-gray hair. Almost in unison, they stepped away from Len, bruised and bloody and in blessed unconsciousness. Officer Lasky—mouth bloodied, eye swelling—and two others picked Len up and deposited him in the back of an off-duty squad car. Lights flashing silently, they drove in line like a funeral procession along the road twisting down Neversink Hill. Sander watched them go, then got back in his car and followed.

Len came to on a metal bench to find Sander Levin sitting beside him. He touched his bruised face, and his hand came away sticky with blood. "I've ruined everything, Sander."

"No, you haven't. Don't say that."

"I've done everything wrong."

"Some things are beyond our control. The downturn in the economy, the boy's body. You can't help these things."

Len laughed, coughed. "Force majeure."

"What?"

"Insurance companies call it that. Acts of God." A bird fluttered down to the window outside, pecked at the dry crumbs of cement, flew off again. He said, "Rachel's leaving me, Sander."

"Ach, Lenny. Ah, no."

"Thank you for helping me. Thank you for coming."

Sander sat beside him on the bench, put his arm around Len, felt the broad back heaving up and down.

"I was thinking I'd stay on a little while longer. At the hotel, I mean."

"I'll give you a raise."

"Okay."

They sat there for a while like that, two men in the darkening room, until it was time for Sander to leave and open the bar.

12. Ezra

1996

The Neversink was closing, and Len was having a final night with friends and family, former employees. Did I want to come? I'd dithered on this point for several months. The last time I'd been, years before, it was too painful to see the state of the place, and this despite the fact that I'd never really cared about the hotel, certainly not like my little brother did. I'd never bought into the mythos surrounding it and my grandparents, never fancied myself the inheritor of an empire. When I left for school, I was happy to renounce an ownership stake in exchange for a modest monthly allowance. This supplementary money has come in handy over the years, allowed me to pursue my interests in academia—take positions not purely based on a paycheck or quick tenure—and indulge in the little pastimes and minor passions for which bachelorhood makes room.

I was grateful for the allowance, but still hated going to the place. In its festering decrepitude, it reminded me of nothing so much as a diseased body—diseased for decades, and now, with its official closing, deceased. Nonetheless, I felt obligated, and with the semester over, I was out of plausible work excuses. I packed my bag, packed my car, left the key for my neighbor, Mrs. Shelden, to feed the cat, turned the thermostat to sixty-two, checked the tire pressure and oil, and set out to pay my last respects, to sit shiva with the Hotel Neversink's corpse.

On the drive down, crossing a rickety one-lane bridge, I noticed a convocation of eagles nesting in a tree by the river. I pulled over, took pictures, and made a note in my birding book. As a boy, I used to watch them with a kind of pure pleasure, struck, as I'm sure most children are, by their plumage and the fantastic gift of flight. I went further, though, bringing home books from the library, science books that explained their descent from dinosaurs, which heightened my ardor. Then, on my thirteenth birthday, I received a pair of binoculars from my father, and, as they say, I never looked back.

How many countless dreary upstate afternoons did I while away, creeping through the forest around the hotel, clad in my boots and hunter's jacket, binoculars around my neck and notebook in hand? When the boy disappeared—I was fourteen at the time—I was encouraged to curtail these excursions, but still I went. On weekends, many miles I would gyre around the Neversink like Yeats's falcon, around a center that, I sensed, would not hold. At eighteen I left for school—Columbia—but continued the habit, as I did through my twenties, my marriage and divorce, my middle years. The life list has grown long, but I thrill the same as I did at fourteen to a new tick, that unique joy only other birders can understand.

I got back on the road with a happy feeling. But as the miles and hours went by and the daylight dulled into a misty upstate dusk, it was as though a thin gauze had been stretched across my vision, and I was once again filled with dread. In the purplish air I could see the Neversink, waiting. I even exited the highway with the fleeting intention of turning around. But no, I'd come this far, was only a hundred miles or so from Liberty.

We ate in the dining room, the twenty or so of us: myself, Len, Rachel and Noah visiting from the city, Susannah down from college, Javits, Sander Levin, and various former employees and longtime guests I didn't know. The pervasive gloom of the hotel is difficult to describe. As Len led our group to the dining room, I caught my breath a couple of times—the cavernous dark seeming to reach out from places deep within itself. Even in the waning days, the Neversink had done a decent trade, and my memories of the place—populated by familiar old-timers and bustling employees and children carrying dripping toys from the pool—were vandalized by this new reality. My memories weren't the only thing vandalized—upon arrival, I'd noticed the handiwork of some local graffiti artists, most notably on the south wing's long side wall, where the word *Mulciber!* was sprayed, ominous and inscrutable, in dripping red paint.

The mood at the table was not exactly bleak, but it was muted. Len seemed like he'd been drinking—when we hugged, I caught the yeasty tang of beer on his breath. An older woman who Len said sometimes helped in the kitchen nervously brought out the plates of food, reminiscent of my grandmother's cooking, though flavorless, as if they'd been run through a dishwasher before service.

But the wine flowed and the chat was pleasant enough. We all caught up, and I found myself glad I'd come, in spite of my misgivings. Dinner finished, we went to the bar, behind which ventured

Sander Levin. He donned his white tuxedo jacket with a courtly little bow, and to a smattering of applause began mixing martinis. I am not much of a drinker, but I was so enjoying the conviviality that I stayed up, talking to Rachel, to Sander, to Len, not really registering the dinnergoers yawning, saying their good-byes, moving to the exit—to the rooms we'd been assigned by Len for the closing. Finally, it was just Len and Sander and me. Sander removed the jacket, hung it over the door, and with a grave look came from behind the bar to shake my brother's hand.

"It's been an honor, Mr. Sikorsky."

Len wiped his eyes, embraced Sander. "The honor's been ours."

I couldn't help being touched by the moment. I shook Sander's hand, and he walked out with the stiff dignity of a soldier discharged from his duty. Somehow, with only the two of us now instead of three, the room felt desolate.

"What are you going to do now?" I said.

"Well, there's a lot to do around here. Have to figure out what to do with the kitchen appliances, art, fixtures." He gestured overhead without looking at the chandelier. "And the golf course is staying open."

I nodded. He said, "What about you?"

"Oh, you know. Teaching, writing articles. Going to a conference in Vancouver in July." I suspected Len wasn't quite sure what my field was, and I was almost tempted to ask him, but I didn't. "I'm going on an expedition in Victoria while I'm there. There's a type of red-throated warbler thought to have been extinct for decades. It's really quite exciting."

He went behind the bar and sloppily fixed us another round, then bent forward on his elbows. "Ez," he said, "I've got some bad news. I have to pull your allowance."

"What?"

"We can't pay you out anymore."

I sipped my martini, which now tasted of spoiled vermouth, water from a vase full of dead flowers. "That wasn't the deal. It was supposed to be for life."

"Well, the Neversink was supposed to be for life, too."

"That's not my concern."

"It is, though, because there's no money to pay you."

"I find it hard to believe there's nothing left behind. And you said you'd be selling off parts of the hotel, right?"

He looked at me with mild disbelief. "I'm selling stuff to pay our creditors."

"Well," I said, "consider me a creditor."

"You always were a cold fish, Ezra, but this is really something." He came around the bar with his sloshing drink, shaking his head as though to the beat of a tune only he could hear. "I'll see what I can do. I know you've always counted on that money. But I have to tell you, if there isn't any—if the golf course is in the red—you're out of luck. It's not as though you signed a contract."

"It was a promise."

"I'll see what I can do."

We drank our drinks, raising them to our mouths with a mechanical air. My brother and I have never been especially close, talked to each other only on occasion, and I felt that distance between us now more than ever before. I didn't really know him, and he didn't really know me. We sat in silence. The darkness of the hotel just past the bar was like a living presence; from somewhere in its depths, a clock ticked like a heart. "Who," I said finally, breaking the awful silence that had gathered around us, "do you think it was?"

"Who who was?"

"The killer."

He looked at me. "How the hell should I know?"

"I'm asking who you think."

"I think some lunatic out there." He swept his arm as though the nearby wall were invisible and we had a vista that stretched all the way through the valley, to the city and beyond.

I should have stopped there. I should have said good night and gone up to my room. But the drink I had in me, the anger I felt at the prospect of being cut off, and the ambience of the place—at any moment you expected a gun to go off, a scream to issue, and Miss Marple to walk through the front door—all combined to produce in me a noxious mirth. "But surely you'd entertained the idea that it might have been someone here."

He didn't respond, bent forward over his drink with a slightly insipid-looking overbite. Even in my drunken state, I understood he was plastered, legless. Doubting he'd remember any of this the next day, I said, "I mean really, two of the killings happened here. Well one, I guess, but still."

"Enough," he said, waving his hand.

"It could be me! Did you ever think about that? I mean, I would have been a little young at the time, fourteen. But old enough. It might have been me this whole time, making the occasional trip up here to visit Mama. The perfect excuse! It's as plausible as anything else."

"Ezra, I mean it."

"Or you! What if it was you? You would have been too young for the first one, I suppose. But how do I know what you've gotten up to since? You've been here the whole time. You were Mama's favorite. If she'd found out, she never would have gone to the police. Ooh, or it could be Javits, Sander—"

Somehow this last was a bridge too far. He grabbed me by the lapels and stood me up. He said, "You are desecrating the last night of this place. Just leave."

So I did. I got back in my car—ill-advised, given the drinks—and drove back the way I'd come. I couldn't say why I'd done it, why I'd pushed him. The money, yes, but there was something else deep inside me—a sadness, a sad anger at always feeling on the outside, though outside is where I've always been happiest. Trees alongside the winding country roads seemed to lean in, grasp at the car, sensing my flagging attention, desiring me upside down in a ditch. When I made the highway, I immediately pulled off into a rest-area parking lot and fell into the kind of dark sleep that enshrouds, after the fact, any trouble it may have contained.

In the morning, the sun slanted viciously through the windshield, turning the inside of my eyes a fragile pink, baking the car's trapped air. It was cooler outside, refreshing to be out of the hot stuffiness, and I walked around on dead legs that eventually began waking to the irrefutable fact of the day. A long sip from the nearby water fountain further revived me. I splashed water on my face and returned to the car, intending to get on the road.

Before I got in, however, a flash of yellowy-green caught my eye. A bird in the trees, one I didn't recognize—I paused, listening to its call, a brief warbling complaint. A juvenile, by the sound of it. Gently closing the door, I retrieved my bag from the back seat, slung it over my shoulder, and crossed the tended lawn beside the granite bathrooms. No one seemed to notice me as I slipped into the woods, heart fluttering like the wings of the creature I pursued, ecstatic at the prospect of adding one more to the life list—that ineffable pleasure only other birders can really understand.

13. Susannah

2001

Her father's call could not have come at a better—or worse—time, depending on how you looked at it. She hung up the phone and, from the island of the sofa, bleared at the wreckage of last night's party. It was always the day after a party here. Bottles and cans littered every available surface; a plastic Dixie cup even floated on top of Cynthia's aquarium, which had miraculously remained intact. A heaping pyramid of cigarettes and ash sat in a makeshift ashtray—a chipped china plate—that she and her roommates, she already knew, would be too hungover to deal with all day. The ashtray would likely resume its function when—unthinkably at this point, but predictably, nonetheless—Seth or Jamie or Cynthia would later bring home some clutch of pretty dilettantes they'd collected while treating their hangover with three-dollar Bloody Marys at Max Fish, and a new party would claw its way up from the grave. Where were her roommates, she idly wondered. Either still in bed, or dead, or vanished at some indistinct point in the night with some loser they now deeply regretted sleeping with—someone so regrettable that they'd start drinking in the afternoon in order to forget they slept with them, thereby setting the stage for sleeping with some other loser.

As if summoned by this line of thought, Seth stumbled wordlessly through the room. She heard him rummaging around in the kitchen, and he emerged with a beer he must have squirreled away during some moment of inebriated cunning. He brought it into the living room. Susannah said, "Jesus Christ, really?"

"What?"

"Back at it?"

He pulled the tab and the beer made a scoffing sound at her quaint abstemiousness. "I need it if I'm going to be worth a damn today."

"What do you have to do today?"

"Nothing. But still."

Nothing: no one Suse knew had to do anything, ever. She'd gotten in with this clique her sophomore year at Brown, a bunch of WASPy theater brats with family money, many of whom could name which year of the seventeenth century their families came over, and in which particular ship. What Suse lacked in this kind of pedigree, she made up for in novelty—not just her Jewishness (though there was, as they said, that), but her family's quirky history, with its tenuous but real connections to Broadway and a lost epoch of entertainers. The Borscht Belt heiress, how fabulous! Post-graduation, a group of them had moved en masse to New York, and now, five years later, they filled their weeks with the occasional purported audition, with acting lessons, with band rehearsals, but mostly with vast quantities of alcohol sometimes accompanied by vast quantities of cocaine and pharmaceuticals. What they did not fill their weeks with were jobs, other than the pretend jobs they assigned themselves—production intern, de facto drug dealer, and in Seth's case, most pliably fanciful of all: playwright.

Seth shook his head like a retriever drying itself after fording a stream and said, "And I'm working, of course."

"Of course. Dante today?"

"And every day."

"How's that coming along?" Seth's project for years had been a stage production of the *Inferno*, adapted to modern times and set in Los Angeles. Suse had often wondered how that would actually work, considering the *Inferno* was just Dante following Virgil around, watching people get tortured (though, then again, she supposed, the *Nightmare on Elm Street* movies). But anyway, Seth had never let her read any of it, assuming any of it even existed.

"Line by tortuous line. Who was that on the phone?"

"My father."

"Really. Long time no speak, huh?" He settled next to her on the couch.

"Since December."

"What did he want?"

"Actually, he asked if I felt like getting out of the city for the summer. Go and help him clean out the hotel."

"I thought it closed years ago."

"It did, but he's thinking about selling it, and there's still a ton of stuff to deal with. My younger brother's away at college, and he could use a hand."

"Cheap labor," Seth shrugged, pronouncing the word *labor* with audible disdain as well as the slight curl of a long upper lip.

"You don't have to always be such a horrible snob, you know?"

"I do, though, it's who I am. I'd have no personality otherwise."

She looked around the room and a fresh wave of disgust washed over her. She wanted to get away from here. But even if she hadn't wanted to get away—even if she had desperately wanted to keep the party going—she was quickly running through the last installment of money her mother had given her, an infusion of cash from her dwindling legacy that may have actually been all there was, though she couldn't bear the idea of asking for more and finding out. Subletting her tiny, exorbitant room for the summer would injure several of these birds with one limp toss of the stone. "I think I'm going to do it."

"You're joking."

"No, I'm not." She grabbed the plate of ashes and carefully walked it through the living room, like a precious heirloom she feared dropping. "I can't stand it here any longer. Some fresh air will be great."

"It'll be great for five minutes, then you'll be bored."

"I don't care. I could use some boredom. Some boring detox and some boring walks in the woods. And are you saying it isn't boring here?"

"Touché."

"Besides, I like seeing the hotel, being in there alone."

"Really?"

"It's creepy and bizarre."

"How so?"

"How do you think? It's a huge abandoned hotel in the woods. The indoor swimming pool alone is the size of a cathedral." She described it as it was the last time she was there, when it finally closed a few years ago. All those empty rooms filled with the presence of a century's worth of guests. Wandering the great halls, feeling not a little like Jack in the Overlook Hotel. A murder had been committed at her father's hotel—and perhaps others in the area over the years, including, almost, her second cousin, Alice—and the killer had gotten away with it, though there hadn't been any new incidents since the eighties. A bad book had even been written about this unsolved case. She went on for a bit, aware of Seth's unusual raptness. "And," she concluded, "there's a ghost."

"Oh, stop." Seth had straightened on the couch. "Who says?"

"Lots of people. My brother, for one. He swore he saw one when he was a kid. For like a year. I mean, come on, a kid was killed there; of course people say it's haunted. But even before that, the guy who built it committed suicide. There were ghost stories about the Neversink from the start."

"That sounds fantastic," he said. "When do we leave?"

Seth rented a car, one-way to Poughkeepsie. "*One-Way to Poughkeepsie*," he said, "now there's a title. Hubert Selby, eat your heart out." She'd argued against the rental since it would be so easy to take the train up to meet her father, but she soon saw the wisdom of Seth's decision: driving across the GW, then up the Palisades Parkway, a green April bucolia took over fast, displacing the gray city behind them. It felt like shrugging off a heavy winter jacket. She was always shocked by how quickly the city—all-encompassing and monolithic when you were in it—disappeared when you left.

As he drove, Seth talked about the positive influence this sojourn, as he called it, could have on his play. The city had been strangling him and he hadn't even known it. Manhattan, when you got down to it, was a dull place, full of dull people who were interested only in themselves. Himself included—it was affecting his work, as he referred to it. Suse didn't say much—Seth didn't need much encouragement—instead focusing her attention on the passing landscape as it shifted subtly from a piney urban verge to a three-lane suburban stretch with manicured Bermuda grass dividers, then to a hilly two-lane.

Having momentarily tired of talking about himself, Seth lit a cigarette and said, "So, your father."

"So, him."

"What's his story now?"

"I don't know. Is 'divorced and depressed' a story?"

"That's everyone's father's story."

"Everyone I know."

"What does he do, now that the hotel's closed?"

"He's been selling stuff off, the last few years. Memorabilia, kitchen appliances, art. He sold the banister last year to a boutique hotel in Beacon."

"That's all? How long can he live on that?"

"Well, there's still family money," she said uncertainly. "And we own the golf course and club there. It's still in operation. I think that's mostly what he does now."

"He's a golfer?"

They crested a hill, hairpinning around a corner on the sudden edge of a cliff face that lacked guardrails, Seth seemingly unfamiliar with the meaning of yellow caution signs. Susannah clutched the car's overhead handle, wondering just how bad an idea this trip would turn out to be. "I don't think he's ever golfed a day in his life."

"How marvelously sad."

Her father wasn't marvelously sad, though—he was just sad. They had left him behind in Liberty when Suse was thirteen, and that was the Len Sikorsky who still held sway in her mind—the version of her father with a still mostly full head of hair and furred forearms bulging with sinewy muscle. He could do forty push-ups with her little brother, Noah, sitting on his back. And he hadn't just been physically strong—the father in her head was quick with a smile and a corny joke, and handier than any man she'd encountered since. (He'd provided a formative model of masculine know-how that tended to make the proudly helpless artistes in her sphere—routinely confounded, as they were, by flat tires or continuously flushing toilets—wholly undesirable to her.) The man who greeted them in front of the old cottage was not that man. This man was both skinnier and fatter, with hunched, pigeony shoulders and spindly limbs framing a pregnant gut. This man wore baggy chinos and a SUNY Binghamton sweatshirt and looked like he hadn't slept in two days, with his bloodhound eye bags and sparse, wiry hair shocked up at angles.

"Hey, sweetheart," he said, and they hugged. He smelled good, though, like soap, not sweat and beer, as she'd expected. He shook Seth's hand, grabbed her suitcase, and lugged it into the house. They followed, sharing a nervous glance.

The cottage was clean enough, yet cramped and dismal. The shades were drawn, or maybe it was the vine that had been allowed to creep all over the exterior of the windows. Boxes were stacked up here and there according to an unknowable grouping logic. It looked like a place someone was in the process of moving into or out of, it was impossible to tell which, but in either case not a place where a person was currently living—a dim purgatory that gelled perfectly with Susannah's sense of her father over the past few years. Len said, "You can stay in your old room, Suse. Seth, you can stay in Noah's, just down the hall there."

"Actually," Seth said, "I was wondering if it might be possible to stay in the hotel, at least for a little while."

"You're not serious," said Suse and her father, more or less together.

"It's just you've told me so much about it," he said to her. Then to her father: "I'd like to know what it was like to stay in such a famous historical site." Seth went on in this buttering-up mode for a bit, and Suse watched her father's tense, battered face soften with pleasure.

"I don't know." He looked at Suse. She shrugged. He said, "I'm not sure it's safe."

Seth said, "You mean structurally, or that there could be a maniac in there?"

Len looked slightly offended. "I'm pretty sure the coast is clear."

"Sorry."

"No, I meant the building's falling apart."

"We'll be careful. It would really be an honor."

"Dad," said Suse. "If you're not comfortable—"

Len said, "It really is a historical site, though I don't know if the building will be granted that status by the National Registry. I've looked into it. At any rate, you're welcome to camp out there for a day or two. I can set the two of you up in a clean room with fresh linens. Though, of course, there's no water or electricity. You can use the bathroom here."

"Would you mind," said Seth, "if I wandered around the hotel now?"

"Be my guest," said Len, wincing at the inadvertency.

Len put Seth in the large corner room of the main building—the Presidential Suite, so-called, since Harry Truman had twice occupied it. It was a huge room, with art deco frieze work and floor-to-ceiling windows that looked out on the strip of forest separating the hotel from the sloping green of hole two. They lit candles and drank margaritas Seth had mixed in one of Len's plastic pitchers. Seth had invited him up to join them and talk, but Len begged off, saying he had work to do—a blatant lie, Susannah knew: he had looked pained even crossing the threshold of his grandparents' empire. In contrast to her father's masochistic desire to preserve the place as a historic landmark, she found herself looking forward to it being razed, expunged from memory.

Seth rose and stretched, saying, "Can you show me where they found the body?"

"What—now?"

"Why not now?"

"It's dark, and I'd have to take you down to the basement."

"Sounds spookalicious."

"Seth."

"Come on, we'll take candles. It'll be like Nancy Drew or something."

Knowing how futile it was to try to talk Seth out of a bad idea, Susannah grabbed a candle and led him down the hall. She didn't want to admit it, but part of her reluctance was simple fright. The flame guttered as they walked down the hall, illuminating peeling wallpaper and a ceiling with brown water damage, like the flesh of rotten fruit. In the stairwell she heard skittering, or imagined she heard skittering, and she certainly smelled something, a pervasive note of earthy decay. It struck her that this was a place they did not belong in now, a place where people should not go.

Echoing her thoughts when they reached the basement, Seth said, "*Lasciate ogni speranza, voi ch'entrate,* am I right?"

The basement walls, unadorned limestone brick, were wet with black condensation—in the candlelight, it didn't *not* look like the walls were sweating blood. Their wary footsteps were amplified by the slate floor, a ticking that seemed to grow louder until they stopped outside the room where Alice had been trapped and the boy's remains had been found. "In here," Susannah pointed.

It was a tiled room, built in theory to butcher and hang livestock in the kashrut manner, a project that had faded with the death of Susannah's grandfather, Asher, since no one else had a burning desire to raise animals on the premises. Instead, it had been used as a de facto dry-storage room, by the hotel and by the murderer, who'd stuffed the boy's body into a cubby meant for cured meats and masked the smell with cleaning supplies.

"Boo," shouted Seth behind her, and despite the predictability of it, Susannah yelped.

"God*damn* it, Seth."

"Sorry, I couldn't resist. This is amazing, though."

"Let's go," she said, and Seth didn't argue. They ticked back down the hall, at a pace that felt deliberately measured, as though in conscious refutation of a desire to bolt breakneck up the stairs. On the first floor, they passed through the cavernous ballroom, far too big for their meager candles. The darkness seemed like a sentient thing, hungrily eating the light.

Seth said, "I can see why lots of people think it's haunted here."

"Yeah."

"Do you?"

The shredded stage curtain flapped in a draft coming from somewhere. "No, not the way you mean."

"What way then?"

"You met my father."

"Very poetic." They started up the stairs to the second floor. "Maybe you should be the writer."

"Maybe so," she said. "But anyway, no, I don't believe in ghosts." But why then, she thought, had she hastened so to escape the basement? Had she felt, or imagined feeling, a cool alien wind on her skin? Had her father felt it, in here by himself, slowly cleaning out his legacy a box at a time? The ghost of his grandfather, their family—haunting her father as he haunted her now.

The work was simple, organized by her father or old Javits, who still occasionally came by and helped out. They were given a task in the morning—collect all the copper bathroom fixtures, for example—then they broke for lunch, usually wilty pre-made egg- or chicken-salad sandwiches from the gas station at the bottom of the hill. After lunch, they resumed the first task, or else were delegated a second, and they stopped around five, at which time Seth would initiate a round of jerry-rigged cocktails that Len would sometimes partake in, though usually not.

Suse was surprised by Seth. She'd assumed he would get bored after a few days and jump ship, a behavioral pattern she'd seen him exhibit with classes in college, art projects, internships, boyfriends, everything. Instead, he seemed both galvanized and relaxed by the work, and the hotel itself. In the evening, after cocktail hour, Seth liked to roam around the place, scribbling in his notebook. He was usually up before her in the morning, too, already showered at Len's and set up in the kitchen, cup of coffee and Smith Corona—one of his many affectations—in front of him. It was more work than she'd ever seen him actually do.

After a month, over an afternoon pitcher of the watery martinis with olive juice he'd thrown together, Seth revealed a page with two words typed in the middle: THE END.

"Really."

"Really. I've blazed through it since we've been here."

"Well, congrats."

"Well, thank you. And I have a crazy idea I want to run by you."

"Oh God." Seth's last crazy idea had been for their apartment to go in together on an ounce of cocaine. That way, he'd explained, they'd have coke for parties, and people who wanted to do some would pay them money. So you want us to become drug dealers, Suse had said. No, no, he'd said, I just want to have drugs and charge people to do them.

"Hear me out," he said. "I want to put on the play, and I want to put it on here."

"Where?"

"Here, at the Hotel Neversink."

"You're joking."

He stood and detailed the plan: With the play finished, they would put up advertisements for local acting talent. A summer-stock kind of thing. After all, he said, wasn't there a rich tradition of that around here? Weren't the Catskills lousy with thespians? Anyway, he said, there were actors everywhere. In fact, he was thinking Susannah could take one of the leads, either Dante or Virgil. Wouldn't that be fun? Hadn't it been a long time since she'd gotten to act? Regardless, he had to do it here. He knew if he took it back to New York, the play would just languish in a desk drawer, never see the light of day. They'd rehearse over the next couple of months and put it on before they returned to the city.

"Put it on where?"

"Yes, if only," he gestured down the hall, "there were an eight-hundred–capacity professional-grade theater located *somewhere* around here."

"The hotel is closed, Seth."

"So we reopen it. For a night."

"My father won't like this."

"You're right," he said, tossing his drink back in one swallow. "Your father will *love* this."

Infuriatingly, Len did love it. He pretended not to, but his crow's feet flexed with gratification as he imagined the building put to use again, filled with people.

"A fitting tribute," said Seth. "Give people a last night to really remember the joint by."

Len said, "Well, it *is* an intriguing idea. Let me think about it."

"Do. Meanwhile, your daughter and I will begin scouring this noble valley for our players."

"Dad," said Suse, after Seth had gone back to the hotel to change clothes, "don't feel like the answer has to be yes, here. Seth is full of great ideas, only most of them are terrible. I haven't even read the play; it might be a joke."

"I think it sounds fun. I might even want to be in it. Dante, right? Maybe I could be one of the damned souls. Which circle would you put me in?"

Looking at him—surrounded by the hotel's multiplicative clutter, clad in tartan pajama bottoms and terry-cloth bathrobe, frowzy head surrounded by a solar system of dust motes in the old house's muted daylight—the answer seemed obvious. "Well, the first circle."

"Which one is that?"

"Limbo."

"Thanks."

"That's the one for virtuous non-Christians," she replied, lamely.

"I think I caught your drift, Suse."

She settled into the ratty armchair in front of the TV and he remained standing, his face cast with its habitual mortified look. She said, "I'm sorry, Dad. But what's the exit strategy here?"

"What do you mean?"

"This can't be it, can it? You're still young."

"I'm fifty-seven."

"Great-Uncle Joe lived to be almost ninety."

"I should move to Boca Raton, maybe? Buy a racehorse?"

"I don't know. But I don't think hanging around here is doing you any favors."

As though casting around for some tiny measure of usefulness, Len lifted a box off the floor near the stairs and set it on another pile of boxes beside one of the old bookcases. When Susannah was a child, the lower shelf had been filled with reference books—almanacs, atlases, and, in particular, *D'Aulaire's Book of Greek Myths*. She'd spent many summer afternoons greedily poring over it, those bright pictures and wonderful, horrible fables.

Len said, "Susannah, I don't expect you to understand this, because you're young and all you see is potential. So it seems like I'm wasting my life to you, and maybe I am. Maybe I've already wasted it. But you can't understand what it's like to have a place in the world, however small. What that means. Living here, running the golf course—that's something. However small and depressing it may be to you, that's something."

"I'm sorry."

"And if you decide to cast me, I'd prefer to be in whatever circle pride is."

She thought for a moment "There's not really one for it. It's behind all the other sins. One through nine, take your pick."

"Nine, then. Put me down for nine."

By June, rehearsals for the play were up and rolling. The cast had been assembled from a motley group of regional actors, or "actors"— it took some stretching to make the appellation fit. Satan—"The Great Producer," in Seth's version—was played by a large landscaper named Dale who had once worked as a clown at children's parties; it was okay, though, since the role's main requirement was the willing-ness/ability to stand on one's head for an hour straight. Len played Homeless Homer, wandering blind and befuddled on the shores of the Lethe, or in this case, the LA River. The plum part of Virgil Merkin was played by a reticent middle-aged paralegal named Virginia, who had actual acting experience in community theater, though this, she said, was by far her biggest role.

Susannah was granted the role of Dontay, and despite her initial doubts as to Seth's talent, she was excited. The play was actually kind of good, a campy and sometimes legitimately funny reworking of the *Inferno*, with lots of Hollywood in-jokes and pop references. Still, it erred on the side of a certain respect for the original, a dark core of seriousness that surprised and pleased her. She'd been worried it would all just be a big joke to Seth, but he'd produced something with a gravity that belied his customary glib engagement with the world.

By July, they were two weeks from opening night and running through the production without glitches, or many of them, anyway, from opening to close. Javits had overseen promotion for the event, and there had been a surprising amount of interest in local papers. The *Hudson Valley Leader* had done a feature, an ode to the late, lamented Neversink. This had, in turn, resulted in a *Time Out New York* piece, which had echoed into a quarter column in the *Times* Sunday Style section: "A Legendary Hotel Gets Its Curtain Call." There was, as they say, a buzz, and Len had been met with a deluge of e-mails and phone calls inquiring after tickets. These questions were difficult to answer, as no one had expected much interest in the production, and ticket planning had not proceeded past asking a local boy to work the front door. Len hired an outside event company that quickly threw up a website and handled phone calls. Within three days, eight hundred tickets had been purchased, and *Dontay Does LA* was sold out.

With this news, rehearsals suddenly became tense, and actorly egos emerged. Virginia complained to Suse that Dale wasn't taking it seriously enough, that he was merely bellowing his lines without inflection; Dale responded that Virginia needed to learn how to project, and she stormed away in tears. Another cast member, Waldron, a sophomore at a yeshiva school in Poughkeepsie, claimed that Cerberus didn't have enough lines. Enough lines, said Seth. You're a fucking dog. Yeah, said Waldron, a dog with two heads, though.

After rehearsal one night, they went down to the Liberty Lounge, a local spot at the bottom of Neversink Hill that advertised "Karaoke Wednesdays with DJ Matt" and "Official APA Action." Seth was in an expansive mood, ordering shots for the cast members and positioning himself in a tall central seat against the wall; the cheap wood paneling reminded Suse of an unsupervised middle school friend's basement where she'd gone to watch R-rated movies.

At the bar, she got them another round of Labatt Blue—the odd default cheap beer in this neck of the woods—and was asked to settle a dispute between Waldron and a crew member, Craig, about which of them was taller (Waldron, by a cowlick). When she returned, as if responding to her general train of thought, Seth said, "Charming place."

"It's fine."

"Oh, it's more than fine, I'd say. It's delightful."

"Have you ever considered giving it a rest?"

"No, I never actually have considered that. Intriguing thought."

She looked around the place—two guys shot pool under a custom Coors Light banner that proudly announced the Liberty Lounge billiards team as regional runners-up. "Just, I don't know. I'm not sure walking around assuming you're better than everyone is the best way to go through life."

"I don't think I'm better than everyone. Brad Pitt, for example. Mother Teresa."

"Ha ha."

"Anyway, you're as much of a snob as I am; at least I admit it."

"I'm not as much of a snob as you are."

"There you are again, not admitting it." When she didn't laugh or smile or respond to this, Seth said, "Okay, what's your problem?"

"Honestly, Seth? I think you look down on everyone. I think everyone's a joke to you. And I think it's going to hurt your work."

"Oh, you're worried about my work. That's what this is about? Why don't you try lightening up for one minute. You're getting to be a real drag lately."

"I think you're going to wind up being a campy hack if you're not careful. Wait—"

But he was already walking out. She thought about following him, apologizing, but the truth was she just didn't feel like it. Someone put "Layla" on the jukebox and she finished her beer, swaying as the haunting, inexorable waves of the final piano chords crashed through the room.

Three days before opening night, Seth appeared in the auditorium bearing a Kinko's box. The group had been lounging on deck chairs in the huge room, with the second circle—the lustful, that is, a group of porn stars from the Valley—practicing the set piece where they blow around the stage in a choreographed dervish. Susannah and Len had been debating a line of Len's in which he, as Homer, tells Dontay to fuck off. Is that really necessary? said Len. How about screw off? Suse told him screw off sounded fifties and weird. Go screw, she said, in a James Cagney voice. Seth handed her a sheaf of papers and she looked up at him. "What's this?"

"This," he said, "is the new script."

"We already have a script."

"This one's better, trust me." He handed it around to the players. Susannah thumbed through hers, confused. She didn't see much difference, or any, in the staging, but the dialogue had been changed, laboriously shifted into a sort of faux Old English. She looked up. "I don't get it."

"Trust me," he said again.

The rehearsal was a disaster. Where lines before had been memorized and recited with relative ease, the actors now read frowning, and poorly, from their sheets. Dale held his script about three inches from his sweating face, attempting to work his mouth around sentences like *Doth thou makest jest at mine torture, at Lucifer Agonistes, ye goode and noble pilgrimmes? Fools! Verily a pox and vexation upon thou and thine.* Even Suse, with her expensive education and experience performing Shakespeare in Brown's Little Theater group (Gertrude, Titania, Ariel), struggled with the pronunciation and syntax. Around the stage they bumbled a-stuttering, Seth watching from the floor with an appraising eye, not displeased. At the end, he thanked them for their hard work, apologized for springing last-second dialogue changes, asked them to learn the new script, and again implored them to trust him.

When the last of the players had exeunted, Suse held up her pages and said, "Okay, Seth. Really, what the hell is this?"

"It's just a rewrite," he said, unable to mask a look of coy mischief on his face—or perhaps he wanted her to see it.

"It isn't just a rewrite. It's farce."

"Well, the play is a farce, so that makes sense."

"The play was just fine before, and plenty farcical." She flipped pages. "*O what ill humours doth befoule this sepulchral zephyre?* Poor Dale is going to swallow his tongue. It's a cruel joke."

Seth rose from the deck chair, where he'd been looking up at her with the patient demeanor of a parent enduring a toddler's tantrum. "Susannah, just remember, this is my play. Okay? You don't have to like every choice I make."

"It's being performed in my family's hotel, and I say we go back to the script, which was good, by the way."

"Oh, it was not. It was kitschy garbage."

"It was fun. This is something else. What is this?"

"Okay, look. When I thought no one would be here, the play was fine. I was just happy to have finished something. But now, there are some real people coming to this, some New York theater people. I heard Lowell Sims might come. And you know, they've seen this kind of thing a million times off Broadway. Lowbrow highbrow, right? It's a formula. Like you said, the last think I want to be is a *campy hack*."

"Seth—"

"But I thought, okay, what about doubling down on that, rendering the thing in high language, as spoken by, you know."

"No."

"Well, the people in it. Locals."

"Locals."

"Right. So it becomes sort of this meta-play about high and low culture."

Suse looked at Seth for what felt like the first time in years—people you've known for a while have a way of adhering to your first impression of them, the early blush of acquaintance and friendship, and you can go years with that afterimage hovering over their actual form. In his later twenties, Seth had gotten slightly fattish—not paunchy, but a kind of white puffiness, like a piece of rice floating in dishwater overnight. At the same time, his features had somehow coarsened, and he looked wolfish to her. Standing in the auditorium, she had a vision of him in twenty years, fat and avid, and in a position of real cultural authority that would lend the weight of actual malice to his habitual archness.

She said, "And in order to create this meta-play, you make the people in it look stupid."

"That would be the common view, I suppose."

"Including my father and me."

"Art is a stern master."

"You're an asshole, you know that?"

"Oh, yes."

She shouldered her bag to return to Len's and said, "I've always defended you. People would say what an asshole you are, and I would say you just don't know him. But people are right. And it isn't about being an artist, it's just being a dick. Talk about common."

She saw that the volley had hit home, and turned to leave before Seth could respond, but he laughed and she waited for it with shoulders tensed. "God, that's rich," he said.

"What?"

"Oh, you know, playing the 'everyone says' card. You want to know what everyone says about you?"

"Not really."

"Everyone says you're a hick. Everyone wondered what you were doing in our group when I brought you in. I said, no, she's funny and nice, and the Catskills thing is a scream. Everyone rolled their eyes, but I defended you. I still do, because *everyone* still wonders what this—I'm sorry—but this rather dull little person is doing hanging around, being gloomy."

"Well," she said, "at least I'm not an alcoholic queen."

"No, you're just a grubby provincial kike."

She walked away and Seth called after her, no wait, he was sorry, he shouldn't have said that. But she was already trudging down the long hallway by the outside pool, where she used to sit and do homework, past the natatorium and the lobby, to the huge front door. Pushing it open, he called a final time—Suse, come on—but his echoing voice was like something she was remembering, something already from the past.

She went back to New York the next day, borrowing her father's old Subaru. Len said what about the play, and she said she had stage fright—that her understudy, Kent, a hair stylist in Tucker's Cove, would do a fine job. Everyone had to relearn their lines from scratch, anyway. Len protested, but not that much, accustomed to this kind of thing after a lifetime of ill-tempered women deserting him. She didn't tell him about Seth, because what was the point, really? "Break a leg," she said.

It took only an hour to clear the apartment of her belongings, which was convenient as she was parked in a delivery-only space. Her other roommates were nowhere to be found, also convenient, both in terms of not having to discuss it with anyone—*everyone*—and also in terms of being able to filch a framed photo of the group in college, which hung askew in the bathroom. She wasn't sure whose it was, or if it was anyone's in particular, but it was hers now.

She stayed with her mother over the weekend, borrowed a little money, and returned to Liberty. Seth, as she'd expected, was gone, had left the day after the show. "How was it?" she asked Len. They were drinking tomato juice in the cottage's overgrown garden.

Len shook his head. "Oh, you should have been here. I'm telling you, it was magical."

"How'd the show go?"

"Eh, the show," he shrugged.

"People learned the new lines?"

"More or less. Dale got some laughs."

"I bet."

"It was fine, I never cared about that."

"Yeah?" The sun glinted off the shiny leaf of some plant. It suddenly felt strange to her not to know more about the flora around here, where she'd grown up. Resolving, from a young age, to escape, she'd apparently refused to take in any information about the landscape or history of the place.

"Yeah. I mean, just looking out at that ballroom, filled with people in formal wear. Filled to the gills." He held his hands out in front of him as though trying to summon the magnitude of the scene for her, then dropped them on his lap in failure. "Oh, it was magical, Suse. A magical night."

"I'm so glad."

"Thank Seth again for me when you go back."

Somewhere nearby, an insect sawed monotonously. She said, "Actually, I was hoping I might stay here a little while longer, if that's okay?"

"Really?"

"Maybe just through the rest of summer, while I figure out what's next. I'm kind of done with New York right now."

"That would be nice."

"I'll keep helping out."

"You can work at the golf course if you want."

"Yeah?"

"Real work, I'll pay you. We need someone to do the books."

"Yeah," she said. "Okay, sounds fine."

"Hey," he turned to her. "The play got me reading Dante; I never had. You know who's in the fifth circle?"

She racked her brain. "The violent?"

"Well, the wrathful. But also the sullen. I thought that was interesting. The sullen stewed below the surface of a muddy swamp. The ancients apparently thought sullenness was anger turned inward."

"What are you saying?"

"Nothing," he said, shielding his eyes and looking up at the sun. "Boy, it's a nice day, huh?"

So she stayed the rest of that summer, saving money to move back to the city in the fall. But then the towers came down, and by the next spring she was living with a local woodworker named Nick, who sold his intricately filigreed cabinets to boutique stores in Beacon and Brooklyn. She did the books at the golf course, accepted a managerial role and pay raise, hired a design firm to rethink the tired clubhouse and pro shop. And in her spare time, she continued helping her father clean out the Neversink.

One day she oversaw a team of workers taking down the chandelier in the ballroom, Len having sold it to a New York antiques dealer. The thing was enormous, bolted to the ceiling with green screws the size of tent pegs—it took five people and a small lift to detach and lower it to the floor. From her vantage on the second story, she saw them put it on a flat wagon, push it out of the hotel, and load it into the back of a truck. As she watched, the pink sun dipped behind one of the larger trees and cast a long shadow on the floor and wall, and it was as though there were something watching alongside her.

She thought of those ghost stories that she'd heard growing up. She imagined it was the ghost. The thought wasn't frightening, as it had vaguely been when she'd described the lore to Seth or other friends over the years. To the contrary, it was comforting somehow—a presence that had been there for so many years, a presence that wanted to stay. Together, they watched the truck wind down the access road, carting away another small piece of home. Together, they moved from the bedroom and out onto the main staircase. Together, they surveyed the Great Hall, the dining room, the lounge, the distant lobby, the drained pool—all these rooms she'd roved as a child, all the while so desperately wanting to leave—and in that moment, she knew it wasn't a ghost she felt beside her, but her tardy love for this great, dead place.

14. Alice

2007

Alice emerged from her psychiatrist's office into the cold damp of London in October. Though the walk home from Dr. Linväld's office would take forty minutes, she preferred it to the alternatives. Despite there being a stop literally outside her front door, the Tube was, in local parlance, a nonstarter; she could barely look at the entrance—like the waiting mouth of a blind, starving monster trapped beneath London—let alone walk into it.

She also didn't drive (owning a car in this city was ridiculous, leaving aside the left-hand-side-of-the-road thing), take the bus (cramped sweatboxes that they were), or cycle (bike helmets looked far too silly). And she hated taking cabs, which entailed talking to the drivers. At minimum, you had to tell them a destination, and sometimes you got a chatty one who wanted to talk about the weather or football or traffic or, God forbid, their family, also a nonstarter. She wanted to talk to people as little as possible lately, including Dr. Linväld, but she'd continued going to see him every week as a nod to the possibility, however slim, that she still might not kill herself.

In this sense, she wasn't sure if continuing her therapy was an act of bravery or cowardice. Or both. Most likely, it meant nothing, as seemed to be the secret—well-kept or open, depending on how depressed she was—about everything. This had, in fact, been the subject of their earlier session. Dr. Linväld—large and bearded (and, despite his Nordic name, black, a point of confusion when she'd shown up for her first appointment eighteen months earlier)—had leaned forward on his desk, head framed by a square halo of diplomas, accreditations, and memberships, and said, "You keep coming back to this sense that everything's meaningless."

"Well, I mean, isn't it?"

"No."

"Oh, okay. Thanks, problem solved."

"Not to most people. Not to me."

"Is it possible you're wrong about that?"

"No. It's not a thing you can be wrong about. Or objectively right about. I don't feel like everything's meaningless, so everything isn't, to me. You do feel that way, so everything is, to you. It's how you feel that makes it real."

"Catchy." He stared at her. He was a very good starer. "But don't you think that's bullshit?"

"No. I wouldn't have said it if I thought it was bullshit."

Opening her mouth to respond, she felt the great heaviness of already knowing what she was going to say, of everything being pre-determined. This sense of merely going through the motions, immensely fatiguing, was something she'd been experiencing with greater and greater frequency lately. It wasn't her main problem, but as a symptom it was rapidly achieving comorbid status with the depression that caused it. She forced herself to go on.

"I know you don't think it's bullshit, but I do think you can be objectively right about it. What's your argument? Okay, some fruity shit about everyone assigning meaning to their lives? But people are right and wrong about things. I mean, some people spend their whole life handling snakes in order to go to heaven, right? Then they get bitten by one and die, and—let's say I'm correct that there's nothing—they've wasted their life playing with vipers."

"They haven't wasted it. They believed in something, even if it was perhaps technically wrong."

"You don't think they would have stopped handling snakes if they'd known?"

Dr. Linväld sighed and looked out the window at the impossible bone-whiteness of Belgravia in autumn. "What's your point?"

"My point is that your best argument for there being a point amounts to just feeling like there's a point, which is a position that deflates the second you poke it. And my best argument is that there obviously, demonstrably, is no point. That you fucking die and that's it. That everyone you know will die, and all their children will die, and their children's children will die, and that's it. That even if you take the really wide-angle view, humankind will get wiped out at some point, all of its art and science and effort with it. If it isn't rogue nuclear weapons, it will be global warming, and if it isn't global warming it will be Ebola, or an asteroid, or the sun dying, or eventually, the heat death of the universe."

"You're saying the heat death of the universe precludes life having any meaning?"

"Yes, that's exactly what I'm saying." She was glad it was Dr. Linväld's practice to sit in chairs, consultation-style. If she'd been lying down, in the Freudian manner, she would have passed out from the strain of speaking.

"I'm taking you seriously here, Alice. It sounds like you're saying the only way life would have meaning is if everyone lived forever. But imagine if that were the case. I grant you, Alice Emmenthaler, eternal life!" He opened both hands at her, like a stage magician executing a corny trick. "Tell me what the point is now."

"There still isn't one. But I don't see how this advances your case."

"Again, I have no case. My life has meaning."

She sighed. "Okay, fine. You win. I feel ridiculous talking about this anyway. I'm forty-three years old, this is stoned dorm-room stuff."

"On the contrary, this is the-deepest-essence-of-being-alive stuff." He tilted his white eyes at her with utter sincerity, and she felt great affection for Linväld—Robert—at that moment. She would miss him. She found she was crying, and he was solicitously offering Kleenex and continuing to talk, thinking, she knew, that she was upset by the conversation. He said, "Alice, at any rate, I don't believe these philosophical issues are what plague you. You are depressed, hence, your life has no feeling of meaning. Most people looking at your life would say it has a great deal of meaning, that you do something that touches people all over the world."

She blew her nose. "I'm not going back on medication."

"I don't see any other course of action, frankly."

She almost said *I do*, but didn't. "I can't write on it. I wind up watching *EastEnders* upside down on my sofa twelve hours a day. You want to talk about there not being a point."

"Let's discuss it next time. Consider it, please. If not, come in with an alternate strategy."

She rose. "I'm not sure I'm coming in again."

"Why not?"

"I just think I need some time off."

He stood and positioned himself, she didn't fail to notice, between her and the door. "That's your choice, but I strongly disagree."

She moved around him, then leaned in for a hug that he returned with stiff surprise. "Thanks for everything," she said, walking away before he could say anything else.

The memory of that embrace now dissolved as a taxi blared by— she'd stepped too early into the street, hypnotized by her own thoughts and by the rain, which was falling harder every minute. To the right, it swept through Hyde Park, dampening the crazies at Speakers' Corner, slicking the black paths of bikers in translucent macs, wetting the stoic ducks that bobbed in the Serpentine. Oil, drawn by the rain to the surface of the sidewalk, shimmered in greasy rainbows. *Cross now*, a woman's voice said, in seeming agreement with the decision she'd come to in Linväld's office: she would kill herself today.

In July, she'd set a date: October 15, two days from now. It had been far enough away that she might be talked out of it, by the world or herself, but it wasn't so far as to make the interim seem impossible to bear. And three months had been enough time to get her affairs in order, as the stock phrase went, though the surprisingly small number of affairs that needed ordering had been depressing in itself. Her parents were installed in an Arizona retirement community, and her sister, Elise, had excommunicated Alice for the sin of using family members in her last novel. In fairness to Elise, "Eliza" had been pretty close to the truth—a monstrous control freak whose primary joy in life was being shrill at and around her children, three boys she'd emasculated so thoroughly she might as well have just castrated them at the bris. There had really just been money stuff to settle, what to do with her savings—grown obese after two best sellers—and arranging for the sale of the apartment. Trust funds, charities, a few pen strokes and a handshake.

That was it. No children, no partner. *No phone, no pool, no pets*, a voice sang idiotically in her head. Marie had left her two years earlier to start a restaurant in Melbourne, Australia. Alice marked Marie's departure as the commencement of this, the Bad Time, as she thought of it, while knowing it wasn't Marie's fault, not really. She'd been depressive as long as she could remember, but there had always been things to fend it off—family, friends, school, partying, sex, her career, Marie. Marie, as it turned out, had been one of the last bulwarks. The other was writing, but that, too, was gone now, destroyed by the drugs Linväld had prescribed. She hadn't written anything in almost three years.

She trudged, head down, through the pissing mist. A takeout carton of curry lay where someone had tossed it, slumped against the brick wall like a drunk, its contents vomited out onto the sidewalk. *Why not today?* she'd thought at Dr. Linväld's, and no good answer had come to mind. There was absolutely no reason why not today. The question was how.

A pub called the Pig and Thistle appeared on the corner. She pushed in, shivering, suddenly aware of the cold. The place was empty, save, at a rear table, an old crone in a plastic rain bonnet, bent to her bitters. Football, inescapably, played on a TV over the bar. The signage of generic pubdom's purveyors—Fuller's, Taylor Walker—were plastered throughout. Over the last decade, Brits had gladly traded the eccentricities of their homey old pubs for corporate uniformity, the same bland menu in each one featuring fifteen-euro fish and chips.

The barman came over, large and smiling through his red beard, a jovial type she would have written and immediately discarded as cliché. She ordered a Johnnie Walker: black, neat, double. He raised a red eyebrow as he poured, then set the glass down in front of her. "That's twenty-seven." She paid with a fifty and motioned for him to keep the change. "I can't take that, miss."

"Take it."

"You American?"

"I moved here ten years ago. Listen, I know about tipping. I'm not trying to demean you, just take it." She didn't know why she'd tried either giving him the money or explaining it, and she could see she'd invited further interaction. But of course, that must have been what she wanted on some level, coming into the pub. So full of shit. She took a long drink. The whiskey tasted good, warmed her chest, did all the predictable stuff.

The bartender peeled off a five, stuck it in the till, and poured himself a small glass of the Johnnie Walker. "Staff discount," he said. "Nice weather, huh?"

"Yep."

"So why'd you move here?"

She forced herself to give the spiel, like pushing a boulder into a sloping ravine. "You remember all those people who said they'd leave the US if Bush won again? I was the only one who actually did."

"No kidding."

"Well, yeah, but that was an excuse. I always liked London."

He continued staring out the window behind her, beaded with crawling drops of rain. "Sorry, but I can't figure moving here. I've wanted to leave ever since I was a kid."

"So leave."

"Not so easy, though, is it?"

"I don't know." Was it easy? What was easy and what wasn't? Things that seemed easy sometimes turned out to be very difficult,

indeed. The easiest thing in the world for her, previously—writing—
was now impossible. And sometimes it worked the other way around,
too: formerly unthinkable things became normalized. Self-
extermination, for instance, an abstracted horror for much of her life,
had in recent years become a subject of practical contemplation. The
question was how. In her last book, one of the supporting cast, a
spurned girlfriend of the asshole sculptor protagonist, slit her wrists
(unsuccessfully) in the bathtub with a jagged piece of solder. This
scene was written after a considerable amount of morbid Googling
that revealed how often this maneuver was botched. It was just too
hard to dig at those veins and really open them up—image searches
turned up forearms and wrists that looked like meat hanging in a
butcher's freezer. So that was out. What, then? Living in England,
guns weren't an option—too bad she didn't still live in America,
where she might have picked up a twelve-gauge on the walk home
along with some jean shorts and beef jerky. And she was too afraid of
pills, of the possibility of brain damage, being locked inside herself
forever—a fate truly much, much worse than death. She'd considered
jumping from something high (London Bridge, falling down), but
there was always the possibility of crippled survival, not to mention
traumatizing onlookers.

"Miss?"

"What?"

"I asked if you were feeling okay."

"Listen, no offense, but I just don't feel much like talking. One
again, single."

He poured it and scrupulously moved to the other end of the bar.
In the space where he'd been standing, her reflection stared back at
her from the lead-lined mirror beside the liquor shelves. She looked at

herself as a stranger might, as the barman might have—middle-aged and darkly complexed, black hair and black eyes, with a faint scar running from temple to cheek. Marie, along with nearly every journalist who'd written her profile, had said it gave her character; it didn't hurt that over time she'd allowed people to conflate the scar with the story of her childhood ordeal at the Neversink. The specter of trauma had affixed itself to her public persona, lending interest and weight to her novels. The scar's actual story—Elise shoving her into a bike rack at their elementary school—was far less catchy. Again she said to the woman in the mirror, you are so full of shit.

But it didn't matter, she thought, averting her eyes, pushing off the stool, and moving back outside. She continued on her way, in a muddled state now that matched the atmosphere. The fuzziness didn't help, though, just made her feel more feebly agitated. For some reason, she'd thought that once she decided to do it, ending her life would be easy, a kind of sighing and letting go. She was surprised to find this wasn't the case. But of course it wasn't. Of course some part of her, the animal part mainly (always more of yourself than you think it is), didn't want to go. And not just the animal part, either. So don't, she thought, cutting north through Hyde Park on Carriage Drive. Even in the rain, people were out trying to enjoy the day—a father and daughter stood together on the bank of the Serpentine, tossing hunks of bread to a jostling flock of geese. On the path above them, a man trembled in place on a unicycle, adjusting his earbuds. Why couldn't this be enough for her? Just the world and its people, straining in their ways to make this moment, that moment, rich or exciting or happy or sad. This, after all, was existence, and if this wasn't enough, nothing else would be.

But it wasn't, and the thought felt hollow and false, like Dr. Linväld's singsong nostrum: *it's how you feel that makes it real.* The thing was, to really love the world she had to be able to write about it, and she couldn't anymore. The feeling that afflicted her movement through life—the fatigued sense of going through the motions—was singularly poisonous to her writing. In thirty months, she hadn't had an imaginative thought—a character, plot point, setting, piece of dialogue, turn of phrase, or orphaned verb mewling in the wilderness of the white page—that didn't feel cribbed from herself. It wasn't that she couldn't write anymore, exactly—she could have written a novel during this time, but it would have been an exercise, like the time in grad school that she'd handwritten Eliot's "Prufrock" just to see what it felt like to put down the same words he had, in the same order.

A year on Nardil had provided relief from the worst of the depression, but it had also soldered the writer's block down at the edges, sealing off important neural pathways. Now she was off the pills, but it was no good. She was broken, alone, useless.

She wiped off her face. Across the bridge, the path she was on curved behind a curtain of trees, after which would come the Bayswater Road, then home. What then? The thing was, the thought of not doing it was worse than the thought of doing it. Or: doing it would be hard, but not doing it would be impossible. That was the thing.

Her phone rang and she stopped walking. It was her agent, Charlotte. Alice winced with guilt at the photo on the call screen as though Charlotte, through some kind of new technology, could see her where she stood in the park, trying to decide whether to answer. "Hello?"

"Alice? Where are you?"

"Out. Walking."

"Did you forget about the meeting?"

"What meeting?"

Charlotte sighed, long-suffering. As a general response it was both justified and irritating, considering the money Alice had made her. "With Mike and Lindsey, concerning your new project."

"Shit."

"Listen, you need to give them something. You can't just string them along forever."

A nearby goose honked, and Charlotte said, "Where are you?"

"The park."

"Can you pop in? We need to catch up, go over a few things."

"I don't know."

"Or tomorrow, if you have other plans."

A violent updraft, like an angry, careening ghost, hit the line of trees under which Alice stood, loosing a welter of fat droplets. "No," she said. "I'll come by now."

The cramped space and spartan décor of Charlotte's office always surprised Alice. It looked more like the workplace of an uncreative middle manager in, say, textiles, than the office of one of London's most successful literary agents. A withered succulent sat atop the file cabinet, and a framed Klee print hung at a slight angle behind the desk. Next to the print, a small window of thick tiled glass obliquely admitted the gray light of the building's interior courtyard. When Alice had asked Charlotte why she didn't move to a bigger, better place, Charlotte had shrugged and said it suited her fine; considering all she really did was read and talk on the phone, she'd debated just working from her Kensington flat.

She smiled as Alice entered, and Alice smiled back, a reflex born of her good feelings for Charlotte and a childish desire to please her.

Charlotte was ten years her elder, and hard not to regard as a fantasy older sister: smart, stylish, and infectiously profane. But as the smile melted off her face, Alice realized coming here had been a horrible mistake. Charlotte was far too intuitive, would probe her in ways she didn't want to be probed, not now.

"Jesus," said Charlotte. "You look like fucking shit."

"Thanks."

"It's not a compliment. You look terrible."

"It's raining."

"Are you drunk?"

"I stopped for one."

Charlotte's phone buzzed. She looked at it and shut it off, placing it facedown. "Alice, I don't know what's going on with you, but you can't get pissed while you're supposed to be meeting with your editors."

"Well, I can, clearly."

"In case you really don't take my point, I'm using *can't* there to mean *shouldn't*. That's not something you should do. You obviously are capable of doing it—"

"I'm sorry, really. I forgot."

"—as you are capable of many other things you shouldn't do. For instance, taking a massive advance on a novel in the works and not delivering anything, not even an outline, for two years. That kind of thing."

"Did you really have me come by to berate me? You could have done that on the phone. Or by e-mail, really."

"No." Charlotte shook her head. Shorn recently of its gray curls, the sheep's wool now resembled a swim cap. "The reason I called was because your therapist, Lindbergh or whatever his name is, called me."

"What?"

"He's worried about you."

From their sessions, Linväld knew Charlotte was her agent, and he also knew she was one of Alice's closest friends. The magnitude of this breach of doctor-patient confidentiality signaled the degree of his immediate concern. "I'm fine."

"You are most definitely not fucking fine. You are about as far from fine as I've ever seen someone be. I think you need professional help."

"I'm getting professional help. Dr. Linväld is a professional."

"I'm talking about hospitals. I've been researching them. There are some really nice places in the country. One in Middlesex that looks like a bed-and-breakfast. They give you a massage every night. I'd like to go there."

"The loony bin, you're talking about."

"What is this, 1950? A mental health facility. For a little while."

Alice got up to leave and Charlotte followed. "Wait, wait. I'd antic-ipated this reaction, too. So the other thing is, if you wanted to come stay with us." *Us* was Charlotte and her boyfriend, Stuart, a talkative barrister and wine enthusiast. Alice pulled on her coat. It was the nicest, most unappealing offer anyone had ever made her.

"Charlotte, no."

"I'm really worried about you, Alice. Everyone is." Charlotte was following her down the hall now, talking and cajoling, following her out of the building and onto the crowded sidewalk, speaking in a strained, quiet tone about how many people loved her and how much she had to live for, and lots of other things like that. It was really quite dramatic, yet Alice still couldn't shake the feeling of going through the motions, or playing something out that was already over. Everything felt like a copy of a copy of a copy. Charlotte's voice faded behind her in a surge of pedestrians, then was blocked out entirely by traffic as Alice cut quickly across the road. She ducked down a side street, then another, and Charlotte was nowhere to be seen. But her phone rang again, and there was Charlotte's face smiling up at her. She tossed the phone into a nearby waste bin. That was all it was, she thought, just a discarding, a throwing away of it all. When you got down to it, it really was simple.

The simpler you could keep it, the better. That was her thinking, standing at her kitchen island, writing the note. She found herself mentally addressing it to Marie, whom she hadn't spoken to in over a year. But that was who she had in mind when she apologized—not her parents, Elise, or her nephews, though they were there, watching in a morose semicircle as she executed the words in her looping cursive; and not Charlotte, who would be terribly upset, but whose ebullient toughness would carry her right through. It was Marie, Melbourne Marie now, bent over a salmon croquette en croute with a small blowtorch, as Alice had most recently seen her on Facebook. *I'm so sorry*, she wrote, picturing that Marie—*I've tried to do better, but I'm just tired and don't see any way forward. Everything seems over now. I hope you know, despite this, how really important to me you were, and that this isn't your fault at all. Love, Alice.*

The writer in her rebelled against the maudlin quality but felt it was probably unavoidable, given the circumstances. She sealed the note in a plain envelope and stood the envelope in a crack in the island's surface, supported at the back by an overripe, wrinkled pear. She didn't want the note to get missed, lost in the macabre shuffle that would follow the discovery of her body, hopefully by her neighbor, a prim scold she'd never gotten along with. In the utility closet, she found a length of nylon cord she'd bought for tying up carpets in the last move. The iron chandelier overhead was obviously perfect, provided it could hold her. Her legs shook the chair beneath her, and for a moment she almost lost her balance, but she steadied herself with a hand on the chandelier. Tugging it first, then putting nearly all her body weight on it, she found it unfathomably secure, fixed to the ceiling with ancient screws of ferrous green. She tied the cord many times around the chandelier's base and began looping a knot on the other end, the one where her neck would go.

As she did, it occurred to her that this was the first time in over a year that the crushing fatigue was gone. Her vivid aliveness in this moment was a terrible joke, but it was also undeniable, as was the grim euphoria that seized her when she worked her head through the noose. *If only there had been someone there to kill her every minute of her life*, she thought—a great line, and true. But even this would lose its novelty, become one more draining thing. That was it, then, all she had to do was kick out, it didn't have to be graceful or practiced, and how could it be? Everyone was an amateur at this—another good line, she thought. Too bad she'd never use it.

Standing on the chair, facing the gray square of her flat's living room window, her view angled down toward Seven Sisters Road. An endless surge of cars, interrupted now and then by people trudging through the drab wet. The pavement flickered blue, reflecting the snazzy signage of a new falafel automat called Izmir. On the left edge of the vista sat the Tube station, constantly feeding on new victims while disgorging old ones. She looked away, at a picture of Marie on the wall, wanting that to be the last thing she saw. She pulled the noose tight around her neck, tensed one leg, and prepared to kick out with the other. This was okay, this was good.

The doorbell rang.

The doorbell rang again. Using the cord for balance, she stepped down from the chair and answered it. "Alice?" Charlotte's voice crackled up.

"Yeah."

"Ring me in."

"I'd rather not, if it's okay."

"I've been calling; this is ridiculous."

"Charlotte, I'm not decent right now."

"So what? When am I decent?"

She held her thumb to the talk button, but couldn't think of anything to say. Charlotte couldn't come up, obviously, and Alice felt that the sight of her agent, damp from the weather and crowds she would have traveled through to check on her disturbed, errant client, would do her in. A passing horn split itself into two versions, one through the window and its staticky twin through the call box. Charlotte said, "Let me up."

"No."

"Goddamn it. Do I need to call the police?"

"And tell them what?"

"And tell them that I think my friend is going to kill herself."

With a mocking look, the noose swung back and forth, bothered by hot air from the nearby vent. When exactly, Alice wondered, did your life become so ridiculous? She took a deep breath and pressed the button. "Why would you say that?"

"Oh Alice, come on. Because of how you've been acting. Because of a million things you've said and done over the last year. Sorry if I'm wrong, but yeah. If I have to stand out here in the rain, that's what I'm worried about."

"I'm not going to kill myself."

"Fucking promise me. You promise."

She didn't want to promise. She wanted Charlotte to go away so she could get on with it, but she didn't see how to make that happen without saying the words, so she said them. "I promise."

"Come to the window, let me see your face."

Alice went to the window and looked down. Two stories below, Charlotte peered up, her red face smudged by worry and wet, the swim-cap hair sleek like an otter's back. Behind her sat the Tube entrance. Charlotte waved and Alice waved back, and Charlotte called up, "Come in on Monday. Promise me."

"I will, I promise," Alice said, knowing that she meant it, knowing that ending things now would be different from two minutes earlier. But why, what really was the difference? She didn't know— there probably wasn't one—and yet she submitted to her sense that it mattered, or to the fact that a part of herself still drew those distinctions.

Charlotte crossed the wet, blue expanse of the road, and Alice stood at the window, watching her enter the Underground, swallowed up. The stairs leading down, the black hole in the earth, made her sick to look at. It flooded her with a sensation that existed in some far border region of memory and sense. She always recoiled when this sick feeling came over her, but this time she did not turn away.

She allowed herself the full memory, to the extent that it still existed in her mind: roaming around the hotel, somehow coming across the basement door and the stairs leading down. Descending them, she descended into the darkness of her own memory, the place where all the lights went out. No, there was an outline there, if she was willing to look. She remembered opening the storage room door and hearing it snick shut behind her. The gray man—for the first time in years she let herself see him. She let that murky underwater light click on, and let him move toward her. She let him look at her face, just as she looked at his. She let him put his arms around her, forty years after he had the first time.

Now, in the bedroom, she pulled on a pair of old jeans and a cable-knit sweater. She tied her hair back in a rough knot, with the false, frightened resolve of a hiker about to take her first tentative step onto the Appalachian Trail or the pilgrimage to Santiago. Into a shoulder bag she threw a bottle of water, a granola bar, a legal pad, and pen. The apartment door creaked open with a surprised, rising note, as though it hadn't expected her to walk through it again. Outside it was raining harder, and as she crossed the street, the canvas TOMS she'd quickly thumbed on plashed in a rut, soaking through instantly. The Tube entrance was in front of her, breathing out heat. The circle with its red and blue, like a hospital sign, warned her away. Why was she doing this? Because a long time ago she'd gone underground, and even though she'd survived, some part of her hadn't come back up; because she sensed a truth down there, perhaps some new story left to write; and because, now, staying aboveground was a nonstarter too. The only way forward, it seemed, was down.

She held her breath, grabbed the handrail, and forced herself to go down one step at a time, passed by a stream of Londoners who regarded her, if at all, as some kind of cripple or defective. Well, what if she was? Her heart thudded wildly in her chest as she reached the bottom, but she pressed on toward a fare kiosk embedded in the tile wall. She managed to get her credit card in but was unable to make sense of the machine's buttons—hieroglyphic squiggles she stabbed at in vain. A rough terror seized the nape of her neck and pulled her toward the white tile ringing the exit. But she couldn't go back—she knew what was there: the jealous noose swinging in the empty room. She slumped against the wall.

"Ma'am?"

Standing over her was a Sikh man, his silken hair wrapped up in a pink turban. He said, "Are you okay?"

"No."

"Do you need some assistance?"

"Yes."

He let her use his card and gently led her through the gate. "Where are you headed?"

She hadn't thought to answer this question beforehand. Which way was Charlotte's? She shook her head, stumped. "Where are you going?" she said.

He cocked his head. "Me? I'm going to work. Lewisham."

"Right, me too. Lewisham."

She clung to his arm, and he helped her down another flight of stairs to his platform. On a wooden bench they waited, and she felt like more of a child than she could ever remember feeling. A train's faraway approach shook the platform, and her heart was the same, juddering at a remove. A wet spot condensed around her feet; the tracks she'd made on the platform's dirty concrete were already vanishing. "What's your name?" she said.

"Phil."

"I'm Alice."

"Good to meet you."

"Thank you for this."

"No worries." He took his phone out, then sighed, seeming to remember it didn't work down here. "You okay now?"

"What do you do, Phil?"

"I'm a med tech." She'd noticed the green scrub pants, but every-one wore scrubs these days. "University Hospital."

"Is it interesting work?"

He laughed. "It's okay. Mostly getting the OR ready for surgery or whatever. You?"

"I'm a writer. Was, anyway."

"I ever read you?"

"I don't know. Alice Emmenthaler?"

He shook his head, the long, delicate nose tapering to nothing at the tip. "Sorry, I go in more for sci-fi, stuff like that. You famous?"

"Yeah."

"No shit."

They sat in a silence broken by the whine of metal scraping metal. Phil opened his mouth, then paused as though trying to decide whether to go on. He said, "Let me ask you something, you being a writer and all. Tell me if this sounds like a book. About two years ago, me and some of the other techs started keeping a photo collection of objects that got pulled out of people's bodies in surgery."

"Really."

"I don't just mean from out of their arses, pardon me, though that does happen. But things people swallow, or get stabbed with, impale themselves. We have to bag and dump the stuff, and me and my mate Keithsey decided hey, let's start taking photos. Like, this one woman, older bird, comes in with a stomach complaint, right? Turns out it was this tiny toy xylophone. Must have somehow swallowed it when she was a kid, had it in there fifty years, no worries, then one day the high-C starts jabbing her." He looked up at the distant glow of the train's headlight in the tunnel, a moment before Alice saw it. "I'd be canned if they found out; it's pretty out of line."

"I won't tell anyone."

He grinned and leaned in. "Thing is, we started an anonymous Twitter, and we've already got like a thousand followers. So I've been thinking, what if we made a book out of it, like a coffee table book."

"You can't be serious."

"I'm serious. I've got some of the photos on my phone here, if you want to see." He pulled them up, proud like a little boy. Pictures of small objects, lovingly photographed, covered in the murk of the human body: a whistle, a can of grapefruit juice, an army figurine. "What do you think?"

"I think it's disgusting," she said. "I think it's great."

He smiled at her reaction, at the smile on her face, and she realized he'd been worried, that he was reaching out to someone who seemed in need of help. "Hey, if you've got time, you could even come by the hospital, and I could show you our little collection."

The train emerged from the tunnel, its yellow light cupped in front like a gift it was bringing from stop to stop. For the first time in so long, the moment she was living in was a new one, and the stale air she breathed was fresh, fragrant as spring. The only way forward was down.

"Yes," she said. "Show me."

15. Noah

2010

When Alice Emmenthaler e-mailed asking if she could interview me about the Neversink, I was surprised. We'd met once or twice at family things, but we'd never been at all close—she was about fifteen years older than me. I knew who she was, of course, but I was a little surprised she'd even thought to e-mail me. And besides, I wasn't sure what I could tell her that would be useful. I didn't know if she knew my story, but in a nutshell: I got out as quickly as I could, and I stayed away. I wrote back saying as much, and she said, well, she was going to be in LA anyway for some business meetings, so would I mind getting lunch. I never mind getting lunch, I said. Where and when?

We met at a Moroccan place near my apartment, in Los Feliz. She looked younger, different than I'd thought from Googling her dust jackets and promo shots. Some people have an energy in person that photos don't capture. I ordered some fruit tea and we sat on the sidewalk, Ernie flattened out at my feet. I'd been up late the night before, doing an improv set, and I guess I was loopy, because when she asked about my life I told her everything: how I've been in Los Angeles for a decade since college, screenwriting and performing, and bartending at the Vermont, how my girlfriend moved away last year and I live with my dog in a little dump in Eagle Rock; how I actually dressed up as the Captain Morgan's pirate for a stretch to make some extra cash—three hundred for a night out at Footsie's or the 4100 Bar, taking pictures and lining up buttery nipples on my cutlass for bachelorette parties; how, for this, I attended the Tisch conservatory at NYU and still pay five hundred a month in loans; and how, in spite of how bleak all of that might sound, I'm happy here. As the song goes, *I love LA*.

Small talk out of the way, it seemed, she set a minirecorder on the table and said, "So, Noah, what was it like growing up there?"

"Liberty or the Neversink?"

"Both."

"I don't know. Weird, but also normal, I guess."

"How so?"

"I mean, you know how, when you're a kid, however things are is normal. You could be growing up on Mars and think that was how it was for everyone."

"Weird how, though?"

"Well, you've been there."

"Yes, I have. I'm going back to do some more research, too."

"It's a creepy place anyway, and then I got older and learned more and more about the history of it—" I trailed off, unsure where I was going with that. Ernie shifted at my feet as if to remind me of where we were—in Los Angeles, on a beautiful day.

She said, "Did you ever see anything strange? Hear about anything?"

"Like what?"

"Anything. Related to the killings."

"Not really. They'd basically stopped by the time I was a kid."

"Were there any theories about who it might have been?"

"Of course. There was always speculation. My dad seemed to think it was an out-of-towner."

"What do you mean?"

"Like someone from the city who visited the hotel on holidays, maybe had family in the area."

"What do you think?"

"What's the book going to be about, exactly? Are you playing detective, trying to crack the case?"

"Not in a legal sense, no. I'm just trying to put things together to my satisfaction. About the killings and what happened to me. But I also want to weave in a history of the hotel through the decades and our family. I'm still figuring it out."

As she described the project, she poured more tea and took a bite of the coiled pastry I'd ordered, the powdered sugar dusting her fingers. Looking at her, I got this weird feeling we were meant to meet up, that this was something important and preordained. When she finally paused, I told her as much, and it was obvious she thought this was stupid. I don't really believe in destiny, but it does feel like sometimes things just line up. Probably all that LA good-energy stuff rubbing off—I know actors who do this thing where they pretend they've already gotten the part before they audition, because it helps them line up their chakras or whatnot. It takes an adjustment to move here from the Northeast, where everything is negative and ironic and self-depre-cating, to get used to this culture of what is—to be honest—sometimes extremely silly optimism. But it's one of the reasons I've stayed out here—because you can choose to be happy, to not lug around your history and family and life story like an overpacked suitcase. The way my father, who depresses the hell out of me, does.

I said some of this, and she said, "What's so depressing about Len?"

"How much time do you have?"

"As long as it takes."

We wound up getting dinner at Casita del Campo, one of my favorite spots. Around the second pitcher of margaritas, the recorder was off and we were just talking. About the world and comedy and LA and writing and so on, and so on. I asked her what had compelled her to write about the Neversink, and she told me how she'd almost killed herself three years before. And how the thing that had saved her was this idea that she had to go down, keep going down. That's how she put it. She said she realized she had to dig into the story of what had happened to her and the hotel and everything, that this would be how she'd move on.

I said, "You should try my technique—just run as far away as possible."

"I did try that. It wasn't working."

Her black eyes reflected the light from a decorative sconce over the table, and I felt this overwhelming desire for her approval, to please her. "Seriously, Alice. I'll help however I can."

After dinner we went back to my apartment and I walked Ernie, then we listened to music and smoked a little grass—I like calling it *grass*, it's so dumb and seventies, and it made her laugh, a pleasing low tone. I put on this Can album, *Ege Bamyasi*, that I really like to listen to baked, and my mind drifted back to her description of herself in that room, how it had ruined her in certain ways forever—*irretrievably*, that was what she'd said. The thought of a perfect, happy little kid being damaged in that way made me start crying—wailing, like I was the hurt child in Alice's story.

"Noah," she said.

"I'm sorry."

"It's okay, come here," she said, and she held my head in her lap while it shook.

We had a good time that week. In some ways—and I told her this after one too many beers by the pool at her hotel—she felt like the older sister I'd always wanted and had never had with Suse, who'd always been distant. That's very kind, she said, and looking me up and down added that I was like the groundhog she'd never had. Funny stuff, I said, maybe you should be the comedian. The next night I bartended, and she came in, ordered a French 75, pretended not to know me at first. On the tip line, she wrote "LOL." We drove her rental out to Malibu and bought cherries from a roadside vendor in Topanga Canyon. I ate them from the bag and threw the pits down the sloping hill, thinking how nice it would be if one of them took root and a cherry tree grew there.

On the day before she was supposed to fly back to London, Alice came and saw me perform at the Laugh Factory. On Wednesdays, they have this five-minute set thing with about thirty comedians, and everyone goes up, one after the other. It's pretty rough, and there's usually a lot of drunks chattering in the front tables, but I did all right, some dumb extended joke about why I quit playing professional basketball, having lost my passion for the game.

Afterward we sat at the bar. She said, "That was pretty good."

"Pretty thank you."

"Pretty you're welcome. I have to say, though, you don't seem like a typical comedian."

"No?" I said. "Lumpy with a Jewfro? I'm the model."

"Yeah, but not unhappy. I've known a few comedians. You're not an asshole and not suicidally depressed."

"You don't have to be depressed; that's bullshit."

"Yeah?" She sipped her drink.

"I mean, do you have to be depressed to be a good welder? A good figure skater?"

"Maybe. And you know that's different."

I laughed. "I like to be happy, sue me."

"There's your problem," she said. "That's why you'll never be good."

Just then, another comedian stopped by and invited us to a party one of the Groundlings was throwing in Coldwater Canyon. We settled the bill, got in the car, and drove up, miraculously finding a parking spot right outside. Everything was light and fun, but I stopped pacing myself and, okay, might have gotten a little bit drunk. On the back porch, as we were sharing a smoke to the strains of Rihanna's "Umbrella," I said, "That's why I'll never be good, huh?"

"What?" She was looking down the steep backyard, a tangled grove of lemon trees and birds of paradise.

"You said I would never be good."

"No. I said trying really hard to be happy is why you'll never be good."

"That's such a fucked-up thing to say." She shrugged, and I went on. "But I guess you're a screwed-up person, right? It's probably why you're so good at what you do."

"You're drunk, Noah."

"That's what you think, though, isn't it?"

In a practiced, casual motion, she flicked the cigarette off the porch and said, "What I think is that people running from themselves don't make good art. I think you're extremely invested in being laid-back and cheerful, and I think that comes at a cost. Maybe it's worth it."

"Fuck you."

"Okay, that's better," she said, and she may have said something else, but I was walking through the scrum of the party, pushing past a couple making out on the stairs and moving down the driveway and street, letting gravity and my drunkenness lower me down the long hill, walking down Hollywood, down Sunset, past the Seventh Veil and a pair of prostitutes on stilt-like heels catcalling me and laughing when I flipped them off, trudging past Kaiser Permanente and the Scientology center, and finally, at three in the morning, collapsing half drunk in my bed to not sleep the rest of the night.

The next day, with a hangover like an itchy wool shirt worn under my skin, I took two Ativan and drove south, all the way down to San Diego. It felt good to escape LA's summer clinch, and cresting the hills in La Jolla, the temperature dropped ten degrees. I parked alongside the Pacific Beach Boardwalk and took Ernie down to the ocean, where we lay in the sand between two rival gangs of sunbathing teenagers.

Sedated by the heat and the sedatives I'd taken, Ernie panting by my side, I drifted into one of those strange zones between sleep and waking. Very clearly, I was back in my old bedroom, in the cottage. It was winter—strange to feel the cold and the warm sand simultaneously—and the wind clattered the shutters outside the window. It sounded like someone trying to get in. I'd childishly begged Susannah to sleep with me on those windy nights, but she'd long ago told me to grow up and shut up, and so I had. And then, one night, came the man.

I was lying sleepless in bed when outside my window was this weird yellow light. My bedroom faced the woods, so I couldn't think what it could be. It got a little brighter, then went dark, and I was about to get out of bed when the window opened. It was so unreal—the hand entering, then the arm, a foot delicately thrown over the sill, a black boot, then the dark figure pushing through and standing there—that for a moment, I hadn't screamed. I'd just stared, knowing I was having a nightmare. But usually the moment you realize you're dreaming is the moment you wake up, and I hadn't. The man had just stood there staring at me, and I at him. Then I'd tried to scream but couldn't, could only lie there silent and shaking.

He approached the bed and leaned over. He put his hands around my neck and began squeezing, suffocating me slowly, and there was nothing I could do about it. I closed my eyes and submitted. Only then did the pressure ease, and when I opened my eyes again he was gone without any evidence he'd been there, other than the barest smudge of snow on the carpet, which melted away. I wasn't able to sleep for a week after that. When I told my parents, they told me it was a nightmare, and that was almost the worst part, that they didn't believe me.

The man returned several more times over the years, then no more. Now, twenty years later, he was back and I was eight again, seeing the glow outside, squeezing my eyes, hearing the window open, willing him away, willing myself to a remote beach like the one I dimly sensed beneath me. Trying to scream but making only a whimper. Thrashing and thrashing, my muscles barely twitching. The man standing there, getting closer, on top now, smiling down at me.

The girls on either side startled up from their sunbathing at the man jumping up from the sand and jogging out into the ocean some twenty yards away. I waded fully clothed out into the waves and must have presented a disturbing enough scene to send a young lifeguard trotting out. He brought me in under his tanned, muscular wing to a smattering of mild applause. People watched for a minute but lost interest as I walked Ernie back up to the boardwalk—just another loony drawn to the beach, nothing to see here. Soaked through, I rolled down the windows and drove, shivering, back to LA. When I got to the hotel, Alice was packing, almost ready to leave.

"Hey," she said. "What happened to you?"

"I told you the first night, I want to help you."

"I think you might be the one that needs help."

"Help me help you help me."

"Come in."

Once again she turned on the recorder, once again Ernie settled under my feet, but this time I had a story for her. How the man started coming at night. How when I told my parents, they said it was a nightmare. And how when I kept having this nightmare, they hired a therapist who diagnosed sleep paralysis. Victims of hypnagogia often, he said, suffer the delusion of someone in the room with them, someone holding them down. He even brought in a reproduction of an old painting called *The Nightmare*, in which a little gray ogre perches on top of a prostrate damsel. A terrifying painting, and a small comfort, considering I knew what was happening wasn't a delusion.

How, after weeks and months of these therapy sessions, I began to believe my psychologist. When the light outside appeared, I closed my eyes and thought about other things—playing on a sunny beach with friends from school—and I could almost convince myself that the footsteps in the room and the hands on my neck were just some other, renegade part of my imagination. After all, if the man was real, why hadn't he killed me, why hadn't he gone after my sister or my parents?

And how, finally, on one morning in the spring, by which point I had convinced myself it really was just a nightmare, the nightmare left something behind: an old military flashlight. A small green metal box with a hinged clip on the rear—it must have slipped from his jacket and fallen under the bed. I pressed the little red button and it turned on, casting the room in the ghostly yellow light that announced his arrival outside my window. It was both terrifying to know the man was real and gratifying to know I hadn't created him, that he didn't dwell in the recesses of my consciousness. I figured I'd tell my parents at breakfast, but I didn't. The flashlight stayed where I'd put it, in my closet, inside a box of old baseball cards.

"Why didn't you show it to them?"

"I guess I knew he'd realize he'd lost it, and somehow that would mean he wouldn't be back. But also, what if I showed them and they still didn't believe me? What if it was like the nightmares? Not having them believe me—to go on doubting myself—would have been the scariest thing of all. Does that make sense?"

She nodded. "It does to me."

I reached in my pocket and pulled it out, the flashlight. I turned it on and the hotel room was suffused with that weird glow. "I've held on to it ever since. After all these years, it still works. To remind me I'm not crazy, to trust myself. Because, you know, I was right. He never did come back after that."

She took the light from my hand and held it in front of her. "I remember this from the basement."

"It's the same person."

"Yes."

She got up and poured us both wine in plastic hotel cups, and we drank together listening to the AC hum. "You understand that what I'm writing will hurt our family, right? I don't want you to be blind-sided. I like you."

"I like you, too." Outside the window, a line of birds perched on the building next door took flight, and their shadows fell like water. "And I don't care if it hurts them."

"No?"

Ernie shifted under me. I wiped my eyes and took a breath. "I think the place is evil. I think they're hiding something; they've been hiding something for a long time. I want to know who did this to us."

She rolled her suitcase down to the lobby, and I followed with Ernie. Her airport Uber arrived and we embraced one more time; then she was gone. I was almost home before I realized she'd taken the flashlight with her.

16. Ensemble

2012

By eight in the morning, the snow had completely blanketed the ground outside the cottage, accumulating overnight on the exterior windowsills and around the edges as well, creating a cozy, enclosed feeling inside. Len looked through one of these snow holes at the side of the Neversink—a pure white blanket now. It covers everything, he thought, inanely. They were big, wet flakes, the kind that stuck instantly; in less than four hours, they'd undone years of neglect, hiding the graffiti and kudzu and ruin—the building looked like a giant overfrosted birthday cake. He'd built himself a fire and put on some old jazz records. *Sketches of Spain, Kind of Blue, Etta James Sings for Lovers.*

Drinking his tea, he hoped the weather would cancel the meeting scheduled later with Alice. She'd called several times over the last month, leaving message after message. But she'd finally gotten him on the line, and he hadn't been able to say no to family. Sure, he'd said, late afternoon on Sunday works. He supposed he owed her that much, despite his misgivings. She was writing some kind of book about or involving the hotel, she'd said, and he suspected, given what had happened to her, that it wouldn't be flattering, her assurances that it would only be "to tie up some loose ends" notwithstanding.

The phone rang, a rare occurrence. Len said, "Hello."

"It's Saul."

"Saul!" Len hadn't seen or talked to Javits in almost five years. His voice was the same, instantly familiar in its brisk nasality. As they caught up on pleasantries, Len walked into the kitchen and put another kettle of water on the stove.

"Len," said Saul, abruptly. "I need to talk to you."

"So talk, we're talking."

"Not on the phone."

"Okay, sounds mysterious."

"Can I come by?"

"What, today? Weather report says twelve inches, maybe more."

"I'm already out. You got time around noon?"

"Hang on, let me see." Len didn't have anything going on until five, when Alice was due. He never, for that matter, had much going on since turning the golf course operations over to his daughter and officially retiring. But it stoked some uselessly tenacious part of his ego to continue keeping up the appearance that he wasn't doing nothing, that he wasn't just drinking tea and listening to Coltrane and watching the snow fall outside. He thumbed through a phone book on the table, riffling the pages, and said, "Yeah, noon works."

"See you then."

Old Javits, he thought. What could he possibly want? Saul Javits, like everyone else, had drifted away with the closing of the hotel.

They'd stayed in touch for a while, having a beer now and then, but at some point Javits and his wife (dubbed "Lady Saul" by Rachel years ago) had moved from Liberty to somewhere farther out in the country, and that had been that. When Lady Saul had died five years ago, Len had attended the funeral, also attended by Rachel. Over a glass of wine at the reception afterward, Rachel and he had agreed that Javits looked terrible, not just haggard from the grief, but old, shockingly old. He could only imagine what the man looked like now, though he supposed he wouldn't have to.

At precisely noon, Javits arrived, and his appearance didn't disappoint. His ancient head poked out of a thick sweatshirt made of burgundy velour, and the effect was that of a large walnut being carried around on a royal pillow. He held a thick manila envelope, which he set on the sofa without comment; Len figured he'd let Javits—a chatterbox who drifted off into wild tangents by way of finally getting to a point—tell him what it was when he was ready. Kicking the snow from his boots, he shook Len's hand, and Len remembered how much he'd always liked Javits, how much he'd really missed him. It all just got away from you.

"Coffee?" said Len.

"How about a beer?"

"I gave that up years ago. Too easy to sit around all day drinking."

"Why not, though? Any reason not to drink beer these days, all day if you want? Who's to stop you?"

"That's the problem. And I was getting fat. Worrying Suse."

"How is Susannah?"

"She's fine. Running the course. Dating a local policeman, if you can believe that."

"Long as she's happy, right? That's what I tell myself, anyway, though I'm not sure I believe it, but what can you do?"

"God, yes. She's thirty-seven, you believe that?"

"My Samara's fifty-something. Unbelievable."

"It's terrible," he laughed, but Javits worried his gnarled hands, and Len saw that something was really bothering him. "You sure I can't get you anything, Saul?"

"Listen, I have to tell you something, and I don't know how to do it. But I don't know what else to do. I couldn't do it over the phone, so here I am. But now that I'm here, I don't know where to start."

The fact that Javits—reliably voluble, even at his wife's funeral—seemed lost for words was frightening. Len said, "What is it?"

Javits took a breath and cast a longing look outside, where snow hung from dead tree branches like clumps of blue spun sugar. "Okay. Has Alice contacted you?"

"Emmenthaler?"

"Yeah."

"Well, matter of fact, we're meeting this afternoon around five."

"Don't do it, call it off."

"Saul, what the hell is going on?"

"Oh, Lenny," Javits hung his shrunken head. "I messed up."

In the distance, up on the hill, snow tumbled off the hotel façade in disintegrating chunks that swirled in the wind as they fell. Len felt a terrible dread, as though something large but hidden was about to clarify itself in his field of vision. He said, "Talk."

And for the next thirty minutes, Javits did. At the end of it, he handed Len the manila envelope. "It's all in there," he concluded. "I'm so sorry."

"Get out of here," said Len.

"Lenny, you know I love you, and I loved your mother. Give me a call after you've had a chance to look at it all, and let me know if I can help with—"

"Get out of here," Len yelled, and there was more, but Javits was already hurrying out the door, already climbing back up the low hill, already getting in his truck, already turning the key and cranking the engine to drown out Len's voice, although Len hadn't come outside, he saw. Was he yelling that loud, or was it still ringing in Javits's head? He peeled out for a few seconds, but gained traction and managed to fishtail up onto the road. It occurred to him, as the hotel, hulking white in his rearview, disappeared behind the trees after the first looping curve, that he'd probably never see it—or Len—again. Balking at that line of thought, he focused his attention on the drive, trying to get home in one piece, the roads on the way back to Newburgh being a mess, a complete mess. He hunched over the wheel, as though the extra few inches might make a difference in his reaction time, but he was going only twenty miles an hour, anyway. And besides, maybe it would be for the best if he just skidded gracefully into the ravine to his right.

"Goddamn you," he said to himself.

He'd betrayed his oldest friend, then delivered news that would probably destroy him. It was Alice's fault. She'd put the seed in his head when she'd gotten in touch a year ago, telling him what Noah had told her, talking about what she'd already figured out. She'd asked him what he knew, and he'd told her he'd look into it, just to get her off his back. The same way he had with that Lucy woman, way back in the seventies, after which he'd left well enough alone, had put it out of his mind and gotten on with the business of life: working at the hotel, raising his kids, grieving Jeanie's death, fixing up the house, helping close the hotel, going on little vacations with Hedda, and for the last few years, living alone as a bachelor. But sitting there at his desk, looking through the yellowy files Lucy had brought by the hotel and that he'd immediately stashed away in the basement— the microfiche copies of newspaper accounts, the police reports—he felt he was, at last, fulfilling his false promise to the woman and finishing the work she'd started forty years earlier. He talked to old cops he knew, retired from Liberty PD, and a homicide-beat writer up in Albany. He went through housing and bank records. He began to put it all together. Was it merely boredom, some lingering bit of ego, a need to feel useful? Whatever the case, what he found was compelling and had the smell of truth about it, some indiscernible character of factuality, the small, strange details that clicked like the tumblers of an invisible lock, and behind it, the echoing memory of Lucy's words: *Children don't just disappear; do your goddamned job.* He'd been so close before, had been on the verge of looking into it, talking to Jeanie about it, but had put it off, telling himself give it a day and see how you feel. And soon thereafter Jeanie was really sick— dying—and he couldn't bring himself to talk to her, and then she was dead, and in a way it had seemed like problem solved, though looking at the evidence spread out in front of him, he finally admitted the truth: he simply hadn't wanted to know, had very much not wanted to know, and not knowing was easy, so he hadn't. Even now, he could barely stand to look at it head-on. But the glittering whiteness of the snow that flew past his windshield was like the truth of the papers that had lain scattered across his dining room table. Going over these facts again and again in his quiet house, he had felt himself in a chain of information passing from the lips of the dead to the ears of the living. A conduit. Many times he considered stopping, but the thought kept pushing him forward that the truth had somehow survived for decades, survived for him to find. It seemed indecent to let this truth dissipate like steam, which it would when he died, and at eighty-seven, how much longer would it be, if he was being honest with himself? For months it ate at him, kept him up at night. At last he called Alice back. Like a dog, he'd done exactly as she'd asked, returning a juicy bone to her waiting hand, and in doing so he'd destroyed his oldest friend.

"Goddamn you," he said again to himself, Alice, Len, Jeanie, Asher, the Neversink, God Himself. And as he did—as though God had heard his blasphemy and responded in brisk, instant rebuke—the road disappeared.

Where it had appeared to go straight was instead a large, flat snow-drift, and in the corner of his eye he saw the road sweep away, up and right. He swung the wheel, but too late, and the car skidded into a wall of snow. For a moment it seemed a surprisingly gentle stop, but then the chassis slammed something hard and Javits's head slammed into the steering wheel. He sat for a few wondering seconds, nose dripping like a leaky faucet onto the vinyl of the seat between his legs. He cautiously stepped on the gas, and the tires whirred uselessly beneath him. The rearview mirror revealed a long white slope that vanished into distant groves of black pine. He'd jackknifed over the top of a sloping hill—not the edge of a cliff, but enough of an incline at the top that the tires had no purchase on the ground. Pulling out his phone, he was unsurprised to find no cell service here.

Hot air from the vent stung his face as he considered his options. The smart thing, he knew, would be to just sit there until another car came along. He closed his eyes and rested his hot, thrumming head on the cool doorframe. Waiting. Since Hedda had died, he felt he'd

been doing nothing but waiting. He'd stopped doing anything—
stopped jogging, stopped fixing the house, stopped gardening,
stopped corresponding with people, stopped cooking and cleaning,
stopped doing anything besides drowsing in front of the TV, talking
to Samara once a week and Charlie once a month. Just waiting—for
the obvious, he supposed. The detective work and Alice and even the
trip to Len's had been the most excitement he'd had in years. Horrible
as it had all been, he'd also felt horribly alive, horribly purposeful.
Busy. Now, here he was, waiting again. Huddled against the door, he
remembered the time when he was five and he'd wandered away from
his mother in a Weehawken Woolworths. What had begun as a fugue
of delighted escape quickly became a nightmare of abandonment, his
dismay impelling him to hide in a dark corner behind a rack of discount coats. He could still feel those coats now, the itchy, cheap tweed
pressed to his face, not bringing any comfort. Then, as now, he'd
eventually had to pull himself together, get to his feet, go get help.
Before he'd fully thought through this course of action, he'd pushed
out the car door and was following his errant tire tracks back up to
the road. The snow crunched, thick and wet beneath his old duck
boots, and he pulled his hood over his head. Hunching forward, the
blood dripped a dotted red line on the white ground. This pleased
him, strangely—walking where the road should be, he seemed to be
leaving a lane marker of his own devising. He felt strong. The temperature was in the low twenties, but after a lifetime spent upstate,
this kind of weather barely registered with him. His wife had grown
infirm, and many of their friends had retired to Arizona and Florida
(a postcard had arrived the year before from Sander, improbably still
alive somewhere down in the swamp where he'd improbably worked
for the last two decades, at his daughter's tropical-plant farm), but

like a stringy old weed, Mr. Javits had somehow gotten hardier with age. Still, it was cold, maybe even high teens, he thought. The teens were when his face began to hurt, and his face was hurting. But then, he'd just hit it on something, hadn't he? The car wreck, he remembered, and looked behind, but couldn't see anything in the whiteness. Where was the car? His breath hung in the air in front of him, like an idea. He would walk to the nearest town, a place called Owananda, he knew, only three or four miles away. He'd been there when he was younger. He could remember a lunch counter there. Speckled Formica. Sparkling chunks of snow tumbled silently off the overhang of a small nearby bluff, and his mind felt like that, like it was sloughing something off, decades of habit and thought, like dead skin. He would get lunch in Onawanda if the lunch counter was open, then hire a tow truck and drive home, if he could. But he didn't even want to go home, he realized. He was glad to be where he was, walking in the middle of the road, where the road should be. A bit of sunlight broke through the clouds, piercing his heart with a shard of derelict joy. To be walking on fresh snow and not a car around—he again felt like a boy, but not the cowering boy in Woolworths; a boy with a whole snow day ahead of him. But God, his head hurt. When he got to Wanadonda he would go to the lunch counter, clean up, and drive home. Back in time for dinner. His daughter had a science project at school he'd agreed to help her with, he remembered now. No, he thought, wait, but Len, he had to meet Len. Where was his car? Stanching his nose with the shoulder of his coat, he stabbed at buttons on his phone.

Someone on the other end picked up. "Saul?"

"Who is this?"

"This is Sander, you called me."

Sander, the name was familiar, but the person it referred to eluded him. Why was this Sander calling him? Play it cool, he thought. "Yes."

"How are you? My God, it's been forever."

"Yes."

"Are you okay, Saul?" Sander held the phone away from his ear and waited, but no answer came. "Saul?"

"Listen, I might, uh, need some help here."

"Where are you?"

"I don't know. I can't find my car. It's okay, though."

"But where are you?"

"I'm sitting down, right now, resting up. I've decided I won't tell Len."

"Len? Tell Len what?"

"Wait, who is this?"

"Sander Levin. You called me. Hello?"

"Sorry," Javits sighed. "I have to go."

Sander looked pleadingly around the room with an instinct to ask his daughter for help—as he still did several times a day after several months—but she wasn't there, of course. Help—his need for it, and her inability to give it to him—was why she'd put him here, at Grovebrook Downes, or as one of the resident wags called it, Brokedown Grove. Louisa visited three times a week, but otherwise it was just him and the nurse who checked on him twice a day. Just him sitting in this room that refused to become an actual place.

It was as though his mind simply couldn't absorb the concrete fact of one more new home. Or maybe it was that he was almost certain to die here, and some obscure part of him could not accept that truth. Whatever it was, this place—a large central room with a kitchen on one wall, bedroom adjoining, and bathroom with bolted steel rails—refused to coalesce into something that felt real. At best, his impression of it was the same as the impression of a weary traveler after a long day's drive checking into a roadside motel; in his exhaustion, this traveler might briefly register the generic details—the TV, the floral bedspread, the cups wrapped in plastic, the chipped cream of the counter, the useless table and chairs—in the few moments before he closed his eyes and fell asleep; likewise did Sander's mind rebel against any real impression, any particularity, of his new, and almost certainly final, apartment.

He pressed the red button on his phone—the flip cell Louisa had bought him years before—feeling unmoored by the call, already plagued by the sense that he'd imagined it. What had Javits—if it had been Javits—said about Len? Where had he been calling from? The words swirled in his mind, but perhaps that was how they'd sounded. He rose uncertainly, grabbing his cane from where it lay beside him on the couch. One of the worst things about getting old was this feeling of uncertainty, never fully trusting yourself. The last time he'd driven—it must have been five years earlier—he would peer left down a clear road for thirty seconds before turning, convinced he was somehow missing an oncoming semi.

Outside the window of his room, the mild March breeze rustled through a line of azalea bushes. He sometimes went out front and sat on one of the benches, the wrought-iron engraved in the middle with *GBD*, for the name of the complex. It was nice here, or nice enough, but it wasn't a real place to him. The strange part was, his memories didn't feel real, either. His childhood; the camps; the decades in Liberty working at the Neversink; even these last twenty-odd years, living near Louisa and her husband, helping with their flower nursery and the grandchildren, then moving in with them the last few. Although particular memories felt sharp and clear, these epochs seemed like other lifetimes. His past and present he saw through smoked glass, and his future did not exist. He was a man out of time.

His thumb moved toward the recent calls list, to his daughter's number, then hovered over the green call button. He didn't want to unduly trouble her or her husband, Ken, who seemed to keep a private list of every call, need, errand, minor request, or inconvenience his father-in-law's continued existence saddled him with. Instead, he scrolled down the list and stopped on the number marked RACHEL S—for Sendak, not Sikorsky, married to some doctor with a West Village practice, like her father. They'd talked a few months earlier, when she'd called to wish him happy birthday, whichever birthday it was. She was the only one he'd kept up with over the years.

She answered on the third ring. "Sander, hello!"

"Hello, my darling."

"How are you?"

Rachel half listened to Sander as she walked through Washington Square to meet up with Elena for lunch. The calls had become less frequent over time, but proportionately more difficult. He seemed increasingly out of sorts, as he did right now, relaying some strange story about Saul Javits. Something about Javits saying something about Len. Rachel was distracted by the drink she was late for, during which Elena—her oldest friend—would be discussing the newly discovered fact of her husband's long-running affair. They would split a bottle of white wine, and by the second glass, Elena would be sobbing into a cloth napkin. Bill, Elena's husband, was what? Sixty-six? Ridiculous. It never ended.

Though, of course, it did—the spectral voice on the other end was proof enough of that. Some part of Rachel was galvanized by the fact that, at her age, people were still sneaking around, cheating on each other. She hailed a cab on the eastern side of the park, told the driver the address.

"I'll call Len," she told Sander, and they said their good-byes.

As the buildings of the West Thirties fanned unremarkably by, the twin concerns of Len and Elena melded in her mind. A long time ago, she herself had considered infidelity, had considered cuckolding Len. As punishment, probably, for marooning her in Liberty with his beavering kindness and his false, foolish hopes about the hotel; in other words, for being exactly the man she'd known she was marrying. It had been her fault, and this had become clear when she'd met Eli, a new internist in her father's practice. Over the last two decades of her marriage to Eli, she had not once been tempted to cheat on him; though this constancy, she admitted to herself, was perhaps owed to worrying about Eli cheating on her. She didn't think he ever had, but he was a doctor, tall and good-looking, with thick gray hair and laughing eyes. He certainly could have, and maybe he was smart enough to have done so and not told her.

Len, she'd never worried about—that was the thing, you wanted to worry about someone, just a little. She called him and got the voicemail. What had Sander been talking about? It only now occurred to her that he may have been calling for an actual reason. She called Susannah.

"Hi, Mom."

"No one says hello anymore?"

"It says who's calling on the phone. You don't have to pretend like you don't know who it is." Susannah had been sitting at her desk, watching the snow and wondering why she'd come in to work. Force of habit, she supposed. And she wanted to check in on Len, make sure he had everything he needed during what was shaping up to be a real blizzard. She worried about him, as she knew he worried about her. Thirty-seven and still single, although she had an idea that Andy was going to propose soon. Len didn't love the idea of her marrying a goy, but that was a different story.

She listened as her mother detailed a strange phone call, Sander needing help in some way—or was it something about Saul Javits? It was unclear. The clock over her desk read 1:45. "Okay, Mom," she said, putting on her heavy coat for the 200-yard walk to the cottage. "I'll run next door and let Dad know."

Outside it had gotten even colder, and she hugged the pleated down to herself like a fond memory of summer. Every year, she'd thought, this will be the last winter, and every year winter came around again. Besides her love life, Len worried about her being unhappy in Liberty, stuck in this podunk town with her fancy education. In fact, she wasn't unhappy. True, if you'd told her younger self that in two decades she'd be working for her father and dating a man who had a nineteen-year-old daughter, she would have jumped off a bridge. But what did her younger self know? Though she did sometimes feel she was wasting her life, she suspected she'd feel that way elsewhere too, and without the familiar comforts of home.

The yellow front light of the cottage burned over a beard of snow. She knocked. She knocked again. The car was here, but no one seemed to be home. Her call went to voicemail. She peeked around the side but saw no one there, just the turntable spinning with the arm disengaged, a cup of tea in its saucer on the couch. Looked like he'd left in a hurry—maybe Javits had picked him up, hence the call?

She pushed away from the window and trudged back up the drive, toward the empty clubhouse. She'd check back again later.

From a window in the Neversink, Len watched her go. His good girl—she could never find out the things he'd found out this morning, as he'd gone through the files Javits had left, the box of files beside him on the ground. It was all there. It covered everything.

He wandered down the hall to the natatorium, everything still and quiet, the windows dampened by the surrounding white. It felt like an old cathedral, a place of former worship abandoned by the old gods and surrendered to the elements. He climbed onto the old concrete diving board and sat, the cold reaching through his thin pajama bottoms. His mind, he realized, was curiously blank, his thoughts dull and sluggish as he found the number on his recent call list.

"Hello," she said.

"Meet me at the hotel. Come in through one of the broken windows at the side."

There was a pause. "Okay."

An hour passed—maybe two, he couldn't say—and eventually she climbed in through the window, looking like the author picture on her last dust jacket. Wearing black, with dark hair and large, alert eyes. They seemed to take in the whole scene as she moved through the room: the rotting hotel, its bathrobed owner splay-legged on the diving board. "Len?" she said, with a look of concern.

"Hi, Alice." He knew he looked insane, but he didn't move. What did it matter?

"What's going on?"

"You know what's going on. You talked to Javits."

"Yes, I did. This was all news to you?"

He laughed. "I'm a fool, what can I say?"

Overhead, a single pigeon beat its wings against the high rafters and Alice looked up at it. "I'm sorry," she sighed.

"Don't write this book."

"Len, it's almost finished. This is just the last part."

"I'm begging you. All that's left are people's good memories of this place and my mother. Please don't take that away."

"You don't get it, do you?" she said, her pitiless expression almost as horrible as anything he'd seen today. "I came here today to see if you knew. And to tell you if you didn't. People should know the truth about this place. People should know what happened."

"Please. We're family."

"I'm sorry," she said again, pausing at the window. "Good luck to you." And with that, she disappeared back into the world.

Len rose and went back down the hall to where he'd earlier set his supplies: two full gas cans, a clutch of rags, and a box of wooden oven matches. In the grand ballroom, a rat skittered into a hole beneath the stage, fleeing the smell of gasoline. Len wiped his face with his shoulder, eyes tearing further from the fumes. How long had it been obvious? Had it ever? Should it have been? Should he have known better or was he destined to be the stooge, an unlucky heir of a cursed fortune?

And her: When the children began disappearing, what had she thought? Maybe she knew, maybe nothing. Maybe like Javits, like himself and Rachel and everyone else—like the police who refused to dig too deep out of respect for the great Jeanie Sikorsky—she'd put it out of her mind, preferring to think it was all either a coincidence or curse. Whatever the case, it had been right there in front of her, but she'd turned away from the truth, the one time her grace had faltered. She couldn't destroy this thing her father had built. It turned out she'd left that to her son.

He climbed the staircase to look down at the Great Hall. Once, when he was a boy, he'd stood there and indulged himself in a grandiose moment of pleasure, knowing one day this would all be his. In his youth he'd been a presumptive magnate; in his adulthood he'd been a struggling businessman; in his later years, he'd settled for the role of caretaker, keeping alive, if nothing else, the memory of happy success, a great family's heyday. Well, that was all over now. It had been over even then, he just hadn't known it—getting the news had been the work of a lifetime.

He dropped the box, poured the last of the gasoline in, and dropped a match. Flames licked greedily up the rags he held to the fire. He tossed a rag into the nearest pool of gasoline and the fire spread with a quiet, sinister evenness. Through the rooms he went, touching the floor with the burning rags, dropping them here and there, trailing the fire as he walked. The Great Hall was ablaze behind him—the dining room, the lobby, the ballroom, the lounge. Standing there watching the fire consume his family's legacy, he saw, for the first time in his long life, who he really was. He was the one to clean things up. He was a janitor. History's janitor.

His work finished, he stepped through a broken window, feeling the cold on his exposed chest, smelling faint smoke. Hearing the distant sirens as he cleared the snow off the car, and seeing the fire engine barrel along Main Street as he drove down Neversink Hill for the last time. For lack of anywhere else to go, he turned north onto 17, into a great line of cars stalled in the storm. Stuck there, just off the exit, he could see the line of heads in front of him craned sideways, watching the black smoke billow off that high white peak. It curled and puffed against the dome of the snowy sky, like someone sending signals, a frantic code, although who was out there to receive it, if anyone, he couldn't imagine.

In the opposite direction, Alice drove back to New York, past an endless line of stopped cars in the northbound lane. Gray-white sludge and dead trees blurred by her window, and she was glad to know she would not have to return here again—the image of Len, slumped in his mangy bathrobe on the diving board like a sick old dog, would stay with her for a long time. He was a genuinely kind, befuddled man, an animal caught in the snare of their family history, and she didn't want to hurt him. But in the end, she didn't care—she couldn't. The story needed to be told, and after years of fending off her editor with outlines and chapters, dribs and drabs, she was almost done. All that was left was to hammer out the last chapter.

She clicked the flashlight on and off as she drove. On and off, on and off, she worked through the material in her mind. She'd let Jeanie, Len's mother, speak last. She was, after all, at the heart of the story, the alpha and the omega. In her image, the Neversink had become great, then ruined. Alice didn't know every last detail, but Javits had given her enough information—birth records and court documents and financial statements and a water-stained journal—to know the truth. And regardless, she thought, putting the flashlight down and both hands on the wheel, it was her story now.

An Ending

I took him back in the end. Of course I did—in the end, what else could I do?

Driving away, I told myself not to look back and then immediately looked back to see his hamper on the hospital's stone steps—the image haunted me every night for the next two years, as did the question of what had happened. Had a nurse or patient found him, brought him inside? Had they, for some unknown reason, been closed that fateful day? Had he frozen during the night, been taken by someone? I did not care what my father said, how it helped the family. It was a sin, a grave sin that I had committed, casting my brother away, and for what?

For money, that was all. Money, and the pride that money brings.

So, shortly after we opened the Neversink, I began to visit Abraham. I'd inquired discreetly at the hospital, bribed a bored clerk with a ten-dollar bill. He pulled a file from a gray-green cabinet and told me the Sussex Boys Home. Steven Andrews, his government name—I went there and found him. He was three, dark-haired and dark-eyed and unusually thin, as though having already cast off his babyhood;

similarly, and in contrast with the howling torment of his first year, he was nearly mute. It took him a month to say anything to me, and nearly a year to learn my name. Jinji, he called me.

They all did, the children at the home. I volunteered there, on and off, for many years, bringing gifts for them all, but really for Abraham: little candies and marbles, tin soldiers and books to read, though Abe had difficulty with words. My hope, each time I visited, was to find him gone, taken by a kind local family, but each time he was still there—a bit older, a bit more silent and morose, increasingly ignored by the staff and the other children. He began to spend almost all his time in a little nook off the main hall, a place I came to think of as his room. There, he had his toys, a blanket, little nonsense odds and ends of materials he'd collected around the grounds. Sometimes things that needed throwing away—a dead baby bird, for instance, its translucent feathers delicately fanned, a tiny drop of ruby blood on its beak.

His favorite possession was a flashlight I brought him when he was eight, a strange old military thing that some guest or other had left at the hotel. After letting it sit in the lost and found closet for a month, I brought it to Abraham. He was fascinated by it, clipping it to his shirt, clicking it on and off, on and off. When I made ready to leave, he followed, as he often did. I knelt and said, "Steven, just remember. Whenever you feel sad, turn this light on and remember that I will always be there. Remember you are not alone."

But he was—as alone as alone could be. Once, I asked a caseworker there why Steven had no friends. She said he was quiet, too quiet, and had trouble carrying on conversations with the other children. Attempting connection, he became frustrated and angry, and turned further inward. I asked a sweet child named Edgar why Steven had no friends, and Edgar said, "He scares us."

"Why?" I said. "He's just a little boy."

"There's something wrong with him," said Edgar, and he said no more.

As I married and had my children, I felt Abe's absence as a constant ache, as painful as if I had given Leonard or Ezra over to the state to spend their days in that gray prison, with its hard tile floor and rows of beds under dull, yellowy light that spilled from the caged bulbs like urine. Part of the pain was the solitary nature of it—I simply could tell no one: not Henry, not Joseph, not Mother, and certainly not Father. There was no confiding our terrible crime in anyone, especially not when the hotel was thriving. So much in our business depended on word-of-mouth, on reputation. I worked so hard to make us worth the trust of our customers, our purveyors, our artisans, our employees. The Sikorsky name meant something: it was an assurance of quality, dependability, and more than that, an essential goodness. If word had gotten out of Abraham's abandonment, we would have been finished—it all would have ended as quickly as it began, and my parents would have died, perhaps deservedly, of mortal shame.

By the time he became an adolescent, I began to despair for him. He would not be adopted, could not fend for himself. What would happen when he turned eighteen? He would be kicked out into the wilderness like a dog, left to wander, to starve and die alone somewhere in bewilderment at his life's brutality. Or—if he was very lucky—he'd be allowed to stay on as a permanent ward of the state, perhaps given a proper closet to live in, pushing a broom back and forth, despised by generation after generation of boys like him, a symbol of their worst potential future. I could continue visiting, continue bringing my little gifts, my flowers and sweaters and toys and candies, but I could not bring him what he really needed: a life out-side the home and a sense of real family.

Finally, in 1943, when he was fifteen, I adopted him. It took a little doing—some money spread around to secure silence, a few forms signed and notarized by a lawyer three towns over, clandestine trips to prepare for his homecoming. On a brisk April morning, I went in, found him in his nook, and led him out to the car. He couldn't believe what I was telling him, that he was free, and the joy on his face was worth the years of torment, every mile we drove back to Liberty rebuking the same miles we'd driven fifteen years before.

On this journey, I explained that I would continue visiting him, taking care of him, but he must never mention me. If he did, I told him—and it broke my heart to make this threat, though it wasn't really a threat, simply the reality of the circumstance—he would have to go back to the home. "Do you understand, Steven?" I said.

"Yes," he said.

I installed Abe in a house I'd found for him, and quietly looked around for work he could do that he might enjoy. I had Michael, the Neversink's maintenance man, privately instruct him in various forms of handiwork. Michael would report back weekly on Abe's progress—he was, it turned out, especially fond of and good at paint-ing. He was not so good at plumbing or woodwork. Occasionally, when Michael had a big project, he would bring Abe—Steven—to the hotel to help him. Now and then, I would see my brother, hang-ing wallpaper, say, or handing tools up to Michael as he fixed a faulty sconce.

Michael became my sole confidante, and he was a good one—quiet himself, unrelated to the family, and utterly loyal. He looked in on Abraham when I couldn't, made sure he had groceries and was staying safe. He fixed things around Abe's house and kept my brother company when he was feeling lonely. Though Abraham enjoyed being alone and was good at entertaining himself—too good, I came to fear.

When the first boy disappeared, like so many other people at the hotel I worried it was a visitor, a guest from the city come to despoil our little Eden. It was not hard to see how, with its ceaseless flow of anonymous visitors and its sprawling grounds, the Neversink could prove an attractive hunting ground for a sick person so inclined. Saul Javits and I talked openly about this possibility, and we made ourselves vigilant to any strangeness, any untoward behavior. But when the next child disappeared in the woods near Liberty, then another two a few years after that, some small part of me began to suspect Abe.

No, *suspect* is not the right word—this thought was too isolated within me, a kernel of doubt buried beneath a heap of blankets, layers of faith and love and all the unexamined confidence that routine and responsibility bring. But did I watch him a bit closer when I visited? Did I ask him what he'd been doing, where he'd been? Did I linger in his bathroom, cast a long look into his bedroom as I passed in the hall? Perhaps. Perhaps it was simply the atmosphere of the time—long gray days of doubt, passing strangers on the street and worrying a little to oneself. Is it you? Is it you? Saul Javits spoke against this, the danger of becoming paranoid, of doubting those closest to you. The worst crime this person can wreak, he said more than once, is to turn us against each other. We must have faith in the goodness of this place, in ourselves.

In my rational mind, I worried about Abe, living alone with a killer or killers somewhere in the town. I worried that people might think it was him, though he seemed to be liked well enough, both

by Michael and by the townsfolk whose houses he painted, whose
rooms he wallpapered, whose gutters and fences he mended. Once,
I sat with him and asked, had he heard of the children
disappearing?

"Yes," he said. We sat in his living room. He turned the TV volume
down, some ridiculous program playing. Strangely, I recall it was *My
Favorite Martian*.

"How does it make you feel, Steven?"

"Bad. It is a bad thing."

"Yes. People in town are very worried."

"I know, they talk about it at the houses where I work."

I turned to him on the sofa. The TV's light played off his black
eyes as though they were made of glass. He was a handsome young
man, tall and thin, unlike anyone in our family, with our blue eyes
and limbs like alder stumps—I sometimes wondered if Mama had
dallied, so unusual were his looks for the Sikorsky line. "You know
you should not talk to children."

"Yes."

"Do you understand why?"

He turned from the television. "They might think it was me."

"Good," I said, and we discussed it no more.

The years went by; my children grew. Ezra went away to college and
Lenny remained to help with the hotel. Those were, mostly, happy
days. My Henry was still healthy, and the hotel was still in its
prime—it seemed we were part of something that could never end,
that was bigger than any of us, bigger even than my papa who had
built the business, or Mr. Foley, who had built the building all those
many years before. The celebrities and the money were nice, of

course, but I never really cared about that. It was the feeling of being part of this great thing that touched, encompassed, so many lives. It was an honor to shake each familiar hand that came through the door, and it was an honor to make new friends—guests for life, as my father said.

My Leonard seemed to feel this as well, becoming an expert on all manner of innkeeping know-how, and I grew older with the assurance, like a hand gently laid upon my back, that the next generation was poised to continue the tradition. Even when Henry died—felled mercifully in his garden by a heart attack—I could stand in our lonely cottage and look at the hotel and think, yes, whatever may come of all of us, this will continue.

I held this close to me until little Alice was assaulted and the Schoenberg boy's remains were found. Then, I knew; oh, I knew. I knew the Neversink was doomed. By the early 1970s, our profits were already declining, and we could not weather such a catastrophe. The short-term curiosity seekers would give way to empty rooms, a feeling of desolation, and the guests would scatter like animals before a storm. Even the sky seemed wicked that awful summer, a yellowy sky auguring sorrow and destruction. The air itself seemed to physically affect me, sap my energy and render me ill. Despite my doctor's verdict—a blood disease, incurable, its slow progression leaving me perhaps a few years to live—I felt infected by evil, or by knowledge of evil.

I knew it was Abraham. I do not know how I knew, but I knew. I lay in bed each night, shivering, seeing him out there in the world, the world I had released him into so many years before. During the day I gathered my strength, and I asked myself how could I know this? It could be anyone in town, anyone in the area, a long-standing guest, even. But somehow, I knew, and on a brisk day in April, I drove down the hill to his house.

I had not been since the year before—before the boy was discovered and before I'd become sick. It seemed to have deteriorated in that time. Litter was strewn about the yard, the paint was blistered off in places, a board in the front steps skewed upward, unnailed. Abraham met me at the door. Despite the shape of the house, he looked the same as always, perhaps a little younger, even. He made me tea and we sat at his dining room table. An auto parts calendar on the wall was open to December, and one date was circled with red pen, annotated with initials.

He drummed his fingers on the table, and I took a sip of my tea. There was an expectant feeling, as though neither of us knew quite how to proceed. "How has it been?" I said, finally.

"Good," he said.

"How is your work?"

"Good, yeah." He seemed distracted.

"Is it you?"

"What, Jinji?"

"Don't lie to me. You must never lie to me."

"I would not."

"Is it you?"

A car drove by somewhere outside in the slush. The smell of mint and slightly dirty water wafted up from my mug. He looked at me, and I at him. How much time passed without him saying anything? I cannot say, though his silence was itself as clear an answer as he could have given. So I did the one thing that I thought might stop him: I told him who he was.

He said, "I don't believe you."

"It is the truth, Abraham." At the sound of his real name, it was as though he were suddenly a baby again. Howling, howling away—tut tut, little chick!

When he finally quieted, I said, "Never again, Abraham. Never again."

These days, I stay here in bed. I see Len and Saul daily, but mostly I am visited by my memories. I think about my childhood, that longest of winters that we somehow endured. I think of the good times here, try to remind myself that they happened, were not themselves lies. And I think about that long, hot day, so many years ago, the employees and townspeople joining together to search for Jonah. Standing before them on the staircase in the Great Hall, looking down and seeing the same expression of determined hope on each and every face—it sustained me at the time, but now the memory haunts me. For there was no hope; there never was. I know that now.

There has not been another disappearance in the last two years, but daily I wake fearing the news of another child gone missing. I want to tell someone the truth—Leonard, most of all—but oh, I cannot. I cannot bear the shame. The truth will be spoken only after I am gone and the hotel is closed.

Outside my window, the Hotel Neversink still stands, but for how long? It is all I have, and yet I see it and think God, please, tear it down. Raze it and burn it and water the ashes, that a field may yet grow in this wicked place.

Acknowledgments

I'm extremely grateful to everyone who helped with the writing and revision of *The Hotel Neversink*: Elizabeth Watkins Price, J. Robert Lennon, Brad Rudin, Lauren Schenkman, Patricia Price, Bill Price, Brownie Watkins, and Ben Felton. Thank you, as well, to Daniel Wallace, Chris Bachelder, Lydia Kiesling, Ling Ma, Michael Goldsmith, and B. T. Coleman, and to the great team at Tin House Books: Diane Chonette, Nanci McCloskey, Molly Templeton, Elizabeth DeMeo, and Yashwina Canter. And I feel honored to work with both Masie Cochran and Samantha Shea, without whom this book would certainly not exist.